I0591969

Paperback: 978-0-578-75813-8
Lightning Source LLC, 14 Ingram Blvd
La Vergne, TN 37086

www.IngramSpark.com

The Misadventures of Snowball

PART I
Gus and the Strawberry Locket

Chapter I

In a lot of ways, strawberries are like friendship. If you try to grow one, you'll often grow many. They are savory and sweet, and if you plant them well, they'll bear fruit. The strawberry plant, if left alone will create more strawberry plants by sending out small shoots. If one wishes one can simply cut off one of these shoots and plant it in a new place and a whole new strawberry patch will begin. Strawberries are easy to grow and you can grow them almost anywhere you like. Springtime, which is when this story begins, is a wonderful time to plant them. They typically prefer to be in the sun and in somewhat sandy places.

Of course, these were not the sort of thoughts going through Angus Finnegan's mind as he was quickly sinking in a patch of quicksand. His thoughts mostly comprised of *Oh Crap!* And *I'm going to die!*

Perhaps I should back up a bit and tell you how Gus managed to get into the pool of quicksand before I continue.

You see, Angus (Gus for short) was smart. Er... Well, he was smarter than most of the peasantry who tried desperately to scrape by as best they could. Gus was a man of twenty-five years, with short brown hair, bright hazel eyes, a ragged assortment of brown and green clothing and a silver locket about his neck that he never took off. He was also no taller than five feet, and could scarcely lift fifty pounds.

Gus was walking along a dirt road through the woods when he decided it was about time he relieved himself. He had been walking for a long while and he could no longer hold it in. He rushed past the pine trees until he found a secluded glen just out of view of the road and dropped his trousers. An immense feeling of relief flooded through him and onto the soil, but that feeling didn't last long. Gus heard a snapping in the branches to his left. He looked around to see what had caused the noise, but there was nothing there. Just the trees.

His attention returned to his business for only a few moments more before some rustling in the bushes alerted him.

"Hello?" Gus called out. "Who's there?" He received no reply and was nearly finished with his business when he heard a huff and felt hot steamy breath on his shoulder. Terrified, he slowly turned his head to see the bovine face of a hulking minotaur breathing down his neck.

For those of you who do not already know, minotaurs are a sort of monster. Considered mere legend and scary-story fodder, these creatures are reported to be half-man, half-bull. They stand over seven feet tall, and are made of over seven hundred pounds of brutality. Most of the stories speak of these creatures in caves or labyrinths and other maze-like places. Decidedly vicious, their horns are sharp and minotaurs often enjoy goring their victims to death with them. Stories of them, as with most monsters, are largely disregarded as myth and frequently end with "and none survived", which of course begs the question: who spread the story in the first place if no one has seen one and lived?

Gus would have peed himself but, luckily, he'd already taken care of that. Instead he ran. Or he would have, but his trousers were down and he fell flat on his face. He scrambled from the ground pulling up his trousers and stumbled and ran deeper into the forest.

The brown, shaggy fur of the Minotaur fluttered in the wind as it pounded after him. With each massive step from the Minotaur, Gus could feel the forest shake around him. Desperately, Gus cut through a tight group of trees that would be difficult to squeeze through for a creature of the Minotaur's size. He smiled to himself as he looked over his shoulder to see his outsmarted opponent. However, his smile turned to a look of horror as the Minotaur simply broke through the trees with his massive bulk, swinging a massive hammer and smashing the trees into kindling.

Screaming in terror, Gus continued his rampant flight through the forest. Sweat was pouring down his neck and he was breathing hard. He noticed a short cliff face up ahead, and decided to make for it. The cliff was only fifteen feet tall, and had many loose rocks littering its surface. With a quick leap he jumped up onto the cliff face and scrambled for handholds as the Minotaur came pounding after him. His first attempt to climb higher failed miserably as the rock he grabbed dislodged from the cliff face. However, he quickly regained his hold and scampered up. When he reached the top, he turned to see his foiled opponent. The cliff face was far too unsteady for a massive creature like that to climb.

"Ha!" Gus yelled at the Minotaur.

The Minotaur gave one go at climbing the cliff face, but the rocks became rubble in his massive four-fingered hands and the creature slid down faster than he could climb up.

"You're not getting me any time soon," Gus taunted with an air of victory. However, his crafty smile soon disappeared. The Minotaur backed up a few paces, got a running start and with all of its strength it leaped off the ground and cleared the fifteen-foot cliff with ease.

"Holy hand-baskets!" Gus cried as the Minotaur snatched at Gus, but Gus was too quick and left a cloud of dust in his wake as he bolted.

The trees were growing thicker the further Gus moved into the forest. He leaped over massive roots that threatened to trip him and ducked under large overgrown bushes that tried to ensnare his head. *What do I do?* Gus thought in a panic, *I can't keep this up forever.* The ever-present thundering of the Minotaur's hooves behind him warned him that he couldn't afford to slow down, even for a second. Up ahead he saw his salvation. A massive tree towered above a large outcropping of rocks and boulders. He darted around the rocks and out of sight and quickly hauled himself up the tree as fast as his arms could take him. When he reached a large branch ten feet off the ground he ran along the limb and into the dense foliage to hide himself. He clung tightly to the branch and held his breath.

The Minotaur ran right beneath him and further into the forest until he was lost from sight. Gus sighed with relief as he clung to the branch. "Ha. Take that you brute. Thought you could outsmart me, huh?"

That's when the branch broke.

Gus and the branch plummeted to the ground. *Strange*, Gus thought when he landed, *the ground doesn't usually feel this wet*. Gus looked down at his torso as it sank.

Now, Gus was not the type to give into fear. No, no. Fear is a very simple kind of word used to describe how one feels about public speaking or falling off large cliffs. Gus was definitely not afraid. Gus was panicked.

Oh crap! I'm gonna die! Gus struggled and struggled before he realized he was only making himself sink faster into the quicksand. He frantically looked around him for something to grab hold of. The branch of a nearby pine stuck out over the quicksand just a few feet away. Gus stretched his arm as far as it would go. His fingertips brushed the bushy needles on the end. "Almost..." Gus leaned forward and sank a little deeper in the quicksand. He grabbed the branch with one hand and, pulling himself a little closer, he grabbed it with the other. With a great tug he pulled with all his might.

The branch snapped.

"Oh, come on!" Gus wailed in desperation. *Wait!* Gus remembered. *I might have some rope in my sack!* He was up to his armpits in the quicksand by then and didn't have much time left before he sank below the surface. If he was going to get his bag up, he only had one chance. He carefully pulled his bag from the mire and opened it. Inside he found a few things. One was a small pouch containing freshly picked strawberries which would be of little help. The other was a torn piece of parchment that read "DON'T FORGET. PACK ROPE AND TENT" in big black letters.

"Help!" Gus screamed at the top of his lungs. "Help!" The quicksand was at his neckline. "Anyone! Please! Anyone!" Gus shouted desperately. "Please, anyone! Help!"

A massive, hairy bulk emerged from the trees. Gus could see the Minotaur's sharp horns and hear its steaming breath.

"Can anybody *else* help me?" Gus yelled. He was sinking even deeper into the quicksand and had to tilt his head back to keep his mouth above the surface. "No no no no no no no no..." Gus murmured as the last of his face sank beneath the quicksand.

A mighty hand grabbed him by the back of his collar and, with a *Splorch*, yanked him free of the quicksand. "Oh, thank you thank you thank you thank you!" Gus cried with joy. But as the muck cleared from his eyes his joy faded. Gus was staring into the fierce brown eyes of the minotaur. "Oh gods! Please don't eat me!" squeaked Gus, "please. Take anything you want. Just spare me, I beg you!"

Without saying a word, the great beast grabbed Gus's still opened sac in one hand and began snuffling around in its contents. "Oh, thank you mister minotAUR-!"   The minotaur carelessly flung Gus back into the quicksand and pulled out the pouch of strawberries.

"Mister minotaur, save me!" Gus pleaded. The minotaur seemed merry as he devoured one strawberry after the next. Gus looked all around him to see if there was another way to escape the ever-consuming pit of quicksand. "Mister minotaur!" The creature ignored him.

"Please..." Desperate and sinking fast, there was only one thing left Gus could think of to save himself, "If you save me, I'll get you more strawberries!"

The Minotaur grunted and focused all his attention on Gus.

"Uh, yeah. I know a place just a few miles from here where they grow whole gardens of them," Gus lied. "I even heard that they serve them mixed with cream."

"Oooooooh!" The Minotaur replied with enthusiasm. "Do they have strawberry cream for me?"

"Uh, yeah," Gus said nervously as the quicksand reached his armpits once more. "A whole cart full!"

"Oooooooh!" the monster replied. "What's a cart?"

Gus slapped his forehead. "I'll show you when we get there, but you have to get me out of this quicksand first."

"Okay." The Minotaur effortlessly plucked Gus from the quicksand from where he stood on solid ground. "We go now. Where is the strawberries?"

Gus sighed with relief. He was safe, at least for the moment. It was lucky the creature could understand him. Though it unnerved him that it could speak. *What have I gotten myself into?* Gus wondered nervously. There was no turning back now. He had to keep going until he could escape the creature. "There's a road I was traveling on nearby. Do you know where that is?"

The Minotaur nodded happily in agreement.

"Well, we need to get back to the road. But before that, do you think maybe I could clean off all this mud?"

The Minotaur shrugged, picked up Gus by the leg and began walking into the forest.

As Gus dangled from the creature's mighty grip, he became very dizzy from the blood rushing to his head. "Mister Minotaur, I am capable of walking on my own."

"Yup." The creature grunted.

"And you don't have to carry me," Gus continued.

"Yup."

"You could put me down." Gus said impatiently.

"Yup." The Minotaur continued walking.

Frustrated, Gus asked, "Why are you carrying me upside down by the leg?"

"Snowball knows the way to a stream. Snowball can get there much quicker than tiny little hooman," the Minotaur explained.

"Beg pardon. Is that your name?" Gus asked.

"Hmm? Of course, Snowball is called Snowball. Why would Snowball not be called Snowball? Silly hooman." The Minotaur chuckled as it shook its head sadly at Gus.

"You're not even white..." Gus noted. "That's... ummm... a strange name for a minotaur," Gus pointed out.

"What's a mean o' tar?" Snowball puzzled as he hopped over a large boulder.

"Minotaur. You. You're a minotaur."

"Snowball is not mean."

"Uh...."

"Snowball is also not covered in tar. See?" Snowball held Gus higher so his face was against the fur in Snowball's armpit. Gus gagged at the foul odor pouring off the creature.

"How much further to the stream?" Gus coughed.

"Almost there." Snowball replied.

When the pair arrived at the coursing brook, Snowball tossed Gus haphazardly into the frigid water. Gus sputtered and thrashed about until he was upright before he splashed water on himself to rinse off the mud. Snowball suddenly became preoccupied with a monarch butterfly that had landed on the branch of a nearby pine.

With the creature distracted and realizing that the current would help him swim faster downstream, Gus seized the opportunity. He took in a deep breath and plunged beneath the cold water. His muscles were screaming at him from the chilling temperature, but he forced himself to swim. He swam and swam and swam… and after five feet Snowball caught him by the ankle and pulled him out of the water. Snowball held Gus up so they were face to face.

Gus gave snowball a sheepish grin. "Please don't hurt me."

"Are you clean mister hooman?" Snowball asked.

"Uh... yeah. Yeah, I'm clean."

"Good! We go to village now!" Snowball's tail wagged with excitement. He carried Gus off into the woods still swinging by his ankle.

"Mister Snowball, sir? Could you please not carry me by the ankle?"

"Why?" the creature wondered.

"Uh, well... You see... The blood rushes to my head and it's hard to think. I don't know if I can remember how to get to the village with the strawberries in it if I can't think."

"Oh! Why hooman not say so? Snowball guess you can walk, but tiny hooman need to keep up with Snowball."

"Yeah. No problem."

Snowball set Gus on the ground, holding his hammer at the ready just in case his guide should try to run away.

"Thank you Snowball." Gus sighed with relief. He eyed the gigantic stone hammer the creature held warily.

"You are most welcome, tiny hooman."

"It's Gus."

"What's Gus?"

"Me! I'm Gus."

"Oh. Okay, tiny hooman." Snowball smiled.

"Gus."

"Oh. Okay, Gus."

Of course, it dawned on Gus just then that sharing his name with his large and dangerous companion might have been a bad idea. But it was too late now so he shook his head and did his best to keep up with the long strides of the Minotaur.

Jagodwine was a small settlement built around a crossroads. It had a tavern, a general store, a smithy and a scattered assortment of residences and farm plots. The town had two main roads that intersected near the general store and tavern and several small side roads that led to the homes of Jagodwine's inhabitants. All in all, its population couldn't have been more than a few hundred.

When Snowball and Gus came upon the first house, the woman who was hanging her laundry to dry dropped her small basket of clothes pins, threw her hands up in the air and ran screaming into the house to lock the door.

"What is her problem?" Snowball wondered aloud.

Gus realized that if the pair of them were seen together the villagers might try to kill the both of them. "Uh... So, Snowball. Listen. I was thinking. Maybe it would be best if I went in to the town first, you know, to let the villagers know that you mean them no harm and that you've only come for strawberries. That way they won't run away screaming and you can get all the strawberries you want."

"Oooooh. That is a good idea tiny hoo- I mean Mister Gus Man." Snowball nodded his head energetically.

"Alright. So, you should wait here and I will go ahead into the village."

So, Snowball waited on the outskirts of Jagodwine while Gus strolled into the village. Once he was out of sight of the Minotaur Gus broke into a dead run toward the center of town. A wooden sign with a white painted goose and the words "Lagle's Tavern" caught his eye. The lively tavern would provide an excellent place to disappear among the rabble. He ducked into Lagle's Tavern and stole into a corner where he could sit out of sight of the doorway. He breathed a quick sigh of relief as the bar patrons ignored him and continued chatting merrily. As he sat there, he thought to himself. *I have to warn these people about the Minotaur, but if I tell them they might throw me out of town and then that monster will smash me to tiny bits. I'll just lay low for a while. Maybe they won't find out I brought him here.* A buxom blonde barmaid in her late thirties interrupted his thoughts. "What can I get for you, dear?" She smiled at him.

"I, uh..."

"Say, I haven't seen you around these parts. You new into town?"

"Um. Yeah, just passing through."

"Well, I'm Miss Lagle." She winked at Gus. The mole on her right cheek made him shrink back a little. "You can call me sugar. What'll it be?"

"I, uh... Some ale please." Gus managed.

"Be just a minute." She left the crowded hall to the back room behind the bar to fetch his drink.

A deep, rough voice tore through the chatter and made Gus sink even further into his seat.

"Well, well, well. If it isn't Gus the Fuss."

Oh, no... Gus cringed.

Ian MacBrody was one of the baddest of the bad. He and his men wandered from town to town, taking what they could and leaving wreckage behind. Unfortunately for Gus, He and Ian had grown up in the same town and due to Ian's large stature and ill temper Gus had always found himself at the wrong end of the stick. In fact, Ian was one of the many reasons he'd left his village in the first place. Ian towered above Gus at six and a half feet, wore filthy animal skins and torn clothes and had the kind of face only a mother could love.

Ian spat on the floor. "Look fellas, it's Gus the Fuss!" Several ragged low-lives slid up behind Ian to take a good look at the minuscule peasant.

Gus did his best not to say anything. Whenever he did it usually got him into trouble.

"Wot's the matter, Fuss? Cat got yer tongue?" Ian ruffled Gus's hair and looked back at his crew. "He's so 'appy to see me, he's speechless." Ian's cohorts laughed. "What brings you into town, Gussy?"

"Just passing through." Gus said meekly, avoiding the eyes of Ian and his thugs and hoping they would ignore him and leave him alone.

"Well that's too bad, ain't it, Fussy. We would love to leave you be and mosey on and all, but there's a little matter we have to address first. Ain't that right, boys?"

"Yeah, that's right." An overweight thug with a low forehead confirmed.

"You see, Gus. There's a toll for passing through town and all. You'll have to pay up if you want to move on."

"I haven't got any money, Ian." Gus told him.

"Well what 'ave you got?" Ian pressed.

"Nothing. I'm broke."

"Well what about this then." Ian reached for the small silver chain that hung around Gus's neck. Gus slapped Ian's hand away and clutched the locket hidden beneath his tunic.

"Did you fellas see that?" Ian asked his men. "Did you all see that?!" He bellowed to the entire tavern. The patrons turned away to avoid any trouble. "He hit me. That's grounds for retaliation that is." Ian grabbed Gus by the throat and hefted him bodily up against the wall. While Gus was thrashing wildly to free himself, Ian grabbed the silver locket and snapped it off Gus's neck.

"NO!" Gus gasped as he struggled futilely against the overpowering grip of Ian's massive arm. Ian rammed his fist into Gus's gut, knocking the wind out of him. He let Gus flop to the floor before he and his men strolled out of the tavern laughing. Tears rolled down Gus's face as he gasped on the floor and watched Ian and his locket walk away.

The silver locket was the only thing of value he had. It had been given to him by Fiona Quinnly, the only woman who had ever paid any attention to Gus. When Gus was getting laughed at by the townsfolk or pushed around by Ian it was Fiona who had been there to give him a hug and tell him it would be alright. They'd been friends since childhood. Sure, she was the daughter of a nobleman and he was nothing more than a lowly peasant, but that had never mattered to her. When Fiona had left the village with her father, she had given Gus a silver oval locket with a small lock of her hair inside. "If you're feeling down don't forget this. With this locket I'll never be far away." She had smiled at him.

Gus was filled with more anger than he had ever felt before. He had to get that locket back. When his breath returned a few moments later he had a massive headache and his vision was blurry from the tears in his eyes. He could still make out the face of Miss Lagle, who was shaking her head and frowning. "You doing alright there, sugar." She helped him up and started to show him to the door.

"I need a room for the night." He protested.

"I can't have you staying here." She refused. "Ian's bad news and It'll make the other guests uneasy. Nothing personal. I have to look after my business."

"What?" Gus was astounded at the lack of hospitality.

"I'm sorry dear. I can't have you staying here. You'll have to ask around town for lodging."

The sun was rapidly descending, so Gus went from house to house to find lodging for the night. He had completely forgotten about the day and his encounter with the Minotaur. All his thoughts were of Fionna Quinnly and the silver locket. His search was in vain as word had traveled fast and everyone had heard what had happened at the tavern. No one would give him a place to stay for fear that Ian MacBrody might take his cruelty out on them for giving shelter to the poor man.

When the sun at last set, Gus crawled into a stable and slept in a pile of straw in an empty stall.

Chapter II

When the sun rose the next morning, Gus was awakened by angry shouts and screams. Groggily he left the stables and headed toward the commotion. There was a ring of villagers, armed with pitchforks and torches, surrounding Snowball in the middle of an old woman's yard. One man, armed with a sword and an air of authority, was shouting fiercely at the Minotaur.

"Leave this town now, you foul monster!"

"Okay, but only if you give me strawberries." Snowball replied.

"We don't have any strawberries for you! Now Leave!"

"Snowball does not believe you. Give Snowball strawberries and Snowball will leave." Snowball shrugged.

When Gus finally pushed through the ring of people, he could see the clearly aging Captain of the Guard trying his best to look threatening before the seven-foot-tall monstrosity.

"Take it easy, Snowball!" Gus cried. "Please!"

"Wait, you know this creature?" The captain said, but his question was drowned out by Snowball's voice.

"Snowball is taking it easy! Old Shouty Man is mean. If he was covered in tar, *he* would be a mean o' tar."

"No, you're the blasted Minotaur, minotaur!" Blustered the captain. "Now get out of my town or we'll remove you by force!"

"Snowball does not think tiny hooman can make Snowball leave. Just give Snowball strawberries."

"Please, Snowball." Gus pleaded. "Do what he says. We don't need any violence. The captain is old. He's probably nearly retired. Just leave him be and let's get out of here."

With a quick lackluster tap Snowball hit the captain on the head with his massive hammer. *Wonk!* The peasants all dropped their implements and ran in terror.

"Ahhh! What are you doing?!" Gus cried.

"Mister Gus Man said that Shouty Man was tired. Snowball helped him sleep."

Gus looked down at the very unconscious old captain in horror. Luckily the captain was still breathing, though his conical helmet had a massive dent in it.

"Snowball, you can't just go around smashing people's heads!" Gus was exasperated.

"Snowball does not understand. Shouty Man wanted a nap. Mister Gus Man said so."

"No! I said *re*-tired. Agh! Forget it. I don't have time for this." Gus threw up his arms and stalked off toward the main part of town once again. Snowball followed him close behind. Villagers peered out their windows as Gus and his companion went by before slamming the shutters closed and locking their doors in fear. Of course, locking a door to keep out a Minotaur is like hiding under a blanket to escape a landslide, but let the common folk have their delusions of safety.

"Quit following me!" Gus shouted over his shoulder.

"But Mister Gus Man said that small angry town has strawberries." Snowball protested.

"Look, I can't have you following me around. Anyone who sees you is going to either run away screaming or try to kill us. If you don't stop follow-" Gus stopped abruptly. He ran it through his mind a few times and then started running back to the tavern. He burst through the door and strode up to the bar.

"Where does MacBrody stay?" He demanded.

"I'm sorry?" Miss Lagle was confused.

"Ian MacBrody. Where does he live?" Gus repeated.

"The men say he and his thugs set up a camp just to the north of town, a little way into the woods."

"Thank you." Gus nodded and left the Tavern once more to find Snowball drinking out of a horse's trough.

"Mister Gus Man has strawberries now?" The Minotaur asked as he pulled his sopping head out of the trough.

"Follow me." Gus told Snowball, and Snowball did just that.

With each passing shrub, every brick in the road, every signpost that seemed to salute their passing, Gus's courage grew more and more. With a beast like Snowball at his back he had nothing to fear. No mortal man could best the creature's strength and very few would stand with courage before the monster. Widows closed their windows and children were hurried inside as the pair strode down the lane towards the outskirts of town.

When Gus passed the last of the houses he took in a deep breath and with a triumphant voice bellowed out "You see that, Ian MacBrody? I'm not afraid of you! You best look out!" He gave a warning finger to the wild woods that lay before him. "Look out, because I've a monster that will make you quake and tremble in your boots! And when we come for you, you had better beg for mercy, for I have brought with me Snowball!" Gus turned and gestured behind himself. "And he will crush..." Gus realized that his companion was nowhere to be seen. He paused a moment and cleared his throat. "Yes... Striking monologue wouldn't you say?" Gus said loudly to anyone who might have heard him. "Yes. I saw that at a play last week. Ahem. I'll just be going now..." Gus sheepishly shrank back down the path.

The lumbering hulk was found sitting on his bottom in someone's garden with something red smeared over most of his face.

"What in the gods' names are you doing?" Gus threw his hands up at the Minotaur. "I thought you were following me!"

"Oh, thank you Mister Gus Man! There is so many strawberries! You are very good, very good. Snowball was smart to follow Mister Gus Man to strawberries." The strawberry patch Snowball sat in looked like it had been picked clean through. A small vine with some leaves hung out of the corner of Snowball's mouth.

"What? When did we pass strawberries?" Gus thought aloud to himself.

"Snowball follow you wherever you go." The creature nodded happily.

"Aghh...." Gus sighed. This monster was certainly a handful. "Listen, Snowball. Some bad men took something from me and I need you to help me get it back."

"Oooh. What did they take from Mister Gus Man?" Snowball's tail thumped on the ground as he stuffed his last handful of strawberries mostly into his mouth.

"It's nothing."

"But you said they took something. Isn't something not nothing?"

Gus groaned. "If you must know it was a small silver locket that is very precious to me."

"What is a lock it?

"Locket. It's a small... It's a little round box that hangs around your neck."

"Does it have strawberries inside?"

"What? No."

"Does it have cream inside?"

"No..."

"Hammers?"

"What, no. Of course not."

"Then why do you want it back so bad?"

"Look, it doesn't have strawberries in it. It's something someone gave to me a long time ago."

"Are you sure it doesn't have strawberries in it?"

"Aghh. No!" Gus started pulling on his hair.

"How 'bout now?"

"Would you stop? Look. I need to get it back. Will you help me?"

"Hmmmm..." The creature scratched at its chin. "Mister Gus Man took Snowball to strawberries, so Snowball will help Mister Gus Man."

As wooden fences passed them by, Gus stayed extra alert as he scoured the roadside for any sign of strawberries, lest he lose his wayward companion once more. His eyes stayed glued to the sides of the road, but Gus saw not a single strawberry plant all the way to the edge of town.

"Well look who it is." Ian chuckled to one of his men as they were walking into town. "It's ol' Gus the fuss. Didn't get a proper wallopin' last time?"

"What luck!" Gus exclaimed. "I've got a thing or two to say to you!"

A perplexed look struck Ian's face.

"Nobody, and I mean *nobody* treats me like that and gets away with it! Now if you hand over the locket right now, I'll let you leave with your lives."

"Are you off your rocker?" Ian laughed.

"Listen you filthy, foul smelling, moronic, most lowly piece of disgusting garbage that ever had the misfortune of coming to the world from the womb of an ugly, misbegotten mother!" Gus felt proud of his scathing insult. "You give me back that locket or else!"

Ian eyed him angrily and tilted his head to crack his neck. "Nobody, and I mean *nobody*, insults me mum. I'll give you five seconds to kiss my boots and apologize."

"I doubt you can even count that high!" Gus shot back. "Fine, if that's the way you want to play it... Get him, Snowball!" Gus shouted over his shoulder at the vacant space behind him, where a powerfully strong minotaur of the Snowball variety should have been. He gulped and started to run but the hand that seized him by the collar shortened his escape by a few miles or so. Ian held Gus up to his snarling face.

"I don't suppose the boots offer is still available?" Gus squeaked.

"Not by a long shot."

It's interesting the sorts of things that go through a man's head when one is participating in a fight (or in this case a beating) in which one has no real investment. Gus's thoughts were an assortment of *I wonder if my broken bones might stab him while he punches me?* or *how many people get pummeled on this road?* and *why does this sort of thing always happen on a Tuesday?*

When the pummeling ceased, and the welts on his arms and legs and the bruises on his eyes and ribs and back began taking on a beautiful shade of sunset purple, Gus lay in a jelly-like pile on the dirt. *Why does this always happen to me?* Gus wondered as he laid there. *Because I'm not big or strong? This sort of thing never happens to anyone else, just me. Why me?*

Everyone else had always stood with their friends or the other townsfolk against people like Ian, but Gus had only ever had one friend, and she was a long way off by now, lost forever to him. He closed his eyes for a while and wished as hard as he could that he would just shrink up inside of himself and vanish without a trace. A thick bead of rain slapped him awake and he looked up at the angry sky. He thought it best to find shelter before it started pouring much harder. Gus pushed himself up off the ground and limped back to Jagodwine where he found shelter in the stable once more.

Chapter III

Catharsis came in with the morning sun like a wave of warm air rolling across the plains. The pain of last night's events had sunk in, and yet Gus was still alive. He still had the capacity to continue the fight, and that brought him a small amount of comfort. Though, like the comfort of a warm blanket, it was quickly torn off when reality set in. About thirty seconds after Gus awoke, he realized that he was very cozy and warm (which was odd since he had been sleeping in an open air stable), and that a massive arm the size of a tree trunk was holding him close. His eyes went wide and he struggled to break free of the grasp, when the arm gripped him tighter and a large and rough voice muttered "Mmmmm... Pillow...".

Recognizing the voice of the creature that was holding him, Gus did his best to wake up his bedfellow. "Snowball. Let go of me, Snowball. Wake up." Nothing. "Snowball, please. It's Gus. You're holding *me too tight.*" The wind was squeezed out of him as Snowball tightened his strong-arm snuggle. *Think. Think!* Gus was desperate. "Snowball, all of the strawberries in town are in danger. You have to save them!"

Snowball sat up like a bolt of lightning and let go of Gus. "Where. Where are you, strawberry man? Snowball... Ugh..." Snowball took in his surroundings and realized he was awake. The Minotaur shivered as he recalled, "Snowball had horrible dream Mister Gus Man. Snowball dreamed that Old Shouty Man had stolen strawberries and made a law against hitting things with hammers. Horrible dream. Snowball was about to smash in Old Shouty Man's head, but Snowball woke up instead."

Glad to be freed from the awkwardness of the Minotaur's embrace, Gus collected himself. "What happened yesterday?" Gus demanded. "You were supposed to follow me to the bandits-"

"Oh, Snowball wanted to thank Mister Gus Man for giving Snowball even more strawberries, but you were asleep so Snowball waited." Snowball interrupted.

"What strawberries?" Gus threw his arms up in exasperation. "I scoured every inch of that road. There were no strawberries on it!"

"Snowball found a pie in a window with delicious strawberries all warm and toasty inside."

"A what? You found a strawberry pie?" Gus was beside himself.

"Snowball even saved some for Mister Gus Man, see." Snowball reached into a small sack that sat nearby and took out a smashed-up gob that at one time had been a slice of pie. "Want some?"

"No, I don't want some!" Gus snarled. "Why can't anything go right? Ever since I met you, things have gone from bad to worse. And what's more is I think I must be going mad, because only a complete nutter would be hanging around a seven-foot-tall monstrosity like you!"

"Is Mister Gus Man okay? Mister Gus Man looks red."

"No, I'm not okay!" Gus snapped. "I wish this whole world would just go away. I wish everything would just vanish and that none of this happened!" He shouted.

Clunk!

A quick smack to the head with a massive stone hammer worked tremendously to calm Gus down. In fact, he immediately crumpled to the ground to take a nice long nap. Snowball thought this to be a very effective means of stress relief for his companion.

"Oh, Gods. My head." The peasant grumbled as he came to, massaging his temples.

"Is Mister Gus Man feeling better?" Snowball said as he offered a hand to Gus.

"You hit me!" Gus realized.

Snowball confirmed with a satisfied grunt. "Better?"

"Oh, Gods... Yes, I'm fine. Just don't hit me with the hammer again." Gus took the creature's hand and staggered about till he got his bearings. He decided to ignore his brutish companion's violent solution to stress in favor of using him to take care of the problem at hand. "Right. Ian. Listen, Snowball. A man named Ian MacBrody took a silver locket from me, and I need you to help me get it back."

The Minotaur's expression was vacant.

"Will you help me?"

Snowball nodded.

"Good. The first thing we need to do is find his camp. It's north of town, probably near the road. If you go there with me there's a bucket of strawberries in it for you."

"Oooooh!" Snowball stamped his foot with excitement.

"Then, if you help me by beating the tar out of Ian and his men, there's a second bucket for you. That's two buckets of strawberries, but you only get them if we get my locket back. Alright?"

Snowball nodded excitedly.

Feeling confident that his plan would work this time, Gus said with determination, "Alright. Let's go then."

The pair strode through town once more. No villagers were seen outside. They knew who was coming down the road and made quick to become scarce. The doors were shut and the small town was eerily quiet. When Gus and the Minotaur reached the outskirts of town, the peasant turned to Snowball.

"Now all we have to do is find their camp. It's probably a way off and it'll take some time to find. But with the two of us I'm sure we can manage by nightfa-"

"It's that way." Snowball pointed straight off into the woods.

"What? How do you know?"

"Snowball has good sense of smell. Eeyan BackBrokey and other smelly hoomans is that way."

Gus raised his eyebrows in surprise. "Well, alright. We'll start off that way, I suppose." Gus began marching off. "And this time you need to stick with me or there won't be any strawberries."

To Gus's amazement his plan seemed to be working. The Minotaur seemed to have no suspicion that Gus couldn't hold up his end of the deal and though Gus felt a little guilty for deceiving the creature, he'd worry about the consequences once he'd retrieved the locket. Snowball followed attentively and was none the wiser.

The pair went straight in the direction Snowball had indicated until they could see several tents around a pit of embers and hear men cursing and arguing about who was the strongest in an arm-wrestling contest.

"That's incredible!" Gus was impressed. "Your sense of smell must be amazing. And we didn't even get lost."

"What is lost?" Snowball puzzled.

"Lost? Lost is when you try to go somewhere but get confused as to where you are going and can't find your way back." Gus explained.

"Snowball is never lost."

"I'm sure you've been lost at least once or twice." Gus chuckled.

"Snowball is never lost." The Minotaur repeated simply.

"Very well. Which way is north, then?" Gus crossed his arm.

Snowball pointed directly north. Gus noted the sun and knew his companion was right.

"Lucky guess. Anyway, that's the camp. I need you to go there and pulverize the bandits, alright? Snowball, where are you going?"

Snowball was sneaking off into the woods after something that Gus could only guess at. He tried to follow but quickly lost sight of the monstrous creature. *Well I guess this will have to wait until I can find my companion first.* Gus thought with a sigh. As Gus came across a very large bush, he heard a rustling. "Snowball?" Gus whispered. "Is that you?"

A large man in furs lunged out of the bush and seized Gus by the shoulders. "Gotcha!"

Ian's man dragged Gus into the camp and shouted for his boss. "I found this one in the bushes. Wot should I do wiv 'em?"

"Tie him up." Ian commanded. The henchman did likewise, binding Gus to a thick tree as Ian helped himself to the roasted elk leg he'd been cooking over the fire. "Maybe we can sell him to a slaver."

They bound Gus to a tree. Ian took a good look at him whilst roast elk grease dribbled down his chin. "You just don't know when to quit, do ya?"

Gus did his best to avoid eye contact.

"I gave you a fightin' chance when we left you in the mud. But did you run away like a good little boy? No. You just came crawling back… Look at me when I'm talking to you!" Ian kicked him in the gut, knocking the wind out of him.

Gus looked up at his captor and managed to wheeze, "give me back my locket."

Ian smashed his fist into Gus's head. "Shut up! Who asked you?" Gus's vision was beginning to blur. Ian took another swat at him, this time striking his ribs. Gus could only grimace in pain as his captor struck him over and over again. His ribs were bruised, his nose bled, he could barely see out of his left eye from the swelling. His whole body was in pain. Just when Gus thought he couldn't take anymore Ian let up.

"You know what. I think I'll have a looksee through your things and see what else is worth takin'. Let's see." Ian started rifling through Gus's pack. "What a load of junk. Nothing... well, that might be useful. Might get a few copper bits for that. What else. See, this is what you get when you mess with *the* Ian MacBrody."

I'm gonna die here, thought Gus. He was hanging by the ropes that bound him and had little strength left. *I have to break free,* he decided. With what little effort he could manage he twisted his arms against his bonds, but to no avail. *If only Snowball were here. I just need him to cut me loose. Then I can make my escape... Wait a minute...*

"Stop!" Gus cried feebly at Ian. "Don't take my stuff. Please. I beg of you."

Ian laughed and doubled his efforts as he ransacked Gus's pack.

"Tell you what. Take it! Take all of it. Just don't take the strawberries! Please, whatever you do, don't take the strawberries!"

"Shut up! I'll take what I want. And when I find those strawberries, I'm gonna stomp them in the mud and take a jolly ol' tinkle on 'em and then feed 'em to ya! How do you like that?" Ian yelled at Gus.

"WRAAAAHHHHHH!" The tremendous war-cry of an enraged Minotaur split through the trees like thunder as Snowball charged into the camp site swinging his hammer left and right. "Leave strawberries alone!"

One swing from the creature's mighty hammer knocked a tent over onto a bandit on the other side who fumbled blindly in the massive cloth and fell to the ground. The next swing of the hammer struck the underside of another bandit's jaw, sending him a good ten feet above the ground before he crashed back down to earth.

"Attack!" Ian shouted frantically at the other bandits. "Monster! Get your weapons!" Ian quickly drew his sword and readied himself.

Another bandit crumpled to the ground from the Minotaur's onslaught before Snowball paused briefly to take aim and swing his hammer like a croquet mallet. The blow struck a charging bandit right in the center of his torso. The bandit flew screaming into the woods a good twenty feet before he was lost from sight.

Suddenly, a whistling bolt sank into Snowball's left shoulder. The Minotaur roared and turned to the man who had fired it who was frantically trying to reload his crossbow. Ignoring the wound, Snowball picked up a large stone from the fire pit and threw it with deafening speed into the skull of the shooter with a *Crack!* The crossbow flew up into the air as the assailant tumbled backward.

Ian seized the opportunity whilst the Minotaur was focused on the crossbowman and slashed at the monster's back with his cutlass. "Gotcha!" He shouted victoriously.

However, the sword didn't cut as deeply as he had intended. Snowball's bovine heritage provided him with an incredibly thick hide, which gave him an uncanny defense against most weaponry. He wasn't impervious, though. The cut, though shallow, still served to make the Minotaur even angrier.

Without needing to look, Snowball swung his hammer around to strike his opponent. Ian quickly ducked underneath and missed losing his head by a fraction of an inch. He had only a split second to recover before the hammer came crashing down toward his head. He dodged to the side, avoiding the blow, before stepping back to give himself room. Snowball roared and came at Ian with devastating force. Ian parried each attack, but the force of Snowball's fury was so great that, strong as he was, Ian's arm began to fatigue at an alarming rate. Knowing that he was done for if he didn't stop the creature's advance, Ian saw an opportunity as the Minotaur brought up his hammer in a powerful overhead strike. Dodging back briefly, MacBrody put one foot on the great hammer when it hit the ground and stabbed his blade into Snowball's forearm, causing the beast to drop his weapon.

"Come on! Have at ya!" MacBrody challenged. "Wot's the matter, monster? Dropped your weapon?" He sneered.

Frustrated, the Minotaur took a few steps toward a young pine tree. The earth groaned as Snowball grunted and tore the tree right out of the ground. Ian's eyes went wide. The bandit leader started to run, trying to get some distance, but Snowball swung the tree, which was so tall it easily reached Ian and knocked him to the ground. Snowball began flailing the bushy tree on top of Ian over and over again. Ian rolled out of the way after the third blow and pushed himself off the ground.

Snowball swung the tree again and Ian tried to parry it out of reflex. With a *thunk!* His cutlass became lodged in the trunk of the tree. Snowball used the tree to wrench the weapon out of Ian's hand. He then turned and threw the tree off into the woods like an enormous javelin.

Ian took up a boxing stance and, with arrogance, challenged his foe. "Looks like neither of us has a weapon, monster. It's just you and me, man and beast. I'll have you know I've bested more than my fair share of tough brutes. I'm not afraid of you."

While Ian boasted, Snowball flexed his massive muscles, pawed at the ground with his right hoof, lowered his horns, and charged.

"Oh, Gods..." Ian was completely unprepared for the goring horns of the Minotaur and only managed to run a few feet before Snowball snapped his head upward and brought his horns up beneath Ian's back, sending him sprawling forward into a tree. Ian's skull hit the trunk hard and he fell to the ground unconscious.

"Snowball!" Gus cried out, interrupting his companion. "Untie me!"

Snowball found Gus tied to the tree on the edge of camp, not too far from where Ian lay. He left Ian where he lay on the ground and returned to the peasant. Using both hands he snapped the rope in two and undid Gus's bonds.

"Is Mister Gus Man okay?" Snowball inspected Gus's numerous injuries.

In spite of the swelling and his numerous injuries, Gus laughed. "I just got to watch my least favorite person in the entire world and his men get beaten so hard their ancestors will feel it. Aside from the bumps and bruises, I'm doing great." Painfully, Gus limped over to Ian and rifled through his pockets. He found some loose change, a bit of dried beef (which he quickly discarded. It was hard to tell if the Minotaur would be offended) and a hunting knife. The locket was nowhere to be found. Ian groaned and began to stir.

"Quickly, Snowball. Grab him."

Snowball grabbed Ian firmly by the arms against the trunk of the tree. "Give me the locket!" Snowball shouted angrily in MacBrody's face.

"...ugh.." Ian groaned.

"You had best give it back." Gus warned. "If you don't, I'll have my friend here pull your arms out their sockets and slap you around with them."

"I'm not giving you nothing." Ian insisted as he became more coherent.

Snowball began pulling Ian's arms to either side, threatening to rip them off. "Give Gus Man locket now!" Snowball roared.

"No. Oh gods, please. I can't give you the locket." Ian persisted.

Snowball growled and pulled harder. The pain that seared through MacBrody's limbs livened up his tongue.

"No. Please don't hurt me. I don't have the locket. I don't have it! Don't rip me arms off! I don't have the locket. Please, I beg you."

"What do you mean you don't have it?" Gus asked.

"I s-sold it." Ian stuttered.

"To who?"

"I don't know."

Snowball growled, giving Ian's arms a tug.

"I don't know. I don't know! You gotta believe me. It was a traveling merchant heading out of Jagodwine. I didn't ask for his name. Please, just let me go." Ian whimpered.

"What do you think, Snowball? Should we let him go?"

"Snowball?" Ian wondered, hearing the creature's name.

"Eeyan BackBrokey would ruin strawberries if Snowball lets him go. Tear his arms off now?"

"Oh, gods." Ian sniveled.

"No, Snowball. Let him go." Gus said with an air of mercy.

Ian sighed in relief hearing that.

"We'll give him a ten second head start, then you can rip his arms off." Gus smiled.

Ian's relief turned to panic.

Snowball released his fierce grip on Ian's arms. Ian turned and ran for all he was worth, snot and tears streaming down his face. A moment passed by before Gus turned to Snowball. "Aren't you going to chase him?"

Snowball shrugged.

"It's been ten seconds." Gus pointed out.

"What's a secuns?"

Gus slapped his forehead. "Never mind. Forget it."

Gus took a sack and collected all the valuables the bandits had on them, which wasn't much, before he started limping back toward Jagodwine. He looked back when he reached the edge of town and noticed that Snowball hadn't followed him. "Oh well." Gus said aloud to himself.

When he walked into Lagle's Tavern, the silence was palpable. The creaking floor boards seemed all too loud as Gus strode up to the bar. The patrons gave him wary glances as they had all heard what had happened to the captain of the guard and how Angus Finnegan had a monstrous cohort doing his bidding.

"I'd like a room please." Gus set a silver piece on the counter.

"I'm sorry, hon." She said quietly. "If I let you stay here it'll upset the other guests. Bad for business."

Gus slapped a second silver piece on the counter. "Give me a room." He said with a little force. "I've had a very rough day and all I'm asking for is a place to put my feet up for the night."

"If Ian shows up to hassle you it'll cause a might of trouble, sugar. Sorry, but-."

Gus rummaged around in the bag he was carrying and slapped Ian's sword on the counter. "Ian won't be troubling you or anyone else anymore. I sent the Minotaur after him and that's the last I saw of him. Give me a room. Please." Gus insisted.

The innkeeper nodded in agreement and took one of the silvers. Gus took back the remaining coin and the sword as Miss Lagle went to fetch a room key.

"Upstairs, third door on the left. There's a wash basin in the closet and you can get water from the well outside. Have a good stay, honey." Miss Lagle nodded in apology. Gus ordered a meal before he went upstairs to get some sleep.

Gus locked the door to his room behind him and collapsed on the bed. The day's aches and injuries slowly seeped out of him. He had gone through all of that trouble and now his precious locket was gone and with it the memories he had of his childhood love. He clutched at his chest in the place the locket used to be as heartache took him and his tears lulled him to sleep.

Chapter IV

Gus awoke to the buzz of angry shouts and people making a ruckus on the streets. Covered in aches and with a groan, he got out of bed and armed himself with a dagger he had taken from one of the bandits. "Oh, what now?" He complained. "Can't a guy ever get a decent night's rest around here?" He headed downstairs with his things and out the front door to see what all the commotion was about.

A size-able crowd had gathered near the market square around a painted, covered wagon. The glare from the sun prevented him from seeing anything through the crowd, but he could make out shouts from the peasantry.

"Let him go!" Came one.

"You had better explain yourself!" Came another.

"The brute won't let go of my leg!" Cried a third.

Gus pushed his way through the crowd, dagger in hand. He feared the worst. Perhaps Ian had returned to get revenge on the village. When he breached the crowd and stumbled out into the clearing, he was dumbstruck. A very distressed, well-dressed man, balding and in his late fifties, was laying on the ground, his leg up in the air and held by the great Minotaur.

"Snowball!" He exclaimed. "What's going on here?

"I'll tell you what's going on." The man cried. "This monster was trying to rob me, and when I didn't comply with his demands, he grabbed my wagon and dragged me here against my will! And now, he won't let me go!"

Snowball shrugged. "Mister Merchant Man is very noisy."

"Snowball, what are you doing?" Gus sheathed his dagger.

"Mister Merchant Man has the locket Eeyan BackBrokey took. Snowball tried to take it back, but Mister Merchant Man would not give it to Snowball. He said I need money, and Snowball said 'what is money' and he said that if

Snowball didn't have money, Snowball couldn't have the locket. So, I brought him to Mister Gus Man."

"Do you really have the locket?" Hope struck Gus like ten thousand beams of sunshine.

"Yes, I have *a* locket. A woodsman sold it to me for a gold piece." The merchant reached into his robes and pulled out the locket.

Gus dug through his loot from the bandits. "By woodsman I take it you mean bandit."

The merchant averted his gaze and scowled.

"Will this cover it?" He offered the merchant a handful of copper and silver coins. "And extra for your troubles." Gus added another silver coin to his hand.

"Yes. That will suffice. Now will you please have him let go of me?"

"Snowball, you can let go of him."

Snowball released his grip. The merchant stood up, dusted himself off, climbed into his wagon and slammed the door shut.

"Why did you bring his wagon?" Gus wondered aloud.

"Snowball did not want to ruin Mister Merchant Man's business, so I brought it with him."

"What happened to the horse that drew it?"

Snowball shrugged. "A tiny hooman took it to the stable."

The merchant soon reappeared and with disgust put the locket in the peasant's hands before disappearing into his wagon once more. Gus nodded and smiled as he clutched the silver locket in his hand.

The crowd parted as Gus began walking toward the outskirts of town with Snowball following close behind.

"How did you find it? My locket, I mean." Gus asked as he walked side by side with the monster.

"Mister Gus Man smelled slightly of strawberries before we got to town. When Mister Gus Man found Snowball with Angry Shouty Man who was tired, Mister Gus Man did not smell like Strawberries."

"I don't understand." Gus puzzled as he tried to work out what Snowball was saying.

"Smell the locket." Snowball shrugged.

Gus put the locket to his nose and took a whiff. He smelled the dust of time, and the silver metal. Confused, he started to put it away, but stopped himself. He opened the locket and smelled it again. Beyond all odds, he noticed the smallest hint of strawberries from the lock of hair Fiona had left him inside the locket.

He was dumbstruck. "That's incredible! You followed that faint a smell?!"

Snowball nodded.

"Why would you do that?"

"That is what friends is for." The Minotaur smiled with his big bovine teeth.

"I don't have any buckets of strawberries to give you." Gus confessed.

"That is okay. Mister Gus Man is friend."

The two walked in silence for a while as they headed out of town.

"There's another village to the north. They may have some strawberries." Gus suggested. "We could try there. What do you say?"

Snowball nodded eagerly.

"I hear there's an inn that bards frequently visit. Maybe they'll be able to tell us where to find some." Gus added.

The pair traveled off into the morning sunrise. Unaware of the great many adventures that lay before them. Who could say where they were heading or if good fortune was in store? Either way the strawberries would be plentiful.

PART II
The Work Out

Chapter V

On any journey it is wise to plan your adventure. Not that every minute need be accounted for, but in order to avoid unexpected and disastrous events, it is a good idea to have an idea where you are going, what you are going to do whilst you go there, what you will do once you get there, and anything else that might come up, such as food, places to sleep, etc.

Snowball thought of none of these things. Minotaurs rarely do. He plodded along behind Gus, eagerly awaiting the next patch of strawberries which was sure to be just around the next bend. Or at least Snowball thought so. Gus had led him to so many strawberries after all. He was sure to find more any minute.

"Say, Snowball." Gus began. "I don't suppose you know where we're going?"

Snowball shook his head no.

"Ah. Well. That... that's definitely... exciting..." He was thinking to himself that the next hamlet or village or city could be miles away and he hadn't even thought to bring food. Fortunately, he'd grabbed something to eat before he'd left the frustrating crossroads of Jagodwine, but who knows how long it might be before he could find more food.

"Do not worry Mister Gus Man." Snowball reassured his companion. "There is a river coming up soon. We will be there in a hour." Snowball put extra emphasis on the 'h' in hour.

"I thought you said you didn't know where we were going."

"Yup." Snowball agreed.

"So how do you know there's a river?"

"Snowball can smell it."

Gus was both impressed and perturbed by how good his companion's sense of smell seemed to be. Smelling a river from an hour's walk away? Now that was impressive. He could only imagine the sorts of smells he would experience if he were a Minotaur. "Well, at least we'll be able to get a drink. But if we don't know where we're going, it could be days before we find a place to get some food."

"Do not worry, Mister Gus Man. Snowball knows where to find an apple tree."

"Oh, can you smell that too?" Gus asked over his shoulder at his Minotaur companion.

Snowball simply pointed to an apple tree sitting by itself in a small clearing just off the road.

"Oh." Gus sounded disappointed. He shrugged and considered himself lucky. "We'll just need to pick a few."

"Oooh!" Excitement exploded out of the minotaur. "Let me."

"Uh..." Curious to see why a Minotaur would be so excited to pick apples, Gus agreed to let him.

Snowball happily trotted over to the tree, looked up into the branches at the apples which were only a few inches above his head, took his hammer in both hands and almost effortlessly delivered a resounding blow to the tree trunk which shook nearly every apple to the ground.

Gus slapped his forehead and sighed. If he was going to continue traveling with such a strange friend, he would have to get used to the monster's titanic strength. Gus wondered what would have happened if Snowball had struck the tree with his full strength. He decided that he didn't want to know. The creature was certainly dangerous. As it was, the two munched happily on some apples until they were satisfied.

Hours later, down the path, as he was trying to get a small rock out of his shoe, Gus wondered what would happen if they actually managed to make it to a town of some sort. Snowball's reception in Jagodwine had been disastrous at best. Snowball was a monster. At least, anyone who happened across the creature would be sure to think so. But then again, there weren't too many who would tussle with a Minotaur. In a way, the creature was insurance from bandits and other dangers along the road. After all, Snowball stood over seven and a half feet tall and was made of over seven hundred pounds of brutality. Besides, Gus had only been to two different towns in his whole life. Maybe people were more tolerant in other cities, more open to new (mostly) intelligent creatures.

Gus glanced over at Snowball who was sharpening a horn on the apple tree.

It was hard to say. Gus had always been taught to be accepting of others. He had also been taught to run for his life if he were to ever cross paths with a monster. As of recently, he'd done both, with varying degrees of success. Then again, maybe the Minotaur had some insight he had not considered.

"Snowball, have you ever been to a city?"

Snowball had somehow managed to get his horn stuck in the tree, and was trying to tug it out with his neck. "What's a city?"

"It's a really big place with lots of houses and walls and people."

"Ooohh! That sounds fun! Lots of pummeling."

"Er... Well, not exactly. You wouldn't be allowed to pummel anything."

Snowball frowned sadly.

"Never mind." Explaining things to Snowball was going to be more difficult than Gus had the patience for. Perhaps he'd have to simply go to the city and hope for the best. Maybe an angry mob wouldn't form and try to run Gus and Snowball out of town. *Yeah!* He told himself. Perhaps things would work out just fine. "What do you think, Snowball? Do you think you can be discreet?"

"Argh!" Snowball had gotten fed up with the apple tree, and tore it bodily from the earth before throwing it into a nearby copse of trees. "Stoopid tree. Snowball's horn is Snowball's!" The Minotaur turned to Gus. "Yes. Snowball can excrete?"

Gus frowned as he rethought his plan. "You know. Never mind. Let's just get moving. I'll think of something later."

Try and try as he might, Gus couldn't seem to figure a surefire way to get Snowball anywhere without causing a ruckus. However, he was certain that if he could find a place that would tolerate the creature, he could put the big brute to use doing manual labor somehow. Then he could make some money and start a new life. Snowball and Gus... wait. No. Gus and Snowball. Brains and brawn. What a pair they'd be.

His fantasies continued until the sun began to set and the concern over shelter for the night grew in Gus's mind. He looked around for anywhere they might be able to sleep where they'd be well protected from bandits or the possibility of rain, but alas there was nothing so well suited.

Snowball showed no signs of stopping, so Gus thought he'd pipe up. "Um. Excuse me, but shouldn't we find someplace safe to rest for the night, or build a shelter or something?" His concern was only met with the perplexed expression Snowball wore. He wondered if perhaps he had used too long of a word in his suggestion, like the word "to."

Snowball responded. "Why?"

"What? Why? What do you mean why?" Gus stumbled to find the words. Of course, this only served to confuse his poor companion.

"Wha...who... Snowball does not understand."

"Do you not understand what I just said, or did you not understand why we should find shelter?"

"Yes." The Minotaur nodded in agreement.

A long sigh left Gus's lungs as he thought carefully about his choice of words. "We need to find shelter."

"Why?"

"Well, because there are bandits and monsters and wolves and tax collectors and rain and wind. If we don't find a safe place to rest for the night, we could have a very rough time out here away from civilization."

Snowball stroked his furry chin and considered for a moment. Then he shrugged. "Snowball is pretty sure that tiny bandits would not attack Snowball at night."

The thought had never occurred to Gus. It would be pretty foolish to approach a sleeping monster with ill intent.

"Also, there are no wolves within a long, long way from here. Snowball would smell them."

He also hadn't considered his companion's sense of smell.

"Besides, Mister Gus Man." He held out a hand as if to feel for falling rain. "It is very nice outside and plenty warm. No one will get rained on. That happens later in the season. In winter, perhaps you would be a hooman icicle, but not today. It is nice today."

Gus hadn't even noticed; the temperature had been so nice he'd felt perfectly comfortable even during their long journey. "I suppose you're right. You know, for a Minotaur, you're pretty smart."

"Snowball is not mean-o-tar." Snowball reminded his companion.

"No. No you are not. You aren't mean nor are you made of tar. Alright, then. Let's find a comfortable place and we'll rest for the evening. Goodness only knows how much more traveling we'll to do before we get somewhere."

They made a small camp, mostly consisting of a fire and a soft pile of leaves to sleep on. It wasn't the most comfortable place to rest, but the country air was sweet and relaxing.

As the two lay underneath the stars, crickets began chirping their cricket song, and for the first time in a long time, Gus felt very at peace out in the open countryside, even in spite of his massive, monstrous companion. He lay there dreamily, thinking of Fiona, the woman he had cared for more than anything, and he thought of the beauty of the stars above and the smells of the forest.

Perhaps things would go right. Perhaps he would be able to find work and make a life for himself after all in spite of the destructive habits and unusual stature of his traveling companion. Things just seemed to work themselves out. All day he had been so worried about food and shelter he hadn't even stopped to notice his good fortune until Snowball had pointed it out to him. It truly was a lovely evening.

"You know, Snowball." Gus said lazily as he lay admiring the sparkling stars above. "It's such a nice night, out here. Don't you think so?"

Snowball grunted in approval.

"And don't you just love the sounds of the crickets chirping. It's so relaxing." Gus closed his eyes and listened to the symphony of crickets playing in the night.

"Oh, yes. It is mating time. Mating is good. Healthy crickets make healthy mating call." Snowball happily agreed. "When Snowball wants to mate, Snowball–."

"Thanks. No. Please. No. I don't want to know. Really." Gus interrupted. "I was just thinking it was a nice night is all."

Of course, the thought that the lovely sounds the crickets were making were actually mating calls disturbed Gus and for a while he had a hard time sleeping. Eventually, he grew weary and as he drifted off to sleep, he thought what a fortunate day it had been. The morrow would definitely be a good day if their fortunes held, and it was a comforting thought to Gus.

The following morning Gus had to peel leaves from his face when he awoke. They had stuck rather fast as he drooled in his sleep. He was groggy and his face felt lopsided as he sat up and tried to determine where he was. He'd slept so well he had forgotten the journey he was on and the strange companion he was traveling with. He slowly acclimatized to the morning and got up from his place of rest. The weather was sunny and bright and it looked to be a fairly good day.

After a short stretch and a breakfast comprised of a few apples Gus had saved from the day before, he and Snowball headed onward.

It wasn't long before they happened upon a large stone bridge crossing the river Snowball had mentioned the day before. The bridge was made of large cobbled stones and stood perhaps ten feet above the water. It was wide enough for a full-sized carriage to cross and sloped gently from one side of the river to the other.

He took a moment to replenish his water-skin and sip a cool, refreshing drink. However, he noticed a strange taste and when he turned his head to mention it to his companion, he noticed Snowball upstream bathing in the water. He spat out his drink in a desperate spray and sorely wished he had something to scrape off his tongue with.

"You know, Snowball. Wherever we go, you're going to have to learn at least a few manners if we're going to get along with everyone." Gus chided his companion.

"What is Man nurse?" The Minotaur asked. "Is that like hooman nurse?"

"No. No, it's a way to act in polite society. To make sure that if problems arise, they can be solved without violence."

"Oh, but Mister Gus Man. Violence *always* solves problems." The Minotaur beamed, pleased at his one-size-fits-all solution.

"No, it doesn't."

"Yes, it does."

"How does violence always solve problems?"

"If Mister Gus Man needs a turnip, he can beat the ground until it gives Mister Gus Man a turnip."

"Alright. And what if I simply need to borrow milk from Mrs. Smithy down the road?"

"You beat her until she gives you the milk."

"And what if she already wants to give me the milk?"

"Then you beat the cow until it is able to make the milk."

"And what if the cow has already made the milk?"

"Then you smash the milk man for not delivering the milk."

"You're impossible, Snowball." Gus sighed as he continued down the road. "We will run into people, though. Definitely." He kicked a rock down the road. "We'll have to deal with people sooner or later if I'm to make any money and start a life for myself."

"And when we do?" Snowball wondered.

"We'll just have to play it by ear."

"Why would Mister Gus Man want to play an ear?"

"Never mind. I was simply saying we'll have to see what happens. It's hard to say how folks will react. Where I'm from, you're a monster and the proper thing to do is run away screaming." Snowball seemed to smile at that. "I'm not really sure what to expect. I'm certain that somewhere there's a place where you won't scare the living daylights out of people. I mean you're fairly harmless."

"And if anyone gets in the way, Snowball will smash them with hammer." Snowball said happily, as once again violence seemed the proper answer.

Gus slapped his forehead and tried to think of some way to make Snowball understand that violence was what made minotaurs scary. He puzzled for a while and decided that teaching through way of example would be best. "Snowball, when things use violence against you, what do you do in response?"

Snowball thought long and hard about it before he determined a good answer. "Snowball beats them with his hammer."

"Right. And so, imagine how other people react when you use violence to solve all of your problems."

Snowball did, for several minutes before he announced "Okay."

"How do they react?"

"With violence!" Snowball said proudly.

"And that's the problem."

"That's okay, Mister Gus Man. Snowball will just beat everyone who uses violence against Snowball."

"Ugh." Gus groaned. "You can't just beat people who don't do what you want."

"Snowball can."

"No, you can't!" Gus raised his voice. "If everyone did things that way there would be no end to violence!"

"Ooooh! Mister Gus Man is right. That would be wonderful!"

"No! That would be horrible! Pretty soon there wouldn't be anyone left." Gus realized it as he said it. "There wouldn't be anyone left to talk to or have fights with. No one to do violence with."

Snowball frowned at the thought of a world without violence.

"There would be nobody to farm strawberries anymore." Gus smirked.

Snowball roared in outrage. "I will smash the violence! For the Strawberries!"

Well at least I have that settled. Thought Gus.

"Does Mister Gus Man think there will be violence if Snowball is not violent in city place with tiny hoomans?"

Gus shook his head and laughed a little. There wasn't much point in planning for Snowball, no matter where they went. He turned to his companion as they traveled onward into the sunny distance. "Let's just play it by ear."

Chapter VI

What separates the bond of true friendship from that of a casual acquaintance is the measure of trust one feels toward another. Trust divides the feeling of predator/prey from two beings and becomes an innate understanding from one person to the other. It is not the product of a single act of kinship, but is developed over time by innumerable acts both sincere and personal. Thus, trust forms true friendship, made of the many ingredients of life, much like a cake.

Gus considered these things in perhaps a less eloquent or profound sense as he lay on the open ground under the starry night sky, his eyes wide open from the sheer vibrations of his companion's cacophonous snoring, wondering why, on this green earth, he had ever thought making the bull-horned monstrosity his traveling companion would be a good idea. The lumbering giant sprawled just a few yards away, draping himself over the ground with no real care.

As Gus's teeth rattled to the tree-splitting, sawmill roar coming from his companion's mouth he thought for a moment that he had made a grave mistake. It was true he was indebted to the great furry creature. The Minotaur had saved his precious locket and delivered the most brutal walloping he had ever witnessed to a band of outlaws. Certainly, if properly directed, Snowball could be a great asset to have along his journey in case of more trouble. The roads in these parts were frequently set upon by bandits. Having him around could come in handy. But this was Gus's journey, after all. He had left his village in search of... of what? He didn't know.

Gus had left home to find his way in the world. To start a new life. He had never really fit in and wanted something more for himself. To accomplish something. To do something with his life. The Minotaur had served its purpose. It had helped him retrieve his precious locket. For that he owed the beast a great debt, surely, but that didn't mean he had to travel the world with such a dangerous creature at his side.

Gus rolled over on his side to glance over at his friend. Snowball was certainly dangerous, but in a gentle way. The monster was almost joyful the way he lived and breathed. Like the innocence of a child locked in a powerfully built frame. As the Minotaur's chest rose and fell it had an almost peaceful quality to it, in spite of the deafening snoring. For a moment the snoring died down and the woodland was quiet and peaceful. This was a companion no more certain of his fate than Gus, lighthearted and free, slumbering peacefully beneath the stars like a gentle giant. For a brief moment, Gus thought almost fondly of the creature.

Snowball rolled over in his sleep and with a grumble brought his hammer crashing down into the earth mere inches from Gus's face.

Gus gulped; his eyes wide.

On the other hand, Snowball was still a monstrous brute with enough strength to pluck a grown tree from the ground. Gus picked up his bedroll and moved over a few yards. It was cold that far away from the fire but at least he was sure his companion's lengthy limbs would not be able to accidentally crush him before morning.

".... Mister Gus Man." The Minotaur began the next morning after their meager supplies had been packed up.

"Please, Snowball, it's just Gus."

"Okay, Mister Just Gus man."

"No... You know what. Never mind. We have a lot of ground ahead of us. Let's just hit the road and get moving."

With a smile, Snowball let out a triumphant roar, and smiling, brought his hammer down on the dirt path with a resounding *whump!* that could be heard from miles away.

Gus jumped and shuddered in surprise. "I didn't mean... not literally!" He sighed.

"Snowball did not hit the road little-ly. That was good hammer smash."

Gus slapped his palm against his forehead. "Literally. It means lit- you know what. Never mind. We have a long day ahead of us. Let's just hit- let's just *walk* down the road here and make good use of the day, shall we?"

"Okay, Mister Gus Man."

Gus started down the path with Snowball for a few moments before Snowball began again.

"Mister Gus Man."

"Yes, Snowball?" Gus said tiredly.

"Where is Mister Gus Man going?"

The question seemed quite simple as the peasant's feet patted along on the rough winding path. The answer, however, was far more complicated. Gus wasn't entirely sure. When he'd first set off from his village, he hadn't time to think much about it. His journey through the kingdom had only lasted about six or seven hours before the Minotaur had surprised him and the fiasco at Jagodwine had swept him up completely. Those first few hours were spent in quiet relaxation walking along the road, thinking only of the freedom of his journey and the end of his life in the small village of Dale.

"I'm going to find some work." He said at last, trying hard to convince the Minotaur as much as himself. "I don't have any money to live on and I will need supplies if I'm going to continue this journey."

"Ooooh!" Snowball's tail wagged vigorously. "A journey. Where is the journey to?"

Again, Gus was stumped. He was leaving home. That much he knew, but he never had a destination in mind. His soul had an aching that spurned him onward but he knew not to where. All he had ever known was the simple life of homesteads and farm hands.

"I don't know." He said, a little disappointed in how the words sounded leaving his mouth. "Maybe I'll find some good honest work and settle down somewhere. Maybe travel to the city and work for king and country."

"Oooh! Where's that?" Snowball's exuberance was growing.

"Snowball, I don't really know. I haven't figured that out yet. I'm a peasant. There's only so many things a man can do with his life. I'm... I am going to find an honest wage and go from there."

"Go from where?"

"I'm going to find some work. That's what I'm going to do."

"Okay, Mister Gus Man," said Snowball with enthusiasm, "we will go find work!"

Gus tripped over a small stone and nearly lost his footing. "We?" He asked, more to himself than to his companion.

Snowball remained silent, sniffing at the side of the road occasionally and staring off into the pines at anything that might catch his attention.

He had never realized just how little he had pondered his situation. The Minotaur had certainly not been figured into his plans. Gus had figured he could find some honest work somewhere but the monster would certainly complicate things. Sure, Snowball was amicable and useful, but would others see him that way? Gus chuckled hysterically to himself. He could try, but chances were he would not be able to find work with that monster close at hand. However, when he turned over his shoulder to look at the creature, he couldn't help but feel sheepish at the thought of asking Snowball to stop following him. Given the situation, Gus conceded and decided to at least try to find work with Snowball. Maybe things would work out. Who could say?

It was nearly half a day before they drifted past some farmland spreading wide across an open valley. Green grasslands rolled like an emerald lake stretched far between banks of evergreen forest. Nestled neatly by a small brook, a small farmhouse sat peacefully surrounded by tilled fields ready for planting.

His stomach grumbled as Gus thought of the mere half loaf of bread growing stale in his pack. He was in sore need of food and supplies and he knew it. This farmland was the perfect opportunity. There was just one problem.

"Say, Snowball, I was thinking," Gus began, "don't you think it might be better if you waited here before we get too close to the farm?"

Snowball cocked his head to one side. "How can Snowball get work if Snowball is not there to get work?"

Gus felt a little sheepish. "Well, about that. I think that the owner of this farm might get the wrong impression if you were to come along with me, is all."

"Do not worry tiny hooman. Snowball is good at interviews."

"Interviews...?" Gus mumbled, mostly to himself.

"Snowball had an interview once. Snowball showed that Snowball is strong and very good at making work happen."

Something told Gus that his friend didn't quite understand the nature of employment but decided not to say anything about it.

"Snowball will show tiny farm person that he is very strong and can do all of the works. Tiny farm person will be impressed. Mister Gus Man will be glad Snowball is there to impress tiny farm hooman. We will get all of the works."

Snowball's eagerness was too much for Gus to refuse, so he shook his head and the pair walked across the open fields to the little farm. He thought for a moment about asking Snowball to walk on all fours in the hopes that the farmer might think him a bull instead of a monster, but he just couldn't bring himself to do it. He certainly wouldn't like it if someone had asked him to walk on all fours.

As they reached the split rail fence, Gus could hear sounds of exertion and the clank of a pickaxe being driven down into the earth. Across a dusty field near a poorly crafted wooden structure hunched a somewhat portly, balding man in sweat-soaked trousers and a loose-fitting tunic. He was breathing heavily and was absorbed in his work as he picked at the ground, digging a short trench. He noticed Gus out of the corner of his eye but continued on with his work.

"I haven't any food to give you." Said the farmer. "Come back in a few months and I might have a scrap or two," the farmer said in a gravelly voice.

The man hadn't seemed to mind that Snowball was standing behind Gus, which for a moment gave Gus a boost of confidence. "I wasn't looking for a handout, sir," Gus spoke confidently, "but for work here on your farm if you could use another set of hands."

The farmer put a hand on his thigh to support himself and let out a heavy breath. "Oh. Well... that might certainly be possible. I can't pay you much in coin, but I can provide a roof and food if you're willing to do some hard work."

Snowball's tail wagged excitedly as Gus replied. "That is fine with me, good sir. I think I might be up for the work, no matter how hard." Gus looked back at Snowball smugly.

"Well, that's a relief." The farmer said with some exertion as he pushed himself up slowly from his stoop. "Though you certainly don't look like a big lad. You see, I had to put the cows down this winter as they fell to illness and I won't be able to get another few head of 'em until June. Which means I'll have to plow these fields by hand. I could use another back to help get the work done."

"Well, at least this way, you'll have two!"

"What? That sure is a lot of confidence from such a little lad. My eye isn't too good anymore. Let me get a better look at you." The farmer finally turned around to size up Gus only to drop his pickaxe and gape as his eyes followed Snowball's immense bulk all the way to the creature's head.

His mouth hung there dryly and his arms went limp by his sides.

Snowball raised a friendly, four fingered hand and waved. "Hello!"

There was a brief moment of complete silence as the monster registered in the farmer's mind.

"Ahhhhhhhhh!" The farmer screamed, turned, threw his hands wildly into the air and ran for all he was worth.

At first Gus thought the man might run into the house for shelter but instead he ran through the property leaped over the fence and kept going. Gus and Snowball stood there watching the man who, for being out of breath only moments before, seemed to find the stamina to continue running far off across the fields until he was but a speck in the distance.

The two of them stood watching in silence as the farmer fled for several minutes.

"He just keeps going..." Gus mused.

"So, do we have a work now?" asked Snowball.

Letting out a sigh, Gus turned to leave. "No, Snowball, we do not have a work. Come on. Let's just go." His stomach grumbled with hunger.

"Maybe Mister Gus Man can take some food to go." His furry companion suggested.

"What?" He was shocked. "No! We are not stealing his food. Even if I'm starving."

"Why not?" the Minotaur shrugged.

"Because. That's stealing!"

"But Mister Gus Man is hungry. Snowball can hear Mister Gus Man's stomach and it is saying to get more food."

"That's not the issue!" Gus started storming off away from the farm quickly. "Let's go!"

"Then what is the shoe?" Snowball wanted to know.

"Stealing is wrong!"

"Why?"

The question seemed so innocent.

"Because that food belongs to someone else."

"Not if Snowball takes it." Snowball pointed out. "Tiny farm hooman does not need food. He is a fat hooman. Mister Gus Man is so tiny he needs to have more food. If Snowball can take food then Snowball can give it to Mister Gus Man."

"That's enough. We are not having this conversation. Stealing is wrong. You shouldn't take things that belong to other people without permission. That's final. Now let's go. We'll just have to find work somewhere else." He said.

Gus led the way off the farm and back onto the road. He was exhausted but he pushed himself onward anyway. They would have a long way ahead of them before another opportunity would present itself and he was both angry and disappointed that the farmer had fled, taking whatever chance Gus had for a good square meal away with him.

That night the dirt seemed harder beneath his bedroll and the small rocks sharper and more eager to dig into his back as he lay to bed. The trees blocked out most of the stars, leaving Gus a most discontented sort. He had finished half of his remaining loaf of bread and his stomach yowled at him sorely for not providing it a proper meal. The fire was burning low under a cool but gentle breeze which provided no real warmth. Gus curled up in his bedroll and tucked himself inside muttering to himself about everything that seemed to be going wrong with his life. It was not long before he muttered himself to sleep and his troubles found their way into his dreams.

When he awoke it was to the sweet aroma of roasted carrots and radishes over a cheery fire in the glow of the morning sun. Wiping the crust from his eyelids, Gus got himself out of bed clumsily and shuffled over to the iron pot dangling over the fire from a supporting branch. He stared at the food groggily for a few moments. It took nearly a full minute for him to realize what he was staring at. He sniffed and cleared his throat. With little to no expression his eyes went from the stew to his companion who had just walked into the clearing carrying a burlap bag laden with cheese, bread and a variety of vegetables. Snowball quickly tucked the bag behind his back and produced with one hand a leek which he tossed into the boiling pot.

"Oh! Hello, Mister Gus Man! Snowball just found some veggie tables in the woods and picked them so that Mister Gus Man's stomach would stop frightening away small little creatures."

"You picked these?" Gus asked as he folded his hands across his chest.

"Yes!" Snowball nodded vigorously.

"And you brought them here." The peasant noted.

"Yes!"

"In a burlap bag?"

"Yes."

"That we didn't have yesterday."

"Yes..."

"Where did you get the bag, I wonder." Gus gave Snowball a wry glance.

"Snowball made it." The Minotaur grabbed a ladle near the fire and began stirring the pot, avoiding eye contact with his human companion.

"Made it?"

"Last night."

"Uh huh..."

"With... What exactly?"

"Snowball made it out of trees."

"Okay. And I suppose you also found the bread and cheese where you found the carrots and radish?"

Snowball nodded and smiled with his big yellow teeth. "Snowball picked them fresh this morning."

"Snowball, where did you get the cheese and the bread?"

"From the bread tree."

"Snowball..." Gus began crossly

"Snowball found a field of wild cheeses."

"Snowball..."

"They were buried with the radishes."

"You stole them!" Gus shouted angrily. "I specifically told you not to steal!"

"Snowball just wanted Mister Gus Man to not be hungry."

"I don't care about being hungry. You took something that doesn't belong to us. I can't eat this!" Gus cried. "We have to give this all back. Who did you take it from?"

"Tiny farm hooman." Sheepishly, Snowball backed away and tried to hide the bag from Gus.

"You went all the way back to that farm?!" Gus was angry, but even more so surprised. That farm was a half day's walk away. "When did you have time to get all of this?"

"During night time. Mister Gus Man was grumbly and asleep."

"And you ran all the way there?"

With a nod Snowball confirmed "Tiny hooman does not run as fast as Snowball. Or walk as fast. Snowball has to slow down a lot. Tiny hooman has tiny legs."

"Yeaagghhh!" Gus threw up his arms in exasperation. "That is... Of all the... Aaaghh!" He stormed around the small campsite, kicking at rocks and muttering to himself with a vengeance. It took a while before his energy faded and at last, he took a seat on a rock and stared with forlorn longing at the bag of food and the boiling pot. "You even took his pot and his ladle..." He said more to himself than to the Minotaur who had returned to stirring the delicious smelling concoction.

"This is how hoomans make food." Snowball tapped the pot with his huge fingernail. "Mister Gus Man thinks it is good?"

"I am not eating it." Gus eyed the soup hungrily, wiping some drool from the corner of his mouth.

"Food will go bad if Mister Gus Man does not eat it."

The Minotaur had a point. Try as he might, Gus could not help but see the logic in it. He could refuse to eat it but it would be a waste of food and he couldn't do that. He thought about insisting that they take the food back to the farmer, but if they did, they would lose yet another day of travel and have no more food than when they started. Even if they did, the farmer would be even less likely to provide a meal for their troubles. Gus shook his head and tightened his lips.

"Alright. Fine. I will eat the food. But only" he said with a raised voice "if you agree that you will never steal anything again!"

Snowball nodded happily with a dumb expression, pretending to understand.

The soup was nourishing and wonderful as the warm contents of a ladle full washed down Gus's throat. He groaned happily as the flavor hit his tongue. He scarfed down half a loaf of bread and a wedge of cheese before he chastised Snowball again. "You know, I take no pleasure in eating this. Mmmmffff.. Mmmmm." He said as he stuffed another mouthful in his cheeks. "You did a very bad thing. We can't just steal from people. Even if we are hungry."

"Okay, Mister Gus Man. Are you full now?" Snowball asked, his tail swishing from side to side.

"Let me have another piece of that cheese."

When the meal concluded, they set off again. The day was sunny and cheerful and Gus noticed a little more spring in his step than the day before, in spite of the theft gnawing at his conscience. Trudging down the path on an empty stomach had proven awful and he vowed he would do whatever he could not to do so again. He merely needed the work to pay for his supper.

Another day of travel passed by and the forests grew thicker as he moved along with his companion. He didn't speak a word about what Snowball had done and the hours passed by quietly save for the sounds of nature and their footsteps on the hard dirt path. Pebbles and rocks and all manner of forest debris passed underfoot listlessly and soon the sun was reclining below the ridge and night began to fade in to a peaceful blanket of stars.

Up ahead the lights shining from the windows of village houses gave reason for relief from the travelers' arduous trek. Before they were spotted by the village folk, Gus and Snowball made camp off in a small clearing in the trees. Gus did his best to get a fire going with the piece of small piece of flint he still had left and with a grumble and a sigh he cooked more of the stolen food over the fire. While he busied himself with cooking, he decided it was a good time to discuss the situation with Snowball.

"We'll make a fresh start in the morning. How does that sound?" Gus asked while cutting a piece of cheese to munch on.

Snowball nodded with enthusiasm and grunted.

"Good. Well, listen. There is something I think we need to talk about. You see," Gus did his best to assume a diplomatic tone, "we may encounter people in this town who are... less than inclined to provide us with work. Well... More specifically, to provide *you* with work."

"But Snowball is very good at the work! Snowball is much stronger than tiny hoomans." Snowball seemed offended.

"Yes, that is true. However, it is not because you aren't a capable minotaur. That isn't the issue. The problem is that you are a minotaur, and minotaurs are... well..." Gus struggled to find a nice way to phrase it, while Snowball remained quiet and attentive. "People are afraid of you. Well, of minotaurs. People are afraid of you because you are a minotaur and minotaurs are... How do I put this?"

"Dangerously handsome?" Snowball chimed in.

"No! Well... I don't know. Maybe for a minotaur you are but I'm not really qualified to say- that's... no. No, a minotaur is what people might call a monster." Gus swallowed the last word, hoping not to offend his companion.

"What is mon-ster?"

The remark made Gus laugh a little. He hadn't ever considered from a minotaur's standpoint that the word monster didn't mean very much. "A monster is a creature that people are afraid of because a monster can do great harm to people."

"Snowball would not hurt even a tiny mouse." Snowball said proudly.

Even then the great beast noticed a squirrel tiptoe closer to the bag of food near the fire curiously. Gus hadn't seemed to notice. Snowball tried very hard to listen as Gus continued but every chance he got he looked at the squirrel while Gus's eyes were averted.

"I can't say I blame them. I mean, you are a very powerful creature. Look at you. Your arms are as thick as my chest. You could pound a rock into jelly if you wanted to. You're cunning, ruthless, and speaking from a spectator's standpoint you are downright terrifying when you fight. Those bandits you fought didn't stand even so much as a chance against the likes of you. It's no wonder people are afraid. As far as they're concerned, you're a rampaging engine of destruction."

"Thank you." Snowball piped in as he still watched the squirrel.

"Nobody knows anything about you, where you come from, what you eat, what you want. Of course, they're scared of you. That's why that farmer ran away from you when I asked him for a job. That's why we need to be careful about how we approach this village for work. I don't think anyone will understand a minotaur wanting to labor for a living. Are you listening, Snowball?"

The Minotaur smiled and nodded, his attention only briefly on Gus before it darted back to the squirrel.

"They are going to be too afraid to give us a job if you are there tomorrow."

"Do not worry, Mister Gus Man. Snowball has good self-control. Snowball will not hurt anything unless Gus wants him to."

56

Whump!

The Minotaur squashed the squirrel with his hammer in the blink of an eye and then smiled at Gus as if nothing had happened.

Gus looked down at the squashed squirrel in disgust. "See. This is what I am talking about. Oh gods," he began muttering to himself again as he paced up and down, "they're never going to give us a job. If they see you, they'll do what anyone would do. They'll run. Or worse... maybe form a mob with torches and pitchforks and axes and goodness knows what else." He turned his attention to Snowball. "You have to stay out of sight tomorrow. If we're going to travel together then you and I need to be smart about this." He paused as he realized that "being smart" might be beyond the means of his companion. "I'll go in to town and ask around for work. You can stay here until I get back. How does that sound?"

With his brow furrowed, Snowball shook his head. "Snowball does not want to wait here like coward from tiny hoomans. Snowball could snap hooman like twig. Why should Snowball be afraid to ask work in town?"

"I just explained that." Gus sighed. "Were you listening at all?"

"Snowball will go in to town with Mister Gus Man. Mister Gus Man worry too much. Everything will be fine and we will get all of the work. Mister Gus Man will see. Do not worry."

Gus could see that his efforts were in vain. He wanted to believe that everyone could see his companion the way he saw the Minotaur, that they could accept him and treat him like they would treat any traveler, but his gut told him otherwise. Then again Gus didn't really know much about the wide world. This was a new place with new people. Maybe, if he was open about it, approaching in broad daylight and shouting friendly greetings, nobody would mind. Maybe they just needed to see Snowball's potential as a source of powerful physical strength and size. If Gus could convince them he was friendly and harmless they might give the two of them a chance.

"Are you sure, Snowball, even if they might not be very friendly to us?" Gus asked.

Snowball gave his famous, energetic nod and settled down on the ground to munch on a carrot from the bag.

Gus tried as best he could to persuade his friend as he packed up the campsite but Snowball would not budge. He was going to town with Gus and that was that. So, once the fire was out and their supplies packed, they headed into town.

The village was a modest one, quaint with cottages and little farms among a crisscross of little dirt roads that led right up to the pines. Wisps of smoke rose quietly from the chimneys while the sounds of wilderness chirruped happily. Pigs and goats meandered in their pens, grazing on weeds while hens clucked and fluttered in the morning light. It was a near idyllic view as the fresh morning brought with it the prospect of new opportunities.

Several villagers were about, tending their livestock and performing the daily chores as Gus approached, doing his best to keep some spring in his step. Today was a new day, Gus told himself, and he was going to be optimistic in spite of the knowledge that just behind him a terror of mortal men lumbered. The villagers were absorbed in their routine until Gus announced himself as he passed a low wall near the first of the houses.

"Good morning!" Gus said as he waved his hand.

A broad-shouldered man with a robust beard turned his attention from spreading feed in front of a group of hens and said "Good morning!" with a pleasant smile. As soon as he saw the great shadow looming over Gus's shoulder his smile fled his face and his hens clucked and scurried in retreat. The color left his features and he immediately turned and hurried himself into the house, latching the door tight behind him. Down the way an older woman and her husband had heard and seen the cause of the commotion. They too locked themselves away in their home and closed the shutters.

Gus lost the spring in his step and stopped in the middle of the road. The waking village suddenly seemed quite cold and the sounds in the forest slowly died. He looked back at his friend who waved a big arm merrily.

"Hello!" Snowball beamed.

The remaining villagers fled to their homes. Windows and doors were closed, latches were latched and in a matter of seconds the village looked barren and deserted.

Determined not to be defeated so easily, Gus continued through the town with Snowball, hoping to find any sign of hospitality among the simple inhabitants. However, no matter where they strayed, no hope could be found and soon the two of them were on the other side of the village staring down another quiet, lonely road.

"Mister Gus Man has found the work now?" Snowball asked.

Clenching his fists and scrunching his face up to contain himself Gus managed to say "No. Snowball. We did not find any work."

The Minotaur remained quiet as Gus worked through his frustration. Suddenly, the peasant spun around to face him.

"This is what I was talking about, Snowball! We can't go on like this. We're never going to find work with you lurking right behind me. These people are scared of you! Look at what happened."

"But Snowball is not going to hurt tiny hoomans."

"Are you? Because they can't tell!" Gus yelled.

"Snowball promises not to hurt tiny hoomans."

"They don't know that."

"Mister Gus Man knows." Snowball tried to point out.

"Do I? Because I don't know. What can stop you from leveling this entire town? Huh?" The peasant threw his fists up in the air and shook them. "You're a monster. These people can't trust you. To them you are a monster. An absolute terror. You remember when we first met and I ran?"

Snowball nodded.

"That's because that's what people do. They flee from things that terrify them. From things like you."

Snowball understood. He nodded and held up a hand. "Do not worry Mister Gus Man. Snowball promises that no matter what, Snowball will not smash tiny hooman village."

"I wish I could believe that. I really do. But we are almost out of supplies and who knows how far it is to the next town."

"Snowball will do whatever Mister Gus Man wants to make him happy." Snowball affirmed with a noble nod.

With a sigh and a grunt, Gus walked off a few paces to clear his mind. He stopped short of a sign post and gave Snowball a wary look. "If I ask you to wait off in the woods, will you do it?"

"Oh yes, Mister Gus Man!" the Minotaur nodded.

"Even if I leave to go find some work in the village?"

"Yes."

"You won't wander off? You promise?"

"Snowball promises. Mister Gus Man will give Snowball strawberries?" The Minotaur's tail wagged.

"No, Snowball. I can't give you any strawberries. Will you do it even if I don't give you strawberries?"

Snowball thought on it for a moment. "Yes."

"You promise?" Gus asked again skeptically.

"Yes." Snowball seemed sure of himself.

"Alright. I will go into town. I want you to walk down that path until you can't see the village anymore and wait there," Gus pointed into the forest, "until I come for you. Do you understand?"

Snowball nodded.

"Alright then. Off you go." Gus said.

Snowball did as he was bade and when he was well out of sight Gus turned with a heavy sigh and headed back into town. Things had just become more complicated. Now, not only did he need to beseech one of the townsfolk to employ him until he could acquire a reasonable amount of supplies, he would also have to convince them that the Minotaur was gone and that the sight of him traveling with the creature was just a big misunderstanding.

Resigned to the arduous task of acquiring work against such odds, the hapless peasant trudged back. After a while some of the villagers peered out their windows to see if the creature had gone. Gus caught sight of the residents as they did so and did his best to act casual. He strolled down the lane until at last villagers ventured from their homes to continue their day's work. They gave him suspicious glances and warning glares as he walked by. He waved in greeting but his amiable gestures were ignored and he continued on until he was nearly at the opposite end of town once again. He was nearly ready to head back to the center of town to try to force a conversation with one of the farmers when he was stopped by a rough faced man with a gravelly voice and a donkey driven cart who was moving some piles of firewood.

"Stand aside." The man said in an unfriendly tone. "You'd best move out of the way before I run you over." He brushed past Gus and continued on his way, the laden cart rocking and rattling behind him.

He was the first person to say anything to Gus since he'd reached the town and Gus was not about to let the opportunity pass him by. Even if the old man was a bit gruff.

"Excuse me, sir. Do you know where I might find some work hereabout in exchange for some supplies and a good meal?"

The old man paused in the road and gave Gus a brief glance from the corner of his eye. "There's nobody here would hire an outsider. What's your business?"

"Oh. I was just passing through and I've run out of food, you see. I'll do whatever needs done if it will get me a few basic tools and some proper food."

"Heh." The old man laughed. "You'd better ask around then. Maybe find someone who will take on a charity case. Heh!"

"Well, you see sir, I doubt very much that I will be able to. These people don't seem to have taken much liking to me. I'm afraid I might have frightened them-"

Gus was cut short by an outburst of cheerful laughter from the old man. He wiped a tear from the corner of his eye and turned to face Gus directly. "Frightened them? Hah! You? What a bunch of sheep. They've been fearful of anything that breathes since a wolf got Farmer Cornwell's prized goat." The old man paused for a moment and rubbed his chin. "That's just the thing to show these cowards that they're all just being paranoid. I'll tell you what. I'll give you plenty of work to go around for the next two days. In exchange I'll fix you up with some proper supplies to send you on your way."

"You mean that?" Gus said, a hopeful smile creeping up his face.

"It'll be hard work!" The old man said with a mean eye. "You'll be sorry you asked for it."

Gus took his hand and shook it vigorously. "Oh, thank you sir! Thank you!"

Chapter VII

The old man, whom Gus later learned to call by the name of Cole, proved himself right. After ten slaving hours of work, which included hefting cords of firewood, cleaning out the stable, cutting down several trees and reducing them to yet more firewood, pulling the weeds from the garden and chasing the pigs back into their pen, Gus was truly sorry. His arms fell limply by his side as he sat down exhausted on a pile of hay in the stable. Cole brought him a plate with bread and some salted pork and an assortment of vegetables and sat it down nearby without a word. Gus only managed to say "thank you" to him before the old man turned and left. He eyed the plate hungrily but his body was a pile of jelly. It wasn't until he'd sat there for a while that he felt enough energy to lean forward and grab up the plate. Once the first bite of pork reached his taste buds, however, he cleaved to like a ravenous wolf.

It had been a productive day. Of that, Gus had no doubt. He had held up his end of the bargain, and so far, the farmer had been true to his word. He had provided some small amount of sustenance through the day to keep Gus's strength up and agreed to keep him in the stable for the night. It would be a bit chilly, but at least he would have a roof over his head. He had also learned a little more about the town. It was called Sunny Pines (not a very creative name in Gus's opinion). It was a small stop on the way to anywhere else but from what he'd heard from Cole, which wasn't much, it hadn't seen too many travelers in recent years. The kingdom was expanding elsewhere and the village only supplied surplus food to the crown every harvest. He had also learned that Cole disliked the townsfolk. He *really* disliked them. Cole had spent the better part of an hour complaining about how weak and indolent the villagers had become while Gus grunted and sweated as he tried with everything he had to reduce a pine tree to splinters. Cole's words were "they're a bunch of ninnies, if you ask me. Lazy and stupid." Gus had no reason to argue with Cole, but he had a feeling Cole was just a grumpy old man who didn't get along well with anyone.

When he'd finished his meal later that day, his eyes closed and he was out before he could even think of returning his plate to his employer. Slumber came heavily and in the peaceful twinkling of night not a dream visited him.

Gus awoke with the break of day as roosters called and the sounds of wild birds rang out through the quite village. He groaned and opened his eyes as he tried to make some sense of where he was. He was quickly reminded of why he wasn't cut out to be a farmer. Every muscle in his body ached and throbbed. Even sitting up took him a few minutes and hurt terribly. By the time he had managed to stand up and begin a morning stretch, Cole was already at hand telling him to get to work hauling a cart of stone to the south fence to finish a wall Cole had started late the previous fall. Gus groaned and shambled in that direction, muttering to himself about restful mornings and taking a break every once in a while.

The cart was heavy and every step Gus took was a strain. He sorely wished that Snowball was with him to help with the heavy load. In spite of it all he trudged on and after stopping several times to catch his breath he reached the wall. It was a low wall that came up only to his hips but he could see where Cole had intended to run it. Far off to the western corner of the property the other corner of the wall stood near a large Fir. There was a wooden fence spanning between the two and Gus assumed the wall was meant to someday replace the fence. He busied himself unloading the rocks and stacking them nearby for easy access. The more he got moving the better he started to feel and soon the hours were rolling by as Cole brought him mortar to seal up the wall.

It was getting close to noon though the sky above remained the same cold gray when Gus became aware that he was being watched. Two women, one in her thirties and one in her forties, stood together by the road with baskets in their hands, bundled up warmly from the cold and whispering to each other. Their stares made Gus uncomfortable. It was as if they saw some foreign beast picking up rocks instead of a simple peasant. He tried to smile politely at them but their expressions only turned more distrusting. Gus decided to pay them no mind. He was there to work for food and supplies, not make friends with the locals. Although, it did bother him a little. He didn't like the idea of townsfolk whispering about him. Soon the women left and he was alone once more with his work.

After a few more hours he heard approaching footsteps and looked up to see two men coming straight toward him from the road. One was older, heavy with whiskers and weight but balding on top, the other a thinner man with a simple mustache and cap. Gus could sense their aggression long before they said a word. They stopped above him, just on the other side of the wall, one with his arms crossed in front of his chest, the other with one hand in his pocket and the other on a thick walking stick. They eyed him intently and waited for him to notice.

Gus pretended to be absorbed in his work in the hopes that they would simply leave him alone, but it didn't last long. Eventually he would have to get more rocks or mortar and he'd have no choice but to look up and then he would have no excuse not to engage them in conversation. Resignedly, Gus smiled meekly and said "Hello. Can I help you gentlemen?"

The heavier one shifted his weight and stamped his cane down in the grass. "What are you doing here?" He asked gruffly.

Gus looked at his wall and then back to the man. "I am helping Cole finish his wall."

"We can see that." The thinner fellow nodded. "What are you doing in our town?"

Gus looked over his shoulder toward the rest of town. "Well... I uh... I was just passing through is all. I don't mean to stay for much longer."

"See to it that you don't. You're not welcome here." The heavier man said.

"Of course." Gus agreed. "I'm sure that won't be a problem."

"Haven't you anything better to do with your time than harass my worker?" Said Cole over the field as he came strolling down in their direction.

Both men stiffened and glared but remained quiet.

"He's just a man looking for an honest day's work. That's more than I can say for the two of you." Cole said with a smirk. "Shouldn't you two be tending to your pigs?"

"He's bad news, Cole." The heavy one said. "He was seen yesterday traveling with that monster. He is in league with that fiendish beast!"

Cole rolled his eyes and snorted. "Oh, please. Not more of this nonsense. You folks with your superstitious paranoia. You'd be suspicious of a cow if it came from out of town. Just take a look at him. Does he seem like a threat to you?" Cole gestured toward Gus who smiled uncomfortably at the men. "Do you really think a guy this small would be in league with some monster? Honestly."

The men shifted uneasily and the skinny one said "He was seen walking through town with a beast the size of a house with fur and horns. He cannot be trusted!"

"With fur and horns, huh? The size of a house? I didn't see anything so large yesterday. Are you sure you didn't just imagine it? You bunch of ninnies. You probably saw a steer. Did you see anything the size of a house?" Cole turned to ask Gus.

"Um. No. Nothing the size of a house." Gus replied quietly. After all, Snowball was large, but certainly not that large.

"There. You see."

"You weren't there." The heavy one insisted. "You didn't see it. It was massive and it was walking right along behind him." He pointed sharply at Gus.

Gus was starting to get a little nervous. He had been walking through town with Snowball close at his heels. He couldn't just explain it away. However, it was clear that Cole was willing to stand up for him for some reason, so he chimed in. "I was running!" He blurted out.

"What? No, you weren't!" The skinny one shouted.

"Yes. I was. I was just as afraid of that monster as you!" Gus lied. "That's why I ran to the other side of town and into the woods, so that none of you would be put in danger. I lost it in the woods after that and doubled back. It's long gone by now."

"I saw you. You were walking." The skinny one insisted.

"Maybe he was." The heavy one began to doubt. "We were quite a way out near the tree line. Maybe he was running."

The skinny one started second guessing himself. "But... but he wasn't moving very fast."

"How could he?" The heavy one asked. "Look at how short he is. Those small legs wouldn't be good for running."

"Gee, thanks..." Gus muttered to himself.

The skinny one paused for a few moments, trying to remember what he saw. "But why didn't the monster catch up with him then?"

"Maybe it was just slow."

"Or maybe," Cole interrupted, "you were just imagining things like you always are. I swear, you're all a bunch of frightened sheep. Now get out of here and leave him alone so he can finish building my wall!"

The two men grumbled to one another but turned and left and Gus returned to placing stones on the wall.

The old man spoke up after a few moments. "Is what they said true?"

Gus turned toward him. "Sir?"

"You came through town yesterday with some kind of creature?"

Gus cleared his head and swallowed. "It's just like they said. I was running from some kind of horned creature covered in fur. I led it through the town and out into the woods where I escaped. I'm just not a particularly fast runner." He looked down at his legs as he knelt in the dirt "See. Short legs." He lied with a half-hearted laugh.

"And this creature was after you?"

"Yes. But he wasn't as big as a house."

"Why was it after you. Do you think it was trying to eat you?"

Gus shrugged. "I think it was after some strawberries I had in my pack."

Cole let out a hearty laugh. "Now I know *that's* not true. You've sure got a sense of humor, lad. And you're sure it won't be coming back?"

Snowball was probably still waiting in the forest where Gus had left him. "Yes. I'm sure. He won't be bothering your village any time soon."

"That's good. Now see to it that you get this part of the wall finished before supper time and I'll have your supplies and a good meal ready for you, understand?"

Gus nodded and watched as Cole headed back to the house. When the farmer was out of sight, he breathed a sigh of relief and continued working on the wall. His thoughts strayed toward Snowball, left standing in the woods. He felt guilty about lying to the farmers but he desperately needed supplies. He told himself that it was necessary and that Snowball would be fine. He laughed a little to himself about the Minotaur. Snowball had likely not stayed where Gus had told him to. He'd probably gone wandering off to find strawberries or something or other. It was possible that Snowball might stray back to the village, but Gus hoped not. At least not until he'd received the supplies he needed. He thought about what he would do once he'd received his payment for the work he'd done. He and Snowball would continue on to the next village in search of... he didn't know. Work would be scarce. Very few people would be likely to employ him with Snowball at his heel. He got the feeling that would never change. If that were the case, what prospects could possibly be in his future? Unless, of course, he and the Minotaur parted ways...

Chapter VIII

The idea seemed so foreign as Gus considered what would happen if he left the creature for good.

When he'd left his home town he had intended to find his fortune by himself. He had never counted on meeting Snowball or anyone else for that matter. He wondered what would stop him from continuing on his own? He could leave Snowball in the woods and travel north instead. Gus would be free to do as he pleased and find work somewhere without worry. The Minotaur did provide some sense of security, however. Not too many wild creatures or bandits would be foolish enough to attack him on the road so long as his furry companion was around. On the other hand, Snowball's presence was a double-edged sword. He could travel from place to place without worry, but arriving anywhere with human inhabitants while Snowball was in tow was dubious at best.

Gus continued mulling over his dilemma as he continued stacking stones. On the one hand, Snowball was not the mean-spirited monster that any human might expect. On the other hand, only Gus really knew that. Perhaps other people might learn to see Snowball as he was someday but that seemed like a long shot. The smart thing to do would be to wash his hands of the creature and move on with his life to spare himself any more trouble the creature might bring him. Yet, Gus felt guilty for thinking it somehow. *Snowball was a menace*, he told himself. Well... perhaps a harmless menace. A menace to strawberry pies and anyone who gets in between one and the Minotaur, maybe.

Gus scratched at his head. He wasn't getting any closer to solving his problem and he was tired from all of the work Cole had tasked him with. He sorely wished Snowball were there to help him. The task would certainly go a lot faster with an extra pair of hands.

It took hours upon hours to build the wall as far as he could. The task would not be completed in a day, however and Gus figured that Cole knew that. When the old farmer came striding across the field, Gus let out a sigh of relief and set down his tools.

"You've done quite a job." Cole said.

Gus looked at his work and disagreed but who was he to argue.

"Come inside for supper. I think our agreement has been reached. I've prepared some goods for you on your journey that will come in handy."

"Thank you, sir." Gus said gratefully.

"Now pick up those stones and get those tools into the shed." Cole barked roughly.

Gus did as he was told and followed Cole into the house.

The meal wasn't fancy but it was filling. Mostly vegetables with a hefty loaf of bread. Cole had butchered a sheep for the occasion as well and Gus thanked him heartily.

"Ah, it's nothing. I'm just glad you gave me a chance to put those ninnies in their place today. I can't stand these folks and their whining and fearfulness. It's enough to put a man right out of mind. Think of this as a way of my saying thanks."

Gus nodded happily and dug into his food and the meal passed quickly. Cole turned him out on his own after providing him with a rucksack stuffed with supplies.

"There's enough in there to keep you warm and dry on your journey and some dried food to keep your energy up."

"Thank you, sir."

"And don't you come back this way again, you hear?" Gus laughed at the old man's compulsory grumpiness and waved goodbye as he set out on the road. He planned to head out of town and as far down the road as he could before sundown.

Instead of returning to the forest, however, Gus reluctantly decided to take the north road out of town. It pained him to do so, but he told himself it would be for the best. If he couldn't rid himself of the creature now it would only get harder in the future. So, he went down the road, step by step. His decision weighed heavily on his mind as he went, but with each step his burden seemed to lighten and fade away. *Such is the way of heavy troubles*, he thought.

As the sun finally sank and all that was left of the light was the pale sky above, Gus reached a fork in the road. There was a signpost pointing in each direction. To the east it read "Province of Kismet" which Gus thought was a particularly strange name. That was the same direction he had sent Snowball the day before. The other sign pointed north and read simply "Respite". He let out a groan of displeasure and plopped down on the ground right there in front of the signpost.

"You're just trying to make me feel guilty, aren't you?" He asked to no one in particular. "I mean, really? Respite? You've got to be kidding me!" He grumbled a few syllables to himself. "Well it won't work. I'm not going to change my mind. I've washed my hands of this mess and I'm done with it. He's a big minotaur. He'll be fine on his own," Gus told himself. Even as the words left his mouth, he knew they weren't true. He shook a fist up at the sky. "It's not fair, is what it is. I'm not going to suffer through this anymore!" He shouted up at the powers that be. "I did my part and tried my best and it's finished. I can't keep going like this. With him. He's a monster and I'm... well I'm just a peasant. I'm little more than an afternoon snack to creatures like him." He said feeling particularly satisfied with himself. "So, you see, there's no use feeling guilty about it. What's done is done. I've already gone north. In fact," Gus scrambled up off the ground and took several heavy steps down the path toward Respite, "I'm already heading down the path. See!" He said, looking toward the sky. He looked back at the signpost and realized he'd accidentally left his rucksack on the ground.

"Oh, for the love of..." He muttered angrily as he trudged back to his pack. Just before he reached to pick it up his foot slipped on a wet patch of ground and he fell over on top of it, knocking the air out of his lungs.

"That's it!" He cried after he'd caught his breath. "I've had it. No more delays. I'm heading north and that's that!"

He stood up and struck his head on the sign and began cursing to himself in pain. Between the signpost striking his noggin and his fall to the ground, the locket tucked beneath his shirt had managed to work its way free and just as he turned and tried to stand once again it snagged on the signpost and snapped from off his neck. Gus winced and rubbed where the chain had dug into his skin and turned to look for the locket.

He was surprised to see that it had snagged on a large splinter on the sign pointing east and dangled there in the fading light.

Gus stepped back and stared at it. He wasn't a particularly superstitious fellow most of the time but with the weight of his guilt and the unlikelihood of his leaving his pack behind, hitting his head on the sign and the locket being stuck to the sign pointing back to his companion was just enough to give him doubt. He snatched the locket from the sign and held it in his hand.

He had met Snowball by a stroke of bad luck. Or good luck... he wasn't sure. The Minotaur had chased him through the woods and scared him half to death all because his pack smelled of strawberries. Gus had fallen into quicksand and nearly drowned but Snowball had saved his life in order to eat the strawberries. Then Gus had gone into town and had his locket stolen from him by his childhood enemy which might have happened had he met Snowball or not. He'd tricked the Minotaur into helping him retrieve it. If he hadn't met Snowball, he certainly wouldn't have gotten his locket back. That was the simple fact. Beyond that, there was little reason to travel with the creature other than he was handy to have around. Nevertheless, Gus did anyway. They were friends. At least, that's what Gus felt in his gut. Somehow, he'd befriended the beast and they were companions.

"Stupid..." He muttered at himself. He clasped the locket back around his neck and snatched up his rucksack. He didn't waste any time rummaging around inside before he found a small lantern and the means to light it. With it lit, he summoned up his courage and marched east down the road.

The road east could not have seemed longer in the dark. Every bend he took, every bump and rock he stumbled over seemed only to lead to more and more shadow covered road. To him it seemed an eternity before he would reach his destination. When he finally found the road he'd set Snowball down he could hardly see save for the light from his lantern. He tried hard to remember what he'd told the Minotaur. He'd asked him to keep walking until he was a long way away, he knew that much.

"What was it again? How did I put it?" He mumbled to himself.

He turned in place, looking down the path in both directions. He certainly didn't see his friend. He chuckled to himself. He'd done such a good job of getting rid of the Minotaur that he'd made it even harder on himself to find the poor beast again.

Suddenly, he returned. "That's right." He said. "I told him to walk down this road until he couldn't see the village anymore. Hooh boy... This is going to take a while." He suspected the Minotaur's vision was more acute than that of a normal human but it was just a hunch. He sighed and resigned himself to walking down the path away from the village. He could make out a few lights in some of the dwellings in between some of the trees, but they were small and faint. In the dark his task would be impossible.

With a stroke of insight, he decided instead to look for the Minotaur's tracks. Snowball was a big creature and standing on his hind legs would be sure to leave footprints in the dirt. Gus pointed his lantern at the ground and began searching. To his relief, the tracks were easy to find. The dirt had been packed hard by foot traffic more than anything else, but fresh hoofprints were cut into the hard soil from Snowball's immense weight.

Gus followed the tracks as they meandered down the way. They were spread wider apart than Gus expected due to the length of the Minotaur's gait, and occasionally Gus would lose the trail as Snowball stepped off the path slightly; most likely looking at a butterfly or grabbing a branch to itch himself with, Gus mused. Gus continued tracking until the path took a bend around an outcrop of rock about ten minutes walking distance from where he'd started. The footprints came to an abrupt end. Gus checked down the path a little way but found nothing. He went back to the outcropping a little puzzled. Surely the village was not that far away.

Then Gus realized exactly why the tracks had stopped. Snowball had followed his instructions to the letter. He had gone until he could no longer see the village. The outcropping was just big enough to obscure the village from sight where he stood. Gus laughed a little but nodded in appreciation of Snowball's precision. In spite of everything, Snowball had done exactly what Gus had asked.

The question was, if Snowball had stopped there, where was he?

He had trusted Snowball to stay put but deep down he knew that Snowball would be hard pressed to follow such an order. The Minotaur was naive and childlike, in a way. His attention span was far too short to wait in one spot for a day. Perhaps he had wandered off to keep himself occupied while he waited.

Gus called out to his friend. "Snowball! Snowball, are you there?"

The wood responded only with the chirrups of crickets.

He called out several more times with no success. Wherever Snowball was he wasn't within earshot. Gus wondered if Snowball had realized he'd been abandoned. He felt a pang in his gut. Snowball had been abandoned. In his heart he knew it was true and what was worse, it might already be too late. If Snowball had wandered off Gus might never see him again. While in a way it might bring him relief knowing that his trouble with Snowball was over, it gave him an overwhelming sense of guilt.

"Snowball, I'm sorry!" Gus cried out to the night. "I'm sorry! Come back!"

The dark wood offered no response and Gus was left with his guilt along that lonely road.

After a while, the hapless peasant decided to head back toward town. It was too dark to set up camp in the forest and he would be less likely to encounter any predators the closer he was to civilization. There was a good spot for a tent in the clearing just at the edge of the tree line near the village. He would pitch his tent in the light from his lantern and look for Snowball in the morning. He wanted to keep searching but, without the daylight to see, his new plan would have to do.

He walked briskly down the path, eager to get his tent up to ward off the cold as soon as he could. He passed the fork where the path turned north and continued on for some time. He knew he was getting close to the village but the lights from the town had already been put out, making it difficult to tell.

He stopped for a moment to catch his breath and take a sip from the water skin that he'd found at the bottom of his rucksack. As he drank, he heard faint voices off in the distance. They were too far away to make sense of the words but they sounded agitated. It seemed too late in the evening for any of the townsfolk to be out and about so Gus headed in that direction to see what was going on.

Up ahead he saw points of light flittering in the forest and ominous silhouettes shifting about. He moved in closer until he could make out the shapes of the villagers. They were standing en masse near a cluster of trees with angered faces and all manner of implements. Some held torches, some pitchforks and other farming tools. They listened anxiously as the heavy man from that morning shouted angrily.

"It doesn't matter if it's gone or not! That monster is nearby. Can't you feel it? It might come back to our village at any moment!"

Several of the villagers agreed loudly.

"We have to hunt it down before it hunts us down. That's the only way we're going to survive. We can't live in fear waiting for this creature to invade our homes and snatch us from our beds at night!"

"Yeah!" Cried the villagers.

"It will burn our village to the ground!" Said one villager.

"It'll eat our children!" Another said.

"If we don't do something it will skin us alive and use our hides for bed sheets!"

A gasp of terror rose from the crowd.

"It's either us or that monster, and I for one choose us!" The heavy man shouted.

They cried out again in agreement.

"Or are there some of you who don't have the stones to do what it takes to keep our homes safe?" He looked around the crowd for any dissenters. Satisfied with the silence that followed he shouted his commands. "Alright! We need to form a line and start marching. The last we saw it was this way. We need to spread out and start marching. The first one to spot it give a holler. Keep your wits about you. This thing is dangerous. We need to work together if we're going to kill this beast! Who is with me?"

"Aye!" They all shouted together. With their last cry they started marching down the path straight toward Gus.

Without hesitation, Gus made the best decision a man can make in such a crisis. He turned and ran.

Think, Gus, think! You have to think of something! The peasant thought feverishly, terrified that they should find his friend. Or worse, find him and string him up. He stumbled and crashed into the brush in his flight and nearly collided with a tree in the dark before he regained his footing and managed to find his way back to the path. Looking for Snowball in the woods in the dark was going to be impossible, especially with an angry mob marching behind him. He had to come up with some way to track his friend without getting caught in the process. *Come on, Gus, think!* Why did he have to leave Snowball behind? Things would have been so much simpler if he had never abandoned his friend.

If only he had a handful of strawberries. The smell would be sure to attract the great creature, though it may take some time. Of course, that was *if* Snowball wanted to find him. Gus doubted Snowball would be able to resist a strawberry though, even if the creature's feelings had been hurt. He had his locket, but the hair only smelled faintly of the red delicacy and that would take even longer for Snowball to track. No, Gus had to come up with something else. Something that wouldn't give away his position to the mob.

By the time he reached the spot where Snowball's tracks stopped, he was no closer to coming up with a solution. He had gained a good start ahead of the mob and it would be a little while before they reached him at the rate they were moving. He stopped to catch his breath and leaned with his rucksack against the outcropping.

"Come on, Gus. You can do this. You just need to think. Where did Snowball go? Or better yet, if you were Snowball, where would you go?" His mind perked up and began working fast. Gus knew Snowball was easily distracted and often very observant of his natural surroundings. Gus had followed his instruction to go until he was out of sight of the village to the letter. He'd also told Snowball to wait there until he returned. Perhaps Snowball had noticed something and gone off to investigate. He raised his lantern to look around but nothing leaped out at him as something the creature would find distracting. Then again, Snowball's other senses were more heightened. Maybe Snowball had heard or smelled something.

Gus took a deep breath and closed his eyes, allowing himself to listen closely and inhale deeply through his nose. To him it just smelled like a forest. As he focused his attention, he could hear the sounds of the nocturnal forest but nothing seemed out of the ordinary. Far away he heard an owl's call and the sounds of crickets but that was all.

Then, ever so faintly, Gus heard a snapping sound. It was far away. At first, he thought it was the sound of the approaching mob, but the direction was wrong. It was coming from further into the woods, off the beaten path. Without anything else to go on and the mob coming his way, Gus decided to follow his gut and head for the source of the sound.

He stumbled through the brush as fast as he could, keeping his ears open for any indication of his furry friend. He pushed through the foliage as fast as he could ignoring the scratches from passing branches, snagging hem and strap and lantern on just about everything one could snag upon until at last he heard a heavy crash off to his right which made him jump. He ducked under a low hanging pine and sped out into a small clearing amid a copse of trees.

"Snowball!" Gus exclaimed.

The Minotaur turned toward his friend. "Hello, Mister Gus Man."

Gus noted the splintered tree that lay nearby on the ground. "Where were you? I thought you would be waiting near the path."

"Oh. Snowball was here!" He replied, pointing at where he stood on the ground.

"Yes... I can see that... What are you doing here?"

Snowball pointed at a nearby tree with a frustrated grunt.

Beyond perhaps the comprehension of the reader, Snowball had, in fact, remained at his spot on the path behind the rocks for an incredible amount of time. He'd stayed there the night before and that entire day right up until about five minutes before Gus had followed his tracks to that very spot. During his waiting he had busied himself by scratching himself with tree branches, picking at his teeth with a twig or two, smelling the air for anything interesting, and occasionally thinking. Yes, that's right. Thinking. Of course, Snowball's thought process is to most people as pouring a jug of molasses is to a steady flow of water. At one point during his attempt at contemplation, Snowball was stumbled upon by a wandering merchant pulling a cart of gourdes. When Snowball had waved a hand and said "Hello tiny hooman," the merchant had yelped in a terrified sort of fashion, dropped his goods, run down the path about thirty feet, turned around while still screaming, returned to his cart and dashed off with it like a bat out of hell. Snowball had found it curious but had made no motion toward the merchant and watched happily as the man scurried off down the road. These sundry activities were enough to keep Snowball occupied for quite some time. Right up until just before Gus had arrived, of course.

Snowball had, by then, busied himself by staring up at the stars in the sky, attempting to count them all with a single four-fingered hand. He didn't get very far as both his number of fingers and ability to count were severely limited. His thoughts strayed toward Gus, whom he was sure was going to show up any minute, just as he'd believed for the last twenty-four hours. While he was deep in thought a sound brought him out of his primitive cognition.

An owl had called out from someplace nearby. "Hoo."

"Oh. Mister Gus Man." Snowball replied, thinking that perhaps he had started thinking aloud and been overheard. "Do not worry. Mister Gus Man will be back soon."

"Hoo." Called the owl again.

"Mister Gus Man." Snowball repeated. He didn't hear a reply right away so he went back to counting stars.

"Hoo." Came the owl again.

"Mister Gus Man. Snowball already told you!"

"Hoo."

"Mister Gus Man!" Snowball said angrily. "Do not ask again anymore."

"Hoo."

Snowball let out an exasperated yell. "Aaagghh. Mister Gus Man!"

"Hoo."

"Mister! Gus! Man!" Snowball roared. He threw his hammer toward the source of the sound and it went sailing off into the trees. Angry and frustrated with the owl, which continued to make its nocturnal calls, Snowball went after his hammer. Once he had retrieved it, he began looking for the source of the sound. It took him some time, but once he had figured out which tree the noise had emanated from, Snowball produced a wicked grin and struck the base of the tree with his hammer, sending a shower of splinters flying as he obliterated a solid chunk of the tree.

The startled owl fluttered up and circled around the tree for a while, eventually returning and perching on a branch high up in the tree.

For a brief few minutes the owl had remained silent as it acclimated to its surroundings once again. Snowball would have left it alone if it had stayed that way but it wasn't long before it called out again. The Minotaur immediately smashed out the rest of the tree trunk and the pine came crashing down to the ground. The owl fluttered to another nearby tree as its perch was toppled. A moment later, Gus appeared.

"Did you knock down a tree?" Gus asked, looking at the debris.

Snowball grunted and nodded and shifted his attention back to the owl in the tree. Gus looked as well, confused.

"Hoo."

"Gggrrraaaaahhhh!" Snowball roared and in an instant the owl disappeared from its branch in a puff of feathers from a perfectly accurate, lightning fast hammer throw. The hammer went sailing off into the night, crashing through the forest but Snowball's expression changed from rage to immense satisfaction.

Gus stood there, dumbfounded. "Uh... Alright then. Well, listen, Snowball. We need to get a move on."

"Okay, Mister Gus Man. Let Snowball get Snowball's hammer." Snowball started off in the direction of his throw.

It took only a few minutes to track it down. They started to head back to the path when Gus heard someone in the distance.

"There! Up ahead! It's a light. I think it's a torch or something."

Gus had forgotten that his lantern was still lit.

"That's no torch. It's the light from the creature's evil eyes!" Came another voice.

"Evil eyes...?" Gus mumbled. "Come on, Snowball. Let's go."

He led his companion back toward the path but stopped when he saw points of light through the trees. He turned the other direction but saw more lights quickly approaching. The torches were growing closer but no matter where he turned, he couldn't see a way out that wasn't blocked by the approaching mob. They were surrounded.

"Snowball." Gus said nervously. "Remember. No violence. Violence will not solve anything."

"Okay, Mister Gus Man."

Soon they were encircled by the villagers in the pale orange glow of torchlight.

"Hold it right there." Said the heavy man, brandishing a torch in one hand and a sickle in the other.

The villagers let out a warning cry in agreement, the business end of their pitchforks and other farm implements at the ready.

"Be careful, men. That creature's dangerous." The heavy man cautioned.

"What do we do with the man?" Someone asked.

Gus turned to Snowball and said quietly. "Don't worry. I'll think of something. There's got to be a peaceful solution."

"He's in league with the creature," The heavy man said. "We'll take him and burn him at the stake. Ready, men? ATTACK!!!"

Gus cried out and darted behind Snowball. "Forget what I said! Violence is the answer. Violence is the answer!"

Snowball grinned and let out an eager roar.

"Just don't kill anyone!" Gus added in a panic.

He was doubtful anyone heard his plea over the Minotaur's roar. As the battle commenced... a battle? Perhaps that's not the best description. A drubbing would be a more accurate account. As the drubbing commenced, little could be heard over the battle cries, terror and clashing of weapons.

Three men immediately charged Snowball with a shovel, a pitchfork, a sledgehammer, and a mighty battle cry. Snowball's massive reach and hefty hammer whipped around before the pitchfork tines could even reach him, sending one man into the next, into the next, and all three went sprawling to the ground. Another man cried out and leaped onto the Minotaur's back with a knife in hand. Before he could bring the point of his weapon down, Snowball struck him in the head with an impossibly accurate back elbow, knocking him out cold. Snowball didn't miss a beat as the next man thrust out with a spear. He let one hand go of his hammer and grabbed the pointed implement, plucking it easily from the assailant's grasp and flinging it high into the trees. The farmer was so shocked he stammered and looked around desperately for something to defend himself with. Seeing nothing, he screamed and turned to flee. Snowball laughed joyfully and grabbed him by the leg before he could take two steps. He swung the man round like a rag doll at an approaching attacker wielding a torch. The two men collapsed in a pile, tripping up another man who was running headlong into the fray with a raised pickaxe.

Meanwhile, one of the villagers, a hunter, took careful aim with his bow and let out a shot aimed at the Minotaur's side. To his dismay, the arrow glanced off the handle of the creature's hammer. He quickly drew another arrow to take a second shot, but by that time Snowball was well aware of him. Before he could take aim, Snowball dashed across the woodland and grabbed hold of the bow in one hand. He held on for dear life as Snowball lifted it up like a piece of dirty laundry, flailing and struggling to keep the monster at bay with his legs.

Snowball let his hammer fall to the ground and grabbed the bow with his finger and thumb. With careless effort he snapped it like a twig and dropped the pieces and the man with it. The villager landed flat on his bottom, and looked up at the creature, pleading for his life. Snowball leaned in close and laughed heartily at the poor villager who scrambled away into the brush to regroup with his remaining companions.

By then those still conscious had formed up to surround the Minotaur. They were careful and waved and prodded their weapons toward the creature. Inch by inch they moved in on him, careful to avoid the creature's grasp and the massive hammer it wielded.

Snowball turned round and round, looking for an opening to continue his attack. The villagers were doing an admirable job of keeping him contained and for a moment he was hemmed in.

You may be wondering what became of Gus during the melee, but like any intelligent man he did the smartest thing he could think of. He dove behind a bush and hid. To his relief, none of the villagers seemed to notice. They were completely focused on his companion instead of him because, let's face it, the Minotaur posed a significantly greater threat. Gus had been watching when his friend became surrounded. The villagers, if only for that moment, had the upper hand. It was then that Gus decided to leave behind his fear and stand up to defend his monstrous friend. He stood up courageously and with great determination hurled a rock at the nearest villager as hard as he could.

The villager yelped in pain as the rock bounced off his shoulder blade and turned toward Gus.

It was all the opening Snowball needed. The Minotaur charged toward the opening, swinging his hammer in a wide arc. It struck a man armed with a lantern and sickle, sweeping his legs right out from under him. He crashed to the ground which knocked the air out of his lungs. The gap in the circle of villagers was just large enough for Snowball to begin his charge. He lowered his head and sprinted round the circle, his great horns plowing to and fro and his hammer swinging back and forth. He bulldozed through half a dozen of them before the circle collapsed, leaving just three of the villagers still standing. When Snowball turned and let out an immense bellow at his remaining foes, they lost their wits and dropped their weapons. Snowball ran toward them and they had no choice but to scrambled up a pine tree and climb as high as they could.

Snowball stopped at the bottom of the tree and laughed up at his quarry. "Hahahaha! Silly tiny hoomans."

Gus jogged up next to him and said "That's enough, Snowball. I think we've won." He put a hand on the Minotaur's massive forearm for him to lower his hammer.

Snowball obeyed and looked up at the men cowering in the tree and asked "Mister Gus Man does not want to get the men down?"

"No, Snowball," Gus answered, directing his voice a little more loudly toward the men up above. "I think they've learned their lesson. The next time someone comes their way I'm sure they'll be a little more careful before they try to attack a peaceful creature like you and a traveler like myself. Isn't that right?" They remained silent so Gus nodded to himself in satisfaction. "Come on. We had better get going. We need to put some distance between ourselves and this place."

"Okay, Mister Gus Man." Snowball nodded and the two headed off to find the path east. Once they had traveled a few miles down the way they stopped and made camp. Exhausted and tired of fumbling around in the dark, Gus quickly fell asleep in his tent and slept soundly through the night.

The next morning, they awoke to a peaceful sunrise coming up through the trees. The sounds of birds and forest animals rustled happily through the air. Gus yawned and found his way out of his tent to find Snowball sitting by the fire, preparing breakfast. Gus thought to ask where Snowball had obtained eggs and several strips of bacon but he decided not to ask and just enjoy the meal. When he'd finished, Gus started packing up his tent. The work went by quietly and Gus felt a little awkward around his traveling companion. After a while he couldn't keep quiet anymore. He cleared his throat and spoke up. "Snowball... About yesterday..."

Snowball listened attentively as he sat on a stump scratching at his hindquarters.

"What I mean to say is, I'm sorry I left you in the woods." Gus knelt down and started rolling up the tent. "You see... I should have trusted you, and I didn't. I thought you would wander off and I was about to wander off myself and there was so much going on..." Gus stopped what he was doing and looked back at his friend. "I even asked you not to kill anyone and you did just that. I will do better to trust you more in the future."

Snowball shrugged and smiled. "Mister Gus Man is good friend."

"Thanks, Snowball, but I don't deserve that."

"Okay."

There was a pause between the two of them. Gus was about to continue explaining himself when Snowball asked "will there be more strawberries soon?"

Gus was a little surprised by the Minotaur's casual response. "That's it? You're not mad?"

"Nope."

"Why not? I left you alone in the woods."

Snowball shrugged. "Mister Gus Man promised Snowball he would find more strawberries. Mister Gus Man will find strawberries."

It took a moment before Gus realized that Snowball really had no idea that Gus had tried to leave him in order to head north. As far as Snowball was concerned, Gus was a man of his word. He'd promised he would come back for Snowball and he had.

"You know, Snowball. That's what we are. Men of our words. We say we'll do something, and by the gods, we do it."

Snowball nodded eagerly.

"And you know what that means?"

"Strawberries?"

"Strawberries."

"Do you know what else that means?"

Snowball thought hard to come up with an answer.

Gus answered for him. "That means that we are, in fact, friends."

The Minotaur smiled and nodded vigorously.

"The two of us are going to find a place where we can fit in and work. How does that sound?"

Snowball grunted.

"Good. So, let's do it. Let's go find a place. There's a place called the Province of Kismet down this road. What do you say we find some strawberries there?"

Snowball's tail wagged with excitement.

"We are going to find something for both of us to earn our keep. I promise."

"Strawberries!"

"Uh... yes. Strawberries."

Snowball pumped his fists into the air, grabbed up his hammer and started down the road.

"Wait. Snowball, I'm not finished packing up the camp."

The Minotaur seemed not to hear over the promise of strawberries and kept marching, so Gus scrambled to get everything together and on his back before he chased after his companion down the long road to Kismet.

PART III
Gainfully Deployed

Chapter IX

Departing from the normal discourse of strawberries and such forth, there comes a time in a man's life when he must face unexpected adversity and rise above the challenges of normal men. It is in such times when his courage is most likely to fail and his luck is at its end. These kinds of uncommon events occur rarely for the common man yet, for a particular commoner, such was not the case.

Gus thought on this subject most drearily, with only a faint wisp of metaphorical cloud hanging over his head, as he passed over yet another low hill and descended into the great Kismet Valley. It was, however, only a wisp of cloud as the sun was much too bright overhead to allow for too much pessimism on such a lovely day. It was also only a mere wisp due in part to Gus's cynical smirk as he realized the poetic irony of his situation. He was a common man and yet, in spite of his lowly upbringing, his life had become an adventure much too far-fetched for a simple peasant.

"Why is Mister Gus Man smiling?" Snowball asked as he plodded along beside his human companion.

Gus couldn't help but let a laugh escape his lips. "Well, you see, Snowball," he said, "I don't know that I can really say. Don't you find it amusing that you and I are here, together, wandering the wilds like a pair of jolly adventurers?"

Snowball gazed at him with a blank expression.

"Right. I don't suppose that you do. For you, this is a typical day, isn't it? Wandering around, looking for food and roving the countryside."

"Snowball sometimes looks for battle instead of strawberries. It is the only thing as good as strawberries." Snowball noted.

Gus raised an eyebrow at his companion. "Is it really? You would prefer to get into fights and brawls than to spend your life in peace?"

"Yes!" Snowball's tail wagged with excitement.

"But you could get killed! Doesn't that frighten you?" Gus asked.

Snowball let out a bellowing laugh that echoed down the valley. "Snowball has not found anything that can beat Snowball in a fight. Snowball is un-mince-able!"

"Don't you mean 'invincible'?"

Snowball snorted and shook his head. "No. Snowball is un-mince-able! Nobody will make Snowball into tiny mincemeat pie. Snowball is much too large to be mincemeat pie."

Gus was about to slap his forehead but stopped himself short. His head was starting to get sore from all the idiotic things the Minotaur had said over the course of the day. Instead, he decided to change the subject. "Since your name is Snowball, and you love fighting, does that mean you like Snowball fights?"

The Minotaur cocked his head to one side, confused by the question. "Snowball just told Mister Gus Man that Snowball likes fights."

"No, Snowball. That was a joke. Get it? Snowball fights?" He waited for his friend to figure it out but it was clear that Snowball didn't get it. "Fights with little balls of snow that you throw at each other?"

The Minotaur looked at him dumbly. "Okay."

"Ugh... Never mind." Gus looked up at the sky as though in search for something else to talk about. He shifted his attention back to the long path in front of him that led deeper and deeper into the valley. "I imagine we'll come across a town before too long. Do you think we'll find some place by nightfall?"

Snowball thought about it for a while. "Snowball does not think so. Snowball does not smell hoomans besides Mister Gus Man."

"Alright. Well... I suppose that's that, then."

"Is Mister Gus Man afraid of dying?" Snowball asked.

Gus was quite surprised by the question. Though he'd been conversing with the creature for some time along the road he had never been asked any questions of depth. "Uh... Well. Yes! Of course, I'm afraid of dying. Who wouldn't be?"

"Snowball." The Minotaur shrugged.

"Well," Gus said, "that might be true in your case, but most of us hoomans- humans," he corrected himself, wincing as he pronounced it like his companion always did, "would prefer to stay alive and so many of us are afraid of getting killed. That's how we've survived so well for so long. Of course, we rely on king and country to protect us from invaders and other things. I would say, for the most part, except for soldiers and knights and so forth, humans fear death. At least a little. We either fight or fly, as the expression goes."

"Mister Gus Man can fly!" Snowball exclaimed.

"No... fly... it's another way of saying 'run away'. We either fight or we run away."

"Snowball wishes he could fly." The Minotaur frowned. Even his horns seemed to droop in disappointment.

"Uh..." Gus tried imagining Snowball soaring majestically across the sky with a pair of feathered wings. "That sounds... mildly terrifying." The only thing he could figure would be worse than a rampaging Minotaur is one that could swoop down from the skies.

The trees had thinned out and the land was mostly grasses and shrubs. They came to a cliff as the valley took a sudden drop above a wide expanse of plains. Far away on the other side, Gus thought he could make out the signs of a small human settlement just before the slope of a large ridge. He stopped a few feet from the edge of the rocks and took a moment to gaze into the distance. Snowball took up a place beside him and looked out over the precipice as well.

"It's quite a way out there. Do you think we can make it there by nightfall?" Gus asked.

Snowball grunted in acknowledgment.

"Can you smell them out this far?" Gus wondered aloud.

Snowball took in a big whiff, his nose twitching almost as if it was feeling the air itself. "Snowball cannot smell Hoomans from this far away. Too much wind between here and there."

Gus reached down and took up a small rock. With an effort he pitched it high and far over the edge of the cliff to see just how far he could throw it. It soared over the ground for a fair while before at last it bounced noiselessly against the dirt below.

Snowball plucked a pebble from the ground as well and followed suit. He made a firm wind-up and threw the pebble hard into the air. The rock flew three times further, striking a low flying grouse squarely in the head, sending it plummeting to the ground.

"I... That was..." Gus fumbled.

"Do not worry, Mister Gus Man. Snowball got it. It was too far away for a tiny hooman to hit anyway." The Minotaur smiled, happy to lend a hand.

"That's not... I wasn't..." Gus could hardly find the words. "You know... I can't say that I'm shocked really. Oh well. At least I know what we'll be having for lunch."

Gus spotted a place where the ground sloped down the cliff a way north from where they stood. They both headed that direction to make their way toward the settlement in the distance. The temperature steadily rose as they continued down to the valley floor and by the time they retrieved the grouse, Gus was sweating. Eager to take a break, he made a small fire from twigs and bushes scattered here and there around the plain. He cooked the grouse as best he could but he found that the bird had little meat. He offered some to Snowball but the Minotaur refused. Instead, Snowball went wandering off across the plains for a while, sticking his head into shrubs and rocky outcroppings. When he returned, he seemed satisfied and by then Gus had finished with his meal.

"Perhaps it would be best if I went alone. We don't know how they are going to react to you." Gus suggested.

Snowball shook his head and stamped his foot. "Mister Gus Man and Snowball the Magnificent will go together. Tiny hoomans will either like Snowball or they will not like Snowball and Snowball will hit them with his hammer."

"I... Uh..." Gus was about to protest but he was starting to get the feeling that Snowball meant no harm. "Wait, did you say Snowball the Magnificent?"

The Minotaur nodded his head and stood up proudly, using the massive hammer as a sort of staff in one hand, striking an inspiring pose. "Snowball the Magnificent is the most magnificent of magnificent mean-o-tars. Snowball knows this."

"How do you even know a word like magnificent?" Gus asked with a bit of a grin on his face.

"Snowball knows lots of all of the words. Snowball learned them a long time ago."

"Ah. I see," Gus folded his arms and nodded skeptically. "And what, pray tell, does it mean?"

Snowball snorted and thought to himself before he came up with a satisfying answer. "Magnificent means that Snowball is *MAG*-nified *IF* he gives off a *SCENT*, and Snowball is lots of scents. Have not bathed in many weeks."

Gus took special notice of the creature's smell and could not help but gag a little.

"So, Snowball has great scent that magnifies Snowball so Snowball is bigger than everything else." The Minotaur explained.

"Uh huh. Alright then. Well," said Gus with a courteous bow, "Snowball the Magnificent. Let's get moving and pray your smell blinds them so they won't be terrified by you in the daylight."

"Okay!" Snowball agreed.

The fire was stamped out quick by the Minotaur's hoof and the two were off once again. To Gus's surprise, they made the journey easily and arrived at the settlement a few hours before sunset. He was also surprised to find that it was not a village but a large camp set up by well-armed men.

Several pavilion tents were erected across the open ground, each surrounded by the trappings of armaments. Weapon stands stood at the ready, banners hung quietly by and many horses were tied at hitching posts throughout the camp. Hearty cooking fires were burning merrily and the sounds of robust conversation held by men at arms babbled throughout. There were many men, soldiers by the look of it, each tending to their duties. Some sharpening their weapons, some working hard to move supplies to large wagons for the night, others enjoying the taste of tender meat cooked on the spit. They wore sandy brown tunics and earthen colored pants, many with chain mail and steel helmets. A large majority of the men bore the emblem of a seven-pointed star on top of a red dragon upon their garments, the same as the emblems on the banners strewn about camp.

Gus and Snowball made it all the way to the first tent before they were spotted. It seemed the men were too preoccupied with their duties to notice the great monster and his human companion. Gus raised a hand in fair greeting and hailed them. "Good day, good sirs."

In a flash the men drew their weapons and stood at the ready to defend themselves or attack at the drop of a hat. Their growls and aggressive stares were so intense that Gus wondered if perhaps he'd made a poor choice of words.

"Good evening?" He gulped.

Within moments a broad-shouldered man with a barrel chest emerged from one of the tents. "What's going on?" He bellowed.

He wore the same sand colored tunic and a breastplate emblazoned with the dragon star emblem, though his clothes were made of fine cloth and trimmed with silver.

He was a handsome man in his late forties with short golden hair and a stern face. He looked as though he had not shaved in several days and he walked with a limp in his right leg. In spite of his staggered walk he moved with authority and a sort of military grace. His right hand hung by a sword sheathed at his hip but he made no move to draw his weapon. It was clear that this man held authority over everyone present.

He quickly took notice of Gus and Snowball shrinking away at the edge of camp and strode through his men, placing himself between the two parties. He eyed the Minotaur warily but did not seem to be intimidated by the size and monstrousness of the creature. He also quickly sized up Gus before he spoke. "Who are you? Where do you hail from?" He demanded.

"My name is Gus. I come from the country. From a small village called Dale. And this is Snowball," He gestured toward his companion. "He comes from... well... he comes from..." He struggled to come up with a good answer.

The man looked to the creature for an answer but Snowball just stared at him dumbly.

"Where do you hail from?" The man asked a little more forcefully.

Snowball looked over his shoulder and pointed the direction they had come from. "Over there."

"Ah. What he means to say," Gus interrupted nervously, "is that we have been traveling from that direction since we left my village."

"But where do you hail from?" The man asked impatiently. "What village, what kingdom?" He gave the Minotaur a sharp stare, expecting an answer but Snowball just shrugged.

"You'll have to excuse my companion," Gus interjected. "I'm not sure if even he knows where he comes from. He was wandering through the woods when I met him."

"So, this creature is your friend?" The man asked, his voice filled with suspicion and concern.

"Well..." Gus took in a breath and cleared his throat, carefully considering how best to answer. "Yes. Yes, Snowball is my friend. We were traveling east in search of work when we ran across your camp. We thought it was a small village from the distance. We did not mean to intrude." He paused to allow the man to say more but he seemed to be deep in thought, calculating something as his eyes took in the two trespassing travelers. "If you don't mind my asking, are you soldiers for the crown?" Gus asked.

The men in the camp laughed briefly. The broad-shouldered man spoke up again. "Forgive me, where are my manners? My name is Garret Thornfall, and these are my men. We are mercenaries from the province of Kismet in the employ of his majesty the King." Garret nodded in respect.

"A pleasure to meet you, Garret. We did not realize you were mercenaries and we certainly did not want to intrude." Gus said as politely as he could. "We were simply passing through." He took note that the men in the camp were now at ease and had sheathed their weapons and returned to their meals, though many kept a watchful eye on the Minotaur.

"Very well." Garret replied. "Welcome to our camp. Please, walk with me." He turned and headed toward the tent he had come from at a leisured pace.

Gus quickly followed with Snowball close behind, not sure what the man wanted.

"You mentioned that you were interested in work." Garret said.

"Uh... yes." Gus stumbled. "We were looking for a way to earn some honest coin."

"Your friend seems strong and able. Have you two seen much in the way of battle?"

"Well. I can't say that I have much experience in that arena but Snowball here is as strong as ten men and three times as dangerous. I've seen him take out a score of bandits in a matter of seconds."

Garret laughed heartily. "I do not doubt it. I can certainly put him to work if he is interested. What say you? Will you join our merry band?" He stopped and turned to face Snowball.

Snowball was surprised and pointed at himself to make sure Garret was addressing him. "Snowball?"

"What?" Garret said, confused. "Did you say Snowball? Is that your name?"

Snowball nodded.

"Er... Yes. We could use a strong creature like yourself for the work we do. What do you say?"

Snowball thought on it for a moment. "Will there be battle?"

Garret nodded, a look of certainty and satisfaction on his face. "As much as you can stomach."

"And strawberries. Will there be strawberries? Mister Gus Man always leads Snowball to strawberries."

The captain raised an eyebrow. "Uh. Yes, I suppose you could afford to purchase some with your wages once we resupply."

Snowball's tail wagged excitedly as he turned to Gus. "We could make good strawberry battlefield work time with mercy-naries."

Gus felt hopeful at the prospect as he considered the benefits of allowing Snowball to do what he was good at while earning the pair of them a decent wage. "Yes. That does sound quite good. I think we would be agreeable to sign on with your company if you'll have us." Gus said to Garret.

Garret took in a deep breath and adopted a look of concern. "While your companion certainly seems to have the strength we need here, I don't know that we would have much use for a man of *your* talents, I'm afraid."

Feeling a bit hurt, Gus protested. "I can pull my own weight. I may not have the skills in combat that you are looking for but I can certainly prove myself useful in other areas."

"Hah." Garret laughed, looking the peasant up and down. "I do not mean to offend, but you leave a lot to be desired. I don't have room for someone of your stature. It is hard work moving a camp or tending to the armaments. Everyone here has to pull their own weight and everyone here is expected to be able to defend themselves. A peasant like yourself would only get in the way and it would put my men at risk if they have to defend you were we to be attacked."

Gus had a hard time coming up with a response. He couldn't help but to see the commander's point. He was small and he didn't have much strength or skill with a weapon. He was about to resign his efforts when Snowball spoke up.

"If Mister Gus Man cannot be part of hooman mercy-naries then Snowball cannot be part of hooman mercy-naries." He said with finality. "Come on Mister Gus Man. We can go find more mercy-naries for battleful strawberry work." Snowball started to head toward the other side of the camp.

Both Garret and Gus were surprised by the Minotaur's objection. Garret spoke up immediately. "Now let's not be hasty friend." He held up a hand and followed after Snowball in protest as the creature started to leave. "I'm sure we can work something out. We could use a monster-" Garret corrected himself, "a mercenary like you. Let's talk this over. Please. Join me in my tent and we can work out a contract."

Snowball stopped and turned around to look at Gus for approval. Gus shrugged a shoulder and gave Snowball a look before nodding toward the tent. Snowball nodded in response and the two followed Garret.

The pavilion was of an accommodating size and had several chests and crates laying inside, as well as a table in its center with a map of the surrounding area spread across it. Other accouterments lay scattered here and there for planning and managing the band of mercenaries. A mostly empty armor stand stood nearby as well with a plumed helmet sporting a large white feather seated at its top. Banners bearing the dragon star emblem hung on either side of the doorway as they entered and Gus noted two armed men standing at attention just outside the tent flap.

Garret went to a chest hidden behind the table and retrieved a set of rolled papers and a quill. He wasted no time spreading the papers over the map and setting the pen within easy reach of his potential recruits. "We can offer you a modest sum for this kind of work, surely. With a creature of your stature," he said nodding to Snowball, "we would normally pay you a triple wage if you can prove yourself on the battlefield. However, given that you are not interested in joining our merry band without the company of Gus here, we will need to make amendments. What say you to twice the normal going rate for you and the normal going rate for him?" He thumbed over to Gus.

"Hey!" Gus protested but Garret didn't seem to hear him.

"Oh. That sounds very good!" Snowball said with excitement. "Snowball would like to have twice the normal rate. What do you pay Snowball with?"

Garrett paused for a moment with a little disbelief. "Why, with coin of course. Each of my men earns a gold coin for every mission we undertake, plus three silvers for every enemy they personally defeat and any plunder acquired during our missions is equally divided among the men based on rank within the company."

"Oooh! And Snowball gets twice that many?"

"Yes. Of course. Provided we are in agreement." Garret gestured toward the quill on the table.

"Wait. Hold on a minute. Don't I get a say in all this?" Gus cut in. "You just said that Snowball would normally earn three times the rate for his size and skill."

"Now, now. Let Snowball here make his own decisions." Garret tried to brush Gus off.

"You just said he could earn a triple wage and now you're only offering double rate. Snowball, would you rather have two times as much pay, or three?" Gus asked.

Snowball thought on it for a moment and then looked at the fingers on his hand. He held up one, then two and paused, his thoughts deeply focused. Then he held up the third finger and his brow furrowed with certainty. "Three times as much pay."

"There, you see." Gus insisted.

Garret rubbed at his beard and then held up a hand. "All right, all right. Three times the normal rate. However!" He continued, "I still have significant doubts about *your* abilities and what you have to offer. I will offer you half the normal rate. I will also not allow you on the battlefield unless you can prove your skills and you will not be eligible for the normal three silver for defeated enemies and you'll only receive a quarter share of the plunder should there be any to distribute."

"A quarter?" Gus was outraged.

Garret slammed his hands down on the table and leaned over to stare Gus straight in the eye with a gaze that put ice in the veins of the hapless peasant. "You'll take a quarter or you'll take nothing. If you want any more than that then I strongly suggest you put yourself to good use and learn how to wage war, for nothing less will earn you a place with my men. Is that understood?"

Gus couldn't find the words and stood there, frozen, desperately trying to come up with a response.

"That's what I thought." Garret continued. "Now, there's just the matter of formalities. I need you to sign your names here on the roster as well as on this form here to indicate that you are liable for your own selves while in this company and any medical attention for injury sustained to you will be paid for in full by you or else taken from your wages."

Snowball grabbed up the quill pen and looked at it curiously. Gus got the feeling he had no idea how to read or write, let alone sign his own name.

"An 'X' on the line will suffice if you are unable to write." Garret told him.

Before Gus could protest further, Snowball had scrawled a crude 'X' on both forms and held out the pen for Gus to follow suit. He considered refusing, but given the situation he saw no other action he could take. The Minotaur would make more than enough for the two of them. Gus would even earn a wage, if only a meager one, which was more than Garret had intended. All told, three and a half times the wage for one recruit didn't sound too bad. Plus, aside from strawberries and a good brawl, Gus doubted that the Minotaur would have much to spend his portion of the money on. Resignedly, he took the quill and wrote his name as elegantly as he could on the contract and the roster. Once he was finished, he handed the quill back to Garret who wrote a note next to each of their names on the roster. He didn't have much time to get a good look but he thought he could make out the word 'juggernaut' next to Snowball's 'X' and 'servant' next to his own.

Before Gus could do more, Garret ushered them out of the tent and immediately shouted some orders to a group of men sitting at a fire nearby.

Chapter X

"Curtis! See to it that these recruits get properly fed and outfitted. We have a long day ahead of us tomorrow and we can't afford to have them on an empty stomach now, can we?"

The man called Curtis stood up from his seat with a "Yes, sir" and quickly approached Snowball and Gus. He was a serious faced man with dark, close-cut hair that had started to gray in places. Curtis stood a head taller than Gus. He had the stature of a soldier and the bearing of a man who had seen much in his life. He wore much the same uniform as the other men though he sported a fine suit of chain mail and his leather boots were well polished. With a stern command he bade Gus and Snowball follow him through the camp.

"How much combat experience do you have?" He asked simply.

Gus spoke up. "Not much. I've been in a few fights." He didn't tell Curtis that he referred to his few encounters where Snowball had devastated a large group of people and he had been standing nearby.

"And you. Minotaur, right? What is your experience?"

Gus got the impression that Curtis felt a little intimidated by the colossal beast.

Snowball simply grunted and nodded his head, a smile on his bovine features.

Curtis caught sight of the hammer that Snowball carried with him in one hand. "I assume that is the weapon you are most familiar with."

"It is." Gus answered for Snowball.

Curtis took them inside another large pavilion filled with weapon racks and armaments. "So long as it's trustworthy then I see no reason you can't use it. I don't have a replacement of that size for a weapon of that kind. What of you? Do you prefer a sword, or have you experience with other weaponry?" He addressed Gus.

Gus didn't know how to respond. He tried to smile and shuffled his foot. "I don't really have much experience with any weapons, I'm afraid."

The look Curtis gave him made him feel very small. "Here. Take this." He grabbed a short sword from one of the weapon racks and handed it to Gus.

Gus unsheathed the weapon and tested it in his hand. It was a functional weapon, but nothing more. The grip and the blade were simple and in-ornate. He waved it around a little bit to get a feel for its weight.

Curtis put a firm hand on Gus's arm to stop him swinging it around. "Careful with that. Come. Let me see how you do with it outside."

They left the tent and Curtis took him to a clearing between two of the tents, carrying with him a longsword of his own. He directed Gus to stand at the ready facing him and told him to hold his weapon up. Snowball stood to the side to watch.

"Let's see if you can perform the basics first. I'm going to come at you with an overhead strike. Try to block it."

"Alright." Gus gripped his short sword tight and prepared himself. "I'm ready."

Curtis took his cue and brought his own sword above his head, making it clear where he meant to strike from. With a quick step forward, he made a decisive strike.

Gus whipped his sword from one side of his body to the other in a high arc, batting Curtis' sword out of the way with a loud *clang!*

"No, no, no. That will not do."

"But you told me to block it." Gus explained.

"I told you to block it, aye. I did not tell you to swat at it like an old woman. Your form is all wrong. You need to block the blow."

"But I did. Your sword didn't hit me."

"You left yourself wide open."

"I did not." Gus insisted.

"Fine. Let's try again. We'll do the same thing."

With a nod, Gus readied himself and they repeated the exercise. This time, when Curtis brought his sword down and Gus knocked it out of the way, Curtis stepped in and bowled into Gus with his shoulder while the peasant was exposed, sending him sprawling to the ground.

Dirt and rocks scraped his arms a little as he hit the ground. Curtis gave him a hand up and got him standing again.

"You see. You leave yourself wide open. You are right, my sword missed you, but that is only one strike. A fight is not just one attack, it is many. Here. I'll show you what to do." Curtis got into a ready stance and lifted his arms up with the sword at an angle to deflect an imaginary blow. "You see. When the sword comes down, you block this way."

"Ah. Alright. I think I see."

They tried the exercise once more. This time, when Curtis brought his sword down, he stopped just as his sword clashed against Gus's. The blow rang through Gus's arms and he staggered backward.

"No, no, no. Not like that. You are trying to completely stop my attack with brute strength. That will never work. You need to keep your sword at an angle." He demonstrated the move. "Your opponent's sword will glance off to the side which will leave him open for a follow up attack. Let's try again."

These exercises went on for some time, first with overhead strikes, then side strikes and thrusts, parries and disarms. Each trial proved difficult for Gus until at last Curtis sheathed his sword and snatched Gus's weapon away from him.

"That's enough for now. I can tell you won't be ready to join us for our next fight. Go make yourself useful and take feed around to the horses. Dinner will be ready for you in a little while." Curtis dismissed him.

Gus left to do what he could around the camp, leaving Curtis with Snowball. He grumbled to himself, disappointed at his performance. He had never held a sword before in his life. They couldn't expect him to take up it just like that. He told himself that he could get the hang of it eventually. After all, how hard could fighting be? It was just swinging swords at someone, wasn't it? Gus went through the moves Curtis had shown him over and over again in his mind as he lifted his heavy bag of feed to pour it into a feeding trough for the horses. He was determined to prove himself useful. He may have been a small peasant but that didn't mean he was useless. "I'll show them I'm worth my weight." He muttered to himself. One of the horses snuffled him out of his thoughts and surprised him enough that he stumbled backward and lost his balance. The feed spilled over the soil and Gus fell to his knees to pick the grains up as fast as he could before anyone noticed.

While Gus tended to his duties, Curtis was busy with Snowball. He cleared his throat as he sized up the great creature, not sure if he could trust the beast to hold itself back if he were to engage in the same exercises he had with Gus. The Minotaur easily stood head and shoulders above Curtis and it was more than enough to make him uneasy.

"Alright, creature. Let's... uh... Let's see what you've got. You already have some experience in a fight, I take it. Let's see how you handle your weapon."

Snowball smiled and gripped his hammer in both hands, readying to strike.

"Hold on! Hold on." Curtis held up a hand. "Let's use a training dummy." He quickly took Snowball over to the edge of a clearing where someone had erected a straw man around a pole to use as practice. "You can use this as your target. Go ahead whenever you are ready." He took several steps back to watch Snowball work.

Snowball shrugged and didn't waste any time. He brought the hammer up and smashed straight down on top of the dummy, pounding the stick straight into the ground and smashing it to splinters in the process. The ground throughout the camp resounded with a thump as the hammer struck and bits of straw and twine flew in every direction. All that was left was a pile of debris.

Curtis gulped and nodded in disbelief. "I think... I think that will do it for today. Very good. I have a pressing matter to attend to. If you'll excuse me." He quickly turned and headed to go speak with Garret about the new recruit.

Snowball wondered briefly if perhaps Curtis was impressed by his abilities but the thoughts scurried from his mind and were replaced by the unusual sights and smells throughout the camp. He wandered off and soon a peaceful night settled over the plains.

A meal was served in short order to the new recruits along with the rest of the men. It was mostly wild game and salted meats served with a bit of oats and a tin of water. Gus didn't care for it much but at least it filled his belly. Later on, Gus had graduated from feeding the mounts to scrubbing the company's armor clean. He didn't much approve of this graduation, nor did he consider it a graduation really. However, his grumbles only got him dangerously close to scrubbing pots and pans and at least scrubbing armor almost sounded dignified and important. After all, dishes were menial labor but armor... armor had an almost regal tone to it. He had cleaved to it with an aggressive (if not downright spiteful) disposition and had managed to clean several pieces of armor to a reasonable shine by the time the sun at last had disappeared beneath the horizon. Gus was determined not to give up, lest his new employers think he was not inclined to do the work. He wanted badly to put them in their place and prove himself a worthy investment. He had just ducked into another small tent to ask its occupant for another piece of armor to shine when he was greeted rudely by the pungent smell of an ale-soaked belch.

"Who are yewww...?" Came the slovenly speech of a disheveled man draped carelessly over a bedroll and chest in the corner of the tent. His limbs spilled loosely around as he tried to get himself upright with little success.

"Begging your pardon, Sir. My name is Gus. I'm cleaning armor. Do you have any in need of service?" Gus held up his brush and pail.

"I don't know wh- anyone who is coming to clean-"

It was clear that the man was not going to get himself upright any time soon as he struggled to support himself with his drunken limbs. He had only managed to get about halfway up before Gus intervened and gave him a hand.

"What- don't help me up. Don't help me- don't... who are you?" The man protested but accepted the assistance. He tottered on his feet for a bit while he tried to smooth out his tunic which had shifted to an odd angle under his belt.

Gus stood back a pace to give the man some room. "My name is Gus," he repeated. "I'm here to clean your armor."

The man swatted in the air with a stagger as if to slap away Gus's hands to keep him from touching his armor. Gus had not moved, however and the man stumbled forward a few steps. "I don't want your armor. Stay away from me." He slurred. He leaned back to prevent himself from falling forward but over-corrected and ended up falling over backward. He landed on his rear with a thud and stayed there, his arms draped over his knees to prevent him falling the rest of the way to the ground. "What time is it?" He asked.

Gus took a look out the tent flap. "The sun set just a little while ago."

The man scratched at his stubbled chin and looked at Gus with a furrowed brow. "It's night time? What happened to morning?"

Gus didn't really know how best to answer that. Instead he asked "Would you like me to come back later? Perhaps tomorrow morning?"

The man gave him an empty stare.

"I'll come back later. Enjoy your evening, sir." Gus turned and left the tent.

Once outside a passing mercenary noticed him and gave him a mocking smile.

"What?" Gus asked.

"Done cleaning the ale and vomit off?"

Gus was a little taken aback. "Excuse me?"

The mercenary stopped and waited for Gus to come a little closer. "Tell me. Which smelled worse, his breath or his body odor?"

"Are you talking about the man in there?" Gus asked pointing back to the tent.

"Aye. He's been drunk nearly every night for months."

"For that long? Really?"

"Aye."

"Doesn't Garret stop him? It doesn't seem like a good way to prepare for a fight. Don't tell me he's drunk on the battlefield."

The mercenary shrugged. "I don't know a man here who has seen him sober since he and the others joined."

"The others?"

"Do you really not know who that is?"

Gus shook his head.

"He's one of the former Knights of Kismet. Regular Soldiers from the Kismet army make up about half of the company at present. They comprised the original troop before more of us joined up."

"The Knights of Kismet?" Gus had no idea what the mercenary was talking about.

"Don't tell me you've never heard of the Knights of Kismet. They're famous around these parts."

"Should I know of them?" Gus shrugged.

"The Knights of Kismet, from the kingdom of Kismet to the south. Well, former kingdom anyway. When their kingdom fell to the current rule, they were left without a king and without a country. So, Garret rounded them up and gave them a purpose. They're quite fierce on the battlefield. The Knights of Kismet were legendary. They never lost a battle. It was once said that no army, no matter the size, could defeat them."

Gus was skeptical. "And that man in there," he pointed again to the tent, "is one of them?"

The mercenary nodded with a bit of a laugh. "He was. He's the only knight in the company. The rest are just soldiers. They used to call him the Knight of the Silver Dragon if I'm not mistaken. It's a shame what he's become."

Gus looked back to the tent with pity on his face as the mercenary said goodnight and turned and left. The night progressed steadily and Gus soon retired to his own tent that he set up on the edge of the encampment.

He slept deeply and soon the morning rose, bringing with it the warm rays of an eager sun.

It took just a few hours for the entire camp to be disassembled, packed and stowed in large wagons. The mercenaries went to it with a will and soon they were marching across the plain.

Gus awoke and emerged from his tent just as the last wagon rolled past in a cloud of dust.

"Oh, for the love of-" He cursed and immediately started packing up his tent and supplies as fast as he could. The work could have gone much faster but Snowball was gone. Gus could see the outline of Snowball's horns rising up above the ranks of mercenaries as they moved into the distance. He bundled up everything with little care and hobbled along as he struggled to get his rucksack on his back. It took a good twenty minutes of running, panting and stopping to catch his breath for Gus to finally catch up with the tail end of the traveling band. He coughed as he pushed through the dust and marched up alongside the first wagon driver.

"Where are we going?" He asked the driver.

The driver, a sturdy, balding man with a bushy black beard, looked down at him with a bit of surprise. "So, you decided to join us, eh?"

"I didn't know we were moving out so early. Nobody woke me." Gus complained.

The driver grunted. "Marching orders were called out this morning for all to hear. Those who can't keep up are left behind."

"I never heard any orders."

The driver shook his head. "You must have been fast asleep."

"I don't suppose," Gus asked between breaths, "you'd let me ride in your wagon for a while?"

The driver shook his head. "No can do. Garret's orders. The men are to march. Keeps 'em in shape. They need to be fit for work each day. Only one who gets to ride in my wagon is me."

"Damn." Gus muttered to himself. "Could you tell me where we're going, then?"

The driver rolled his eyes. "Look. If you want to be a part of this company, you need to pull your own weight. Go ask someone else."

The driver whipped the reins and pulled ahead of Gus leaving the peasant in a cloud of dust.

Determined not to be defeated so easily, Gus jogged ahead to try to find Snowball. After several minutes of searching he finally spotted the towering beast trotting alongside the cavalry. The Minotaur was trying to hold a conversation with one of the horses when Gus managed to catch up to him.

"Snowball!" Gus called out.

"Oh! Hello Mister Gus Man." Snowball answered.

"Why didn't you wake me up this morning?" He asked, a little hurt.

Snowball thought about it for a moment but could only shrug and give Gus a big, toothy, minotaur smile.

"Ugh... Never mind. Forget it. Listen, I don't know where we're going. Do you know?"

"Yes." Snowball replied with a nod.

Gus waited for Snowball to continue explaining but the creature simply kept on walking with the same dumb expression on his face. "And?" He asked at last, "where are we going?"

"We are marching southeast. Tiny hooman mercynaries are supposed to go find renegade solders."

"Renegade solder?" Gus gave Snowball a blank stare, trying to figure out what Snowball had meant. "Do you mean renegade soldiers?"

Snowball nodded. "Yes."

"Tiny Garret hooman said mercy-naries are supposed to rout the renegade solders."

"Renegade soldiers" Gus corrected.

Snowball didn't seem to hear. "It is a long way to where we are going. Maybe half a day of marching."

"Do we know why they've become renegades? Did they betray the crown?" Gus asked.

Snowball simply shrugged. "Solders are pillowing across the country."

Gus nodded. "So, we are going to fight some renegade soldiers a half day's march from here because... they pillow... Wait. Do you mean pillage?"

Snowball nodded.

"Alright. I understand the mission, I think. Thank you."

Chapter XI

They marched on just as Snowball had said, across
the plains past rolling hills and occasional shallow ravines. By
the time the group stopped for a rest they had been marching
for hours. Gus took the opportunity and plopped down on the
ground to rest his feet and repack his gear. His tent had nearly
spilled out of its loose binding several times and his rucksack
sat funny on his back due to the rushed packing earlier that
morning, causing his back to be ache for most of the march.

While he sat, Gus took in what he could of the
scenery. There was a quiet beauty to his surroundings and for
a brief moment he felt a peaceful breeze pick up and then
quietly die down. After several minutes, once he'd finished
repacking his gear, he took note of the mercenaries' formation.
Cavalry rode to one side slightly ahead of the marching group.
Next, the mercenaries carrying spears. Behind them the
swordsmen and next the archers. Supplies were carried in the
rear by the wagons rolling side by side. It would make a tight
squeeze if the company had to pass through a ravine or circle
around a mountain on a narrow path, Gus thought.

After a good while the band continued onward
through the plains. It was another long march but there was a
distinct tension in the air and casual conversation had died to a
dull murmur every once in a while. As they reached a low hill,
Garret rode ahead of the rest of the men and lifted up a hand.
At his signal, the wagons stopped and twenty of the men
stayed behind as well as three of the cavalry. The rest of the
company continued on as the sun rose high above their heads.

"We'll be entering combat soon." Came a grumbling
voice next to Gus.

"Is that why everyone's so tense? I suppose we're
nearly there, aren't we?" Gus noted, more to himself than
anyone else. He looked over at the man who had spoken and
found that he was addressing the supposed "Knight of the
Silver Dragon", though the man looked sloppy and hungover.

The knight scratched at the stubble on his chin and mumbled something to himself before he answered. "We're about to face our enemy. You're no soldier, lad. You'd best wait behind with the camp."

"What? I will not." Gus protested. "I aim to earn my keep just the same as any man here. I mean to prove that I can handle myself and be a valuable member. I have no intention of being stuck scrubbing armor and cleaning up after the horses."

The knight huffed in reply. "You're going to prove yourself, eh? And how do you plan on doing that with no weapon?" He asked.

Gus looked down at his waist and went pale. Curtis had taken away the sword from the day before. He panicked and started rummaging through his pack for the knife he'd taken with him. He pulled it out but the look from the knight made him flush.

"Put that away. You're embarrassing yourself." The knight sighed. "Come on. Here. Take mine." He unstrapped a spare short sword from his right hip and handed it to Gus. "Take good care of her. I expect to see her back once we've won."

Gus took care to strap the weapon to his waist and when he looked back up to thank the knight he was already lost among the other mercenaries. He made certain to position himself near Snowball before the fighting started. He didn't know much about military matters but he figured he'd rather be next to the strongest person on the battlefield than anywhere else, and considering the size and potential skill of all present, Gus assumed that was Snowball.

The group continued their march forward over the next rise and down a gentle slope. Far in the distance hundreds of renegade soldiers could be seen. They marched in formation, baring banners and dressed for combat. As the mercenaries continued forward the enemy changed its direction and formed a skirmish line.

"Steady on, men!" Garret barked at the front of the line from horseback. "Form up."

The men jogged to their positions, the cavalry at the front to lead the charge. Next was Snowball and behind him the rest.

Gus noted that the rest of the men stood about a pace and a half behind him. It was as if they thought Snowball deserved to be his own rank and file. Of course, that meant that Gus was also part of Snowball's line. His knees trembled and he swallowed his courage as he stared at the enemies across the field. Much like their own company, someone rode in front of the renegade soldiers, barking orders and inspiring the men. He only half paid attention to Garret, his head spinning as he tried to grasp what was about to happen. All around him horses shifted, men steadied themselves, and the air went still, save for the challenging voice of the commander.

"... And you will be victorious, men. Remember, these are our enemies. We shall show them no quarter!" Garret shouted, lifting his sword high into the air.

The men shouted back fiercely and beat their shields with their swords. His forces ready, Garret turned and faced the enemy, pointing the tip of his blade to the sky.

Across the battlefield the enemy commander did the same. With nearly perfect unison, they leveled their swords at one another.

"Charge!"

Before Gus really knew what was happening, he and the mercenaries were running headlong toward the enemy yelling and screaming. He was surprised to find himself shouting his own war cry but he did it anyway. It sounded perhaps a bit terrified but that didn't matter.

In a matter of seconds, the opposing forces crashed against one another like colliding waves. The cacophony of banging steel rang out over the field like a maddening symphony. Men rushed through gaps between mounted cavalry and soldier and mercenary as they met in fierce combat.

Gus kept as close to Snowball's hindquarters as he could, in as noble a fashion as possible, which to the casual eye may have seemed like cowering.

The Minotaur... well, he did what minotaurs do best. He smashed through the ranks like a boulder, sending a group of fifteen men flying.

"So sorry!" Gus apologized frantically as men were battered left and right by the creature's mighty hammer.

As Gus and Snowball pressed far into enemy ranks, the opposing forces began to close behind them. A soldier with a sword caught sight of Gus as he felled one of the mercenaries with a decisive blow to the neck. He dashed forward and thrust his weapon at the peasant's gut.

With surprising agility, Gus pushed the blade aside with his own and wormed his torso out of the way. The tip missed him by just a few inches but that was all Gus needed. He was both proud and terrified in that moment, for he had bought himself just a few seconds but the soldier was already upon him with another strike.

However, the attack never struck home. On the back-swing of an attack aimed at another soldier, Snowball's hammer struck him squarely in the side of the head and sending him to the ground.

For a brief moment Gus wondered if his companion had done it intentionally or if it was merely an accident.

The fight continued on for what seemed in those few minutes like ages. Renegade soldiers pressed into the mercenary troops hard, bringing many to their knees and sending many to their graves. All the while the Snowball front pressed into the renegade soldiers further and further, no man standing against the rampaging creature for more than a handful of seconds.

Suddenly, Garrets voice could be heard over the battlefield. "Fall back! Fall back!"

Gus managed to hear the voice through the din of shouting and swordplay. He looked to his surroundings for a way back to their comrades but they were hemmed in on all sides. He took a risk and slapped Snowball's hip to gain the creature's attention and threw an arm in the direction of the retreating mercenary band. "We have to go back, Snowball! We need to fall back!" He shouted.

Snowball finished bopping another soldier on the head with his massive hammer and looked out over the swarm of enemy soldiers. With a deep understanding of what needed to be done, Snowball nodded in agreement. He grabbed Gus by the belt of his trousers with one hand, held his hammer in the other, lowered his head and charged headlong shouting "MOVE!"

The renegade soldiers found Snowball's command to be rather agreeable and shifted, stepped, leaped and dove out of the way as his hooves pounded over the dirt. One foolish soldier thought himself particularly strong and made the mistake of standing up to the beast. Snowball did not slow even for a moment as he blocked the soldier's sword blow with his hammer and whipped his great horned head wildly, sending the soldier a good twenty feet into the air. Their path clear, Gus and Snowball made haste to return to their forces and soon they were running with the pack the way they had come.

Gus looked behind himself as he hung from the Minotaur's hand by his belt. The renegade soldiers had taken the opportunity to regroup and form another line to march after the mercenaries. He could tell it wouldn't be long before they caught up with their mercenary group. "Hey, Snowball. Let me go."

The Minotaur did, still running all the while, and Gus fell face first into the dirt, his feet tumbling over his head. He got up quickly, wiping the dust from his face and rushed ahead toward Garret who rode in the center of the retreating band.

"Why are we falling back?" Gus asked as he kept pace with the commander.

"They knew we were coming and caught us in a pincer movement. We've taken too many casualties. The enemy has too much momentum. We need to regroup."

Gus thought about the soldiers in pursuit and spoke up. "They'll catch up if we don't do something." He pointed out. "They're faster on foot than we are."

Garret spoke in frustration. "I know that. We have to find some place to dig in and hold their line."

Gus looked at the landscape they were marching across. "There's nowhere to dig in."

Garret's expression turned to one of pointed anger. "Do you have a better idea?" He spat at the peasant. Garret was about to snap the reins and drive his horse onward, leaving Gus in his wake, when to his surprise the peasant talked back at him.

"Actually, Sir, I do," Gus replied.

Garret was angry and wanted to ignore him but Gus's boldness was just enough to prevent him from leaving.

"There's a hill up ahead. We passed it a little while ago on the march. If we can reach it and climb to the top, we'll have the high ground. You can set up the archers and form a line to hold off the enemy. If we can hold them off until nightfall the enemy will cease pursuit. That should give us enough time to set a trap."

Garret eyed the peasant warily. "If we cannot outrun them, we'll be dead long before then. As you said, they are closing in."

"Then we need to move faster." Gus repeated himself. "It's the only way."

"Your input is noted," Garret said coldly. "However, I will not take military advice from a novice and I certainly will not take advice from a peasant." He spurred his horse onward to the front of the column, leaving Gus behind.

Gus didn't know what to do. They were hopelessly outmatched. These men were used to combat but they did not have the speed of their pursuers. If he couldn't get Garret to listen then they were all doomed. He was contemplating splitting off from the main group to save his own skin when he heard someone shouting over the men.

"Mercenaries!" The voice echoed over the troops. "The enemy is in close pursuit! If we cannot move faster, they will catch us. There is a hill just ahead. If we can reach it, we will stand a chance! We will be victorious yet! Now, come on! Double time! Move, move, move!"

Just like that the mercenaries picked up the pace. Their footsteps doubled and their fevers rose. They jogged ahead, nearly at a run, thundering over the earth. Each man breathing hard with red-faced determination.

Gus was impressed with their mettle, though he thought he could see fear in many a man's eyes. He gritted his teeth and ran along with them. It wasn't long before his lungs burned and sweat drenched his brow. He couldn't remember exactly how far the hill was but he prayed they would reach it soon or else he'd collapse before he ever got there. They ran for what seemed an eternity. Every second that passed was another he was grateful his legs had not failed him. He could not see the hill over the other men. At one point he glanced behind him to see how many of his comrades were moving slower than he was. He was gladdened that he still managed to keep pace with the middle of the pack, however all gladness was flushed from his face as he saw the glimmer of steel pressing in hard on their heels.

The renegade soldiers were closing in. It seemed only a matter of minutes that separated them. Gus couldn't quite see their faces but he easily made out the swords they carried by the sunlight glinting off of them. There number was far greater than he had realized and gave him good cause to run faster. Up ahead he could see the hill and the first of the men running to its top. He was almost there!

He heard an anguished cry from behind him as one of the mercenaries was overtaken by the enemy. He looked back just in time to see a well-aimed broadsword swinging down at his shoulder. Gus cried out and dove forward to the ground to avoid the blow. He knew it would only buy him a few seconds and then the enemy would be upon him, hacking their swords into his body. His hands covered his head and he tensed up as the enemy's sword flew toward him.

He heard another anguished cry, then another. He heard footsteps and shouting and all manner of steel clashing upon steel until at last the sounds of battle began to fade. For a moment, Gus feared the whole of the mercenary band had been overtaken and would soon be wiped out. However, he heard a set of footsteps stopped right beside him. He dared not move, hoping that perhaps the enemy thought him already dead.

"Get up." Came a familiar voice as something hard prodded Gus in the back. It was the Knight of the Silver Dragon staring down at him. "There's no time for cowardice on the battlefield! Come on." The knight reached down and grabbed Gus by the arm, hoisting him up on his feet.

Gus became keenly aware of the arrows whipping overhead at the enemy as they retreated, their shields up to deflect the incoming missiles. The forward part of the mercenary band had reached the hill and the archers had formed up while the rest of the band caught up.

He kept his head low as he marched up the hill and out of the line of fire. He collapsed on the ground, his heart still pounding, breathing heavily. A few minutes later, after his pulse had slowed to a mere stampede, he saw a shadow looming over him from behind. It was Garret and, from what Gus could tell, he wasn't looking too pleased.

"On your feet, peasant." The commander said coldly.

Gus got up off the ground.

"We've made it this far and managed to force the enemy to regroup for now. The archers can hold their forces at bay but there's no guarantee the enemy won't attack again before nightfall. Eventually we're going to run out of ammunition."

"So, what is the plan, Captain?" Gus asked.

"You tell me." Garret said gravely.

Gus felt very uneasy as the captain led him to the top of the hill behind the archers, far enough away that no one would be likely to hear him.

"We can't hold this position forever. So, either you have a plan or we leave tonight and leave you behind. Understand?" Garret spat.

Gus suddenly felt the pressure of everyone on that hill riding on his tiny little shoulders. It took a moment for him to wrap his head around what was happening. With a force of will, he swallowed and summoned what tiny scraps of courage he had left. "If we're lucky they won't attack until dawn, correct?"

Garret raised an eyebrow but said nothing.

It looked like it was up to Gus to make a decision. "Er. Um. Well, assuming they don't attack immediately since we have the high ground, we need to make use of the cover of night to dig a trench in the field just in front of our hill. When their cavalry charges, we let loose some arrows to keep their attention up and not on where they're riding. It might not catch all of them but it could be enough to stop some of the horses and give our men on the ground a chance to charge in and attack."

Gus paused to give Garret a chance to disapprove but the captain simply continued listening. He continued, "next, once the cavalry has been dealt with, they're going to form up a line to march against us. By then we will be dangerously low on ammunition, as you said. With a unified line, we're done for, so what we need is to punch through their line to divide their forces. Then what's left of our own cavalry can sweep in from the left and the rest of our men can attack from the right. They'll be forced to fight on two fronts with

Snowball in between them." Gus was met with a look of surprise from the captain. "Well?" He asked. "What do you think?"

Garret mulled it over for a minute before he said with a bemused smile "It's a good plan. You're in charge of making sure we make it until nightfall. Understood?"

"Yes, sir!" Gus said with enthusiasm.

As Garret was turning to leave, he added, "You're on your own finding a shovel."

"Wait, what?" Gus called out after him. However, Garret made no reply. He merely waved a hand lazily over his shoulder to dismiss the peasant and went about to make his rounds with the remaining troops.

Gus knew his plan was sound and he was certain it would work. There was just one flaw: None of the mercenaries had a shovel. Determined not to be defeated so easily, Gus scoured their position on the hill for anything he could use to dig a formidable trench. He even considered using a sword or an axe to break up the ground but there was little to no chance that any of the mercenaries would put their only weapon to use for such a purpose. After half an hour of searching and asking for help Gus was left with little more than his own two hands to dig a trench deep enough to stop a herd of charging cavalry.

"What's the matter?" One of the mercenaries called. "Haven't started digging yet?"

The other men laughed at the peasant's plight. The sun was already setting.

Gus flushed and balled up his fists as the mercenaries mocked him. He wanted to shout a clever retort back at them but he had no ammunition to work with. In anger he grabbed up his lantern and marched out to where the trench would need to be dug. If they were just going to laugh then he was going to have to prove them wrong.

Of course, these are the sorts of irrational thoughts that pass through the mind of an angry man. There was no way Gus could dig such a trench by himself without any tools. Even if he worked at a fevered pace with a shovel it would take all night to dig a stretch big enough. However, Gus was not concerned with such logistics. He took his little knife and stabbed into the dirt and grass to loosen the soil, pawing it away with his other hand.

Bits of laughter filtered down to him from the mercenary camp and at first Gus paid no mind to their jests. After the sun was down and his work was lit only by the fading light and the amber glow of his lantern the laughs and jeers that carried into the night air began to sting and Gus started to realize just how futile his efforts were and how foolish he was behaving.

After a few hours the camp grew silent as the men got what rest they could before the morning came. Gus had managed to dig a hole about two feet wide and two feet deep that ran little more than an arm span. By then he was exhausted. His fingers stung from the dirt and his knife had grown quite dull. He collapsed against the side of his trench and took a break. "Forget it. I'm never going to finish this damned thing." He said quietly to himself.

"Hello, Mister Gus Man!" Snowball said happily as he stood over his companion.

"Hello Snowball..." Gus sighed, feeling thoroughly defeated.

"What is Mister Gus Man doing?" The Minotaur asked.

"I'm digging myself a hole..." Gus said, referring more to his own foolishness than the trench he had started.

"Why?"

"To make myself look like an idiot." Gus groaned. He got up off the ground and sat down on the edge of the hole. When he saw that Snowball was still looking at him with curiosity he explained. "If we can dig a trench here, there's a chance we can survive the enemy. They're camped less than a mile away but it's far enough that they won't be able to tell what we're doing under the cover of darkness. The trench will help stop the enemy riders from charging into our camp and obliterating us in one go. We just have to finish it before the morning comes or we'll all be killed. It's a good plan, Snowball," Gus said throwing his arms down helplessly, "the problem is there's no way I can dig this hole big enough by myself and I don't even have a shovel."

Snowball patted his good friend on the back (making Gus wince with each blow) and smiled. "Oh! Do not worry Mister Gus Man. Snowball will help dig long hole thing!"

Gus looked at his companion with a bit of confusion. Snowball didn't have a shovel, or any other useful implement to use for that matter. He got up out of his hole and stood back to watch skeptically as Snowball sized up the hole. When the Minotaur nodded assuredly and grabbed hold of his hammer with the hefty head down toward the earth, Gus realized a profound truth. When you're as big as Snowball and all you have is a hammer, life's problems start looking an awful lot like nails.

Snowball gripped his weapon like a croquet mallet and, with an enthusiastic wind up, he swung down at the side of the hole. The earth exploded up in a cloud and took a sizeable chunk out of the ground.

At first, Gus was hopeful that this method would work but after a few more swings it became apparent that the massive hammer would be a poor tool to complete the trench in time. However, Snowball's massive strength and powerful weapon started giving Gus ideas. If all he had was a hammer... what he really needed *was* a nail!

Gus picked up his lantern and held it aloft to see further around the area. He could barely make it out in the dark but he found what he was looking for. "Come on, Snowball!" He said excitedly.

They both rushed over to a small copse of young trees where Gus found a birch as big around as his arm. "Snowball, we need to get this tree down! I'll go get an axe!"

Gus rushed off to the camp. He found a battle axe resting on the ground near a snoring mercenary. He figured it wouldn't be missed and the mercenary would forgive him for using it if it helped save their entire company so he took it. When he returned to the birch tree with the axe to chop it down, he found a hole where the tree had been. Nearby the tree lay, roots and all next to Snowball who stood looking to Gus for further instructions.

"Did you just..." Gus decided it best not to even think about the kind of strength plucking a tree from the ground would take. "Here. Take this." He handed the axe to his companion. "We need to sheer off the branched and cut right here close to the roots."

After a series of powerful and precise cuts, they were left with a relatively straight tree trunk cut down to a point at the top. Snowball nodded and smiled, pleased with his handiwork as he handed Gus the axe.

Working together, Gus directed Snowball to place the tip of the tree in the hole against the sidewall. "Alright. Now I'll hold up the tree and you hit that end there. Understand?"

Just like that, Snowball hammered the tree into the earth like a great nail, keeping it at a shallow angle. Once the tree was almost completely under the earth, Gus had Snowball stop. "Alright. Do you think you're strong enough to lift it now?" He asked.

For a moment he was afraid it would be too much strain on Snowball. However, Snowball grunted with a nod and took the end of the tree in both hands, straddling the hole. With incredible power and the veins in his arms bulging, Snowball lifted with his great legs. The earth seemed to groan and crack with the impossible force of the Minotaur's strength and with a sudden give, the earth split and the tree ripped a long hole the span of several tall men.

"Haha!" Gus laughed with triumph. "It worked! Quickly! We need to dig the hole a lot longer."

Through the night, Gus and Snowball worked, using the tree as a lever to tear the earth and loosen the soil. When at last the tree trunk snapped under the massive pressure the trench was just wide enough to work for Gus's plan. Tossing the timber aside they worked together to remove the loose soil from the trench. Gus pawed from one end with his hands with no great speed. However, Snowball more than made up for it, battering soil from the hole with his hammer with great joy. When at last the sun began to spread its morning light above the horizon, Gus sat exhausted with Snowball beside him staring at their handiwork proudly. Much to Gus's relief, the earth Snowball had knocked around with his hammer had fallen evenly in brown clouds around the trench, making it difficult to see through the grass. Beyond his own belief, they had succeeded in making it a formidable trench.

"Well, Snowball," Gus said to his friend, "I think this plan just might work."

Chapter XII

They got up and found the captain who had just stirred from his sleep. When Garret walked to the front of the camp to view where the enemy had set up for the night, he saw the trench carved neatly across the ground before the hill. His jaw dropped.

"Well," Gus puffed out his chest, "What do you think? Shall we give it a go?"

"I... Uh... Well, that is..." Garret was dumbfounded. He met Gus's gaze and nodded in disbelief. "I suppose... Yes. We shall. How did you..." His voice trailed off.

"We'll need to get the men up to speed on the plan before the enemy gets organized." Gus continued.

"Yes... Yes!" Garret snapped out of his daze. "Gather up the leaders of each unit! We don't have much time."

"Yes, sir!" Gus beamed. He did exactly as the captain asked and rounded up the head of the cavalry, the archers and the ground forces, though he met with skeptical looks from each of them. After explaining the plan, the men scrambled around the camp to prepare.

While they were busy with preparations, Gus took advantage of the time to do the one thing he needed to do. He sat down on the ground to rest. He was beyond exhausted. His head felt like a great weight on his shoulders, his muscles ached in places he didn't know he had and his eyes felt like they were about to fall out of his head. His head nodded and he fell asleep.

It didn't last for very long. He was torn from slumber by his body being jostled to and fro. "What... What is...?" He was incredibly disoriented. He saw the ground moving from underneath him as he rocked back and forth. As his senses sharpened, he became keenly aware that he was moving backward and there was a pressure across his chest. He looked down, perplexed, as he saw a bovine tail swishing beneath his feet. "What is going on?" He said in a sort of groggy panic.

He felt around on his chest and his fingers gripped the leather straps holding him in place. When at last he saw the all-too-familiar hammer head swinging to the side just barely into his view he realized.

Someone had strapped him to Snowball's back!

"Aaaahhhhhhh!" He cried in panic as his companion charged into the fray, knocking renegade soldiers left and right.

The battle had already started!

"Gods, why!" He screamed as the din of battle drowned his plea.

His unique perspective of the battle was one of bewildered terror. Gus saw men sprawling to his left and right as the Minotaur ran forward knocking enemies out of the way. He saw renegade soldiers turning their attention to the cavalry as it pressed in from his right and the infantry charging in from his left.

As his companion charged ahead, he could see soldiers pressing in toward the Minotaur's rear, desperate to stop the rampaging engine of destruction. They were running to catch up to the beast, weapons drawn and, unfortunately, heading right toward Gus.

As they closed the gap and came within weapon's reach, Gus realized they would have to cleave through him to get to the Minotaur's back. He looked down. He looked left, he looked right. His hands groped for something, *anything* to defend himself with. His fingers closed around a handle at his waist and he drew the sword the Knight of the Silver Dragon had given him. He'd forgotten to remove it when he'd fallen asleep and as luck would have it, it was still strapped on.

"Hah!" He belted as he swatted away a spear that came quite close to piercing his heart. "Aha!" He cried. He'd meant to sound like a fierce warrior but it came out more like a cry of desperate panic. He swatted the spear away again as the soldier continued running after him with determined fury.

"Why would you do this?" Gus yelped as he and Snowball tore across the battlefield. "Who straps a man to a minotaur's back when he's sleeping?"

Suddenly, he spun around. Or rather, the Minotaur did. Snowball had reached the far edge of the advancing army's forces and had turned to face the soldiers behind him.

Gus saw the enemy commander sitting atop his horse with plumed helmet staring curiously at the harnessed peasant. He smiled sheepishly and waved a hand. "Hello."

The commander soon disappeared behind a line of infantry as they closed in around Snowball. Gus saw a line of men charging right at him with swords drawn. For several minutes, Snowball spun and turned, swinging his hammer about like an angry hawk darting through the sky. The whipping hammer smashed into armor and sword and legs and all manner of enemy. The furious onslaught gave Gus little room to get his bearings. As the world blurred around him all he could do is swat away steel as it came too close for comfort.

Foe after foe fell to his monstrous companion and before Gus knew it the sharpened swords aimed at his poor peasant body grew fewer and fewer until at last he could see through his dizzied vision that Snowball stood victorious in a field of unconscious men.

"What..." He held back his gorge as the dizziness caught up with him. "What's happening?" He burped. "What's going on, Snowball?"

Suddenly, a resounding cheer arose from the battlefield.

"What was that? Did we win. Did we beat them?" Gus asked.

Snowball grunted and began walking back toward the hill. Gus was squirming, trying to see around the Minotaur but to no avail. Snowball came at last to a stop and Gus saw a few mercenaries standing in the corners of his vision.

"Victory has been won this day!" Garret shouted to his men. "Take care of our wounded and plunder what you will. Tonight, we celebrate!"

The men gave a loud cheer.

"You have done very well this day!" Garret said. "We could not have emerged victorious if not for you."

Gus assumed the captain was addressing Snowball. After his up close and personal ride along the creature's devastating onslaught, it was a wonder they even needed the other mercenaries. Surely, the Minotaur had defeated more men by himself than perhaps the entire cavalry put together.

"You have proven yourself valuable to our..." The captain fell short. "Would you please turn around?" He asked impatiently.

Snowball turned and suddenly Gus was facing the whole of the mercenary army. They stared at him with respect, many nodding in approval. Gus went wide eyed as he realized that Garret had been addressing him.

"You have proven yourself valuable to this company. You will be promoted to the role of tactician from here on out!" The captain said for all to hear.

Gus was speechless as the men cheered him on. It wasn't long before he was unstrapped from Snowball's back. At which time he stumbled about, dizzy, embarrassed and discovering all sorts of places that hurt. A few of the men congratulated him personally. Most were too busy tending the wounded or thanking their captain who was all too happy to take credit for their victory due to his wise choice of tactician.

To Gus's relief, casualties were very few that morning. Most of the men who had perished had done so the previous day before the company began its retreat. The mercenary group gathered what they could from the battlefield and buried their dead on that hill. Once a word was said for those who had fallen, the company marched to meet up with the wagons. Gus noticed that they left their slain enemies where they lay in the open. He also noted, quite curiously, that the mercenary company did not fly their colors during the fight. Banners and flags had been stowed in the wagons. He wondered why they had the banners at all if they didn't intend to use them in a fight but he soon put it out of mind as he helped move the company's supplies.

They traveled for several hours, making camp further south on a small, flat piece of land by a shallow stream. It was cozy and a dense tree-line nearby gave them plenty of cover from the wind. It was there that the men set up camp and celebrated.

The sounds of cheers and laughter rang from all corners of the camp. Gus helped himself to a roasted boar's leg as he sat down around one of the many fires. In spite of the revelry, he found he was quite alone. The other men kept their distance. He was relieved as his furry companion sat down beside him, causing the log on which he sat to quake.

"Snowball... I've been meaning to ask..." Gus began, not sure how best to word his complaint. "Were you the one who decided to strap me to your back?"

Snowball shrugged. "Mister Gus Man was going to be left on the ground and puny hoomans would walk all over you. Besides, Snowball was going into battle and would not be able to protect Mister Gus Man if he was sleeping."

"So, you tied me to your back?" Gus raised an eyebrow.

"Mister Slushy Man thought it was a good idea." Snowball beamed. "Snowball thought so too."

"Mister Slushy Man?" Gus tried his best to figure out what Snowball meant but it was anyone's guess. "Who is Mister Slushy man?"

Snowball pointed a finger across the camp at a group of mercenaries feasting around another fire. "Mister Slushy man."

"You mean the Knight of the Silver Dragon?" Gus clarified, picking out the only familiar face among them.

"Yes. Mister Slushy man."

"How is he Mister Slushy man?"

Snowball shrugged. "He talks all slushy."

Gus couldn't help but agree with him but he was no less upset. "Wait. You took the advice of a drunk!"

Snowball nodded vigorously. "Mister Slushy man is a great warrior, full of blood and battle. Has good advice."

"No!" Gus said, exasperated. "That was terrible advice! I have bruises in places a man should never have bruises. I can hardly walk without pain in my sides." Gus lifted up the sides of his shirt to reveal the large purple patches left by the straps. "See! It hurts to laugh. It hurts to breathe even! Were you thinking about my well-being at all?"

Snowball nodded happily.

"Ugh..." Gus gave up. There was little point in arguing with the Minotaur. From the creature's perspective, Gus was safer on his back than anywhere else on the battlefield. Although he hated to admit it, Snowball had been right. It probably was the safest place for the Minotaur to defend, even if it was an uncomfortable, nauseating ride. "Look. Just don't do it again, please." Gus asked of his friend. "I've had enough posing as a rucksack for one lifetime."

Little more was said as Gus devoured his boar's leg until he and Snowball were joined by an unlikely figure.

"Mister Slushy man!" Snowball greeted him with excitement.

"I see you've made a new friend..." Gus mumbled, less than enthused to be sharing a camp fire with the drunken knight that had been the inventor of his unorthodox battlefield experience.

The Knight of the Silver Dragon staggered over, a pint held carelessly in his hand, sloshing some of its contents over the side. He fell, more than sat, down on a crate to join them. With a grand gesture of welcome he raised his pint, nearly teetering off the back of his seat, and offered a toast. "Here's to a cereblation! Vic-tree in the name of the people that we. That. That we are. Here's to vic-tree!" His speech was so slurred from drink Gus could hardly understand him. "Whasss that look for? We won! Thasss all that matters." He stifled a belch, much to Gus's disgust.

"Sir Knight," Gus addressed him.

"Hold- Hold on a minute." The Knight held up a hand in protest. "We're friends, aren't we? We should be friends."

Gus rolled his eyes. It was clear to him that this supposed knight was well beyond modest inebriation. He didn't much care to endure the knight's company but, lacking friends among the mercenaries, he resigned to tolerate his presence for a little while. Other than being an irritant, he wasn't doing anyone any harm and there was sufficient reason to celebrate after all.

"Wait. What was I talking about?" The knight asked.

"Listen, Sir Knight," Gus tried.

"There! That was it. I'm not Sir Knight. That's not my name. I'm not that name." He shook his head loosely. "Thasss-my name is not that. Don't call me that." He said.

"Then what should I call you, Sir Kn-"

The knight held up a hand in warning to stop Gus from continuing. "My Name is Ethan," he said. "Sir Ethan Wallard, Knight!" He proclaimed with a flourish, standing up with a hand raised to the heavens, "of the Silver Dragon!"

He declared his full name and title with such unexpected clarity that Gus was taken by surprise. He waited for a moment to see what Sir Ethan would do next but when the knight relaxed into the same drunken, wavering posture on his crate Gus was left with the same feeling of disappointment in the knight's tiresome drunkenness.

"Sir Ethan," Gus corrected himself, "you are very drunk."

The knight waved a hand to dismiss it.

"How is it you managed to survive the battle, anyway?" He wondered aloud.

Sir Ethan tried to come up with an answer but even he was confounded by it.

"Oh! Mister Slushy man is not wobbly on the battlefield. Mister Slushy man fought very well!" Snowball commented.

That was certainly a surprise coming from the Minotaur. Perhaps the knight had some sort of clarity he gained through combat. Gus doubted it, but at the same time Snowball had a better view of the fight than he did. Maybe it was true.

"How is it that a knight like you ended up like this?" Gus asked, gesturing at Sir Ethan's wavering posture.

Ethan was a little taken aback and pouted, crossing his hands across his chest, spilling more of his drink on the ground. "How very rude! There's nothing wrong with me at all." He said.

"You used to be a knight of some renown was my understanding." Gus recalled his conversation with one of the men.

"I was!" The knight insisted. "I fought for king and country with the best of them. Those years in service to the crown were filled with honor and glory!"

"But now?" Gus asked. "I mean, look at you. It's downright pitiable! Your honor and glory are no sharper than your sentences."

"Whasss that sssssposed to mean?" The knight slurred.

"You're a drunk, sir." Gus said simply. He felt a little mean saying it but he was growing more and more irate with Sir Ethan.

"And what would you have done?" Sir Ethan challenged. "My kingdom is dead now. My king is slain and the knights of Kismet are disbanded. The kingdom of Kismet is no more." A note of deep sorrow fell into his voice. "What else am I supposed to do?"

Gus was silent. He'd never heard of Kismet when he'd lived in his little village and certainly hadn't known the tragedy that had befallen it. The problems of the kingdoms at large were foreign to him. "Tell me then. What happened to your kingdom?"

Sir Ethan swallowed and set down his pint. "The king of these lands led a campaign against my people. They stormed the castle, killing many of my fellow knights. They killed my liege before my very eyes. We were outnumbered and outmatched. I did the only thing I could. I fled. I ran for my very life. They left Kismet broken and without a king. Now they serve their new king and what once was Kismet is now gone." Ethan stared off into another time, memories filling his vision with images of the past. "If only you could have seen it. It was beautiful."

Gus noticed his voice grow calm and clear, the drunkenness disappearing as he spoke.

"Endless seas of golden grains grew in the countryside. Lush verdant forests surrounded those lands, filled with wild deer and pheasants. We used to hunt in the woods when the season was right. In one day, we would come back with enough meat to feed a village, there was so much game. I remember the sunrise as it crested the hills in the east. It was like golden fire coming down from heaven. It was so peaceful. We were a peaceful people, building paradise with our own sweat and hard work. And we had succeeded. Never was there a place in this world so free from the troubles of our time." He slowly returned to seeing his companions around the campfire. "That's what I swore to protect," He said. "And now she's gone, ssswallowed up by a con- by a conquering king." He sighed and took up his pint, taking another swig. "What would you have done?" He asked again, more to himself than to anyone else.

Gus was at a loss for words. What little bit of revelry he'd had for their victory that day was lost in the sorrow of Sir

Ethan's tale. He finished his last few bites and turned in for the night, leaving the broken knight reminiscing by the campfire.

Chapter XIII

The next three days were spent marching through the countryside to the southeast. Gus and Snowball kept mostly to themselves, striking up conversation with the other mercenaries only as necessary. They were heading toward a larger town with a trade industry of good repute. The company was in need of supplies and new recruits to replenish their ranks.

They arrived mid-day in the bustling burg of Carath amid caravans from all corners of the map. In the market square, people were shouting, smiling, bartering and haggling over this, that and everything else. Colors of all kinds could be seen in the stalls and carts of those wishing to peddle their wares. It was a simple burg built with rosy stone native to the area and with the flourishing trade industry it would see such development in years to come.

It took quite some time for Gus to take it all in. The most trade he'd ever seen had been from travelers that would pass through every spring and fall season on their way to somewhere else. The sheer volume of colorful fruits and vegetables, cloths and accessories was enough to overload his senses. He was almost awestruck. His wonderment made the jostles and bumps from those who passed around him go unnoticed and it wasn't until someone asked him hurriedly to move that he realized he was standing right in the flow of foot traffic.

He looked around for the other mercenaries but very few could be seen. Most of them had gone to the taverns and only a handful were shopping to spend their hard-earned pay.

The captain and a few of the mercenaries would be busy selling what loot had been taken from their enemies and Gus had a feeling that the employer who had hired the company to attack the renegade soldiers in the first place would be in town to deliver payment for a successful job. That left Gus with ample time to do as he pleased until later that night. However, being a small peasant in a highly populated market was enough to make him uneasy.

He looked around for his companion but the towering Minotaur was nowhere to be seen. Lacking the confidence to navigate the city himself, he decided instead to search for his friend. At first it was quite difficult to see anything over the crowd of people so Gus looked for a good vantage point where he could see more of the city. It took him a few minutes walking down the main street before he spied a grassy hill with a tall maple standing just off the gentle slope. He could see a path winding up to it from the next intersection so he turned and headed that way. At the top he found a stone bench beneath the tree and he climbed on top of it to get a better view.

There was very little to see. Crowds of people went about their business and wagons came and went. Gus spied several merchants filing into a tavern on one of the streets. After a few minutes of looking he was startled by a young boy staring up at him.

"What are you doing?" The boy asked.

Gus felt somewhat embarrassed but, being that it was just a child he simply answered "I'm trying to get a better view."

"What are you looking at?" The boy asked inquisitively.

"I... Uh..." Gus wasn't sure how to answer without startling the young lad. "I'm looking for my friend. He seems to have gotten lost. Or... well. I have gotten lost and I need to find him."

"I can help you find him!" The boy offered with excitement. "This may seem like a big place, mister, but it isn't. There's lots of people who come and go but I seen most of this city myself. What does he look like?"

"Errr..." Gus gave the boy's offer a second thought. "Well..."

"I know loads of people here. I'm sure he won't be hard to find."

"No. I don't think he'd be hard to find either..." Gus said dryly.

"So, it's settled then!" The boy said. "What's his name?"

"Well..." He couldn't very well ignore the boy's eagerness, in spite of the fact that the child's parents would most likely be appalled if he came anywhere near such a monster as the Snowball. "I can tell you this... he..." Gus thought carefully, "he has a great big horned helmet. Yes. And he's a giant. Biggest fellow you've ever seen. Fills up a door-frame and more."

"Wow!" The boy's eyes went wide with wonder. "How did you lose such a big fellow?"

"How did I lose such a big fellow?" Gus kicked himself. "Well," he said to the boy, "like I said, I think I may be the one more lost. Listen, he wears furs from a dozen animals and he almost looks like a bull under all that armor. If you find him just let him know that Gus is looking for him. He'll know what you mean."

The young lad nodded eagerly and dashed off into town. Gus decided not to wait around and headed in a similar direction. The longer the mercenaries were in the city the more likely Snowball would set off a panic among the residents. He had to locate the big guy before that happened. He'd never heard of a minotaur wandering about a city in a peaceable fashion and he had the feeling nobody else had either.

He searched and searched as the sun arced across the sky but to no avail. As he was passing down a lane just off the main thoroughfare, he heard a great crash and wood being splintered. He rushed around the corner as fast as he could, his pulse racing, afraid Snowball had decided to use his hammer on something. Or worse, someone. To his relief it was merely a crate that had fallen off a passing wagon and broken into pieces. Straw and splinters lay littered among a pile of strewn grain that had spilled from several sacks.

He turned and headed back down the alley to continue his search. As he got more and more lost among the twisting turns and alleys that cut their way in between the houses he came across a courtyard with a stone fountain at its center and several overhanging trees. While he was glad to be out of the maze of interweaving alleys, he felt even more isolated from the rest of town. As he passed into an alley across the courtyard, he heard a distinctly familiar voice.

"Payment in full. That's the deal." It was Captain Garret.

"That would normally be acceptable but it is a considerable investment." Someone else was talking to him. "Full price up front would be too great a risk. I have no doubt we can deal, but without a guarantee it can't be done."

Garret frowned. "We run a dangerous business. What should I tell my men? That they won't be paid if we fail? Mercenary work isn't cheap."

"I understand, I understand." The second voice plied.

Garret and the other man walked casually into the courtyard. Garret's companion was a thin faced man with a bald head, dressed in a simple, cream colored robe. He stood a few inches shorter than Garret who seemed to look down upon him with disdain.

Something in Gus told him to take shelter and retreat down the alley to avoid being seen. Perhaps it was just that Garret was clearly in the middle of a private deal. Or, perhaps it was the feeling in his gut. Either way he remained out of sight as they passed by.

"Payment in full." Garret repeated.

"I'm sorry, but I cannot. We'll pay you for half. Once the job is complete you can claim the rest. Are we agreed?"

Gus crept to the corner as they continued on down another alley to catch more of their conversation.

"You're certain that they are transporting the goods in three days."

"You have my word, sir. You have my word." The bald man insisted.

"I shouldn't need to tell you the consequences if you're lying to me." Garret warned.

The bald man waved a hand to dismiss the comment. "Really. There is no need. Business is good. We both have great things to look forward to. I can assure you this one will be a walk in the park."

"It had better be. That last one cost me more men than I care to think about. These are people's lives on the line."

"It is a grisly business," the bald man sighed, "but such is life. I trust you'll be able to recruit the necessary replacements."

Garret shook his head with disappointment. "I'll need to complete this next job with what men I have left before I can afford more."

Gus continued to follow them, unable to help himself, as they passed around a corner down the alley. He kept a reasonable distance, lest they should turn and see him.

"Were the casualties really that bad?" The bald man asked.

"Yes." Garret said simply. "The Kismet soldiers are hearty and strong but their numbers are growing thin."

"I see. It is unfortunate, then."

"It matters not. We are still making progress."

Gus wondered what Garret meant by that but he could no longer turn his ear to their conversation. Garret and his associate had reached a wide street where there were no places he could hide. He watched them carry on, exchange a handshake, part ways and disappear into the crowd. He couldn't help but feel somewhat guilty, eavesdropping like that. His parents had raised him better than that. He was kicking himself a little for doing so but all the same he couldn't shake the feeling that something had compelled him to listen on like he had. He decided it best to put it from his mind for the time being. Garret ran his company and provided the work and it was not Gus's place to question what went on in private conversations that didn't include him. Instead, he returned to his search for his monstrous companion. It was uncanny that Snowball could remain unnoticed in such a place and the fact that Gus had not been able to locate him was of equal concern. He decided to head to a tavern, hoping that the Minotaur had perhaps gone for a drink with the other men.

Evening came and Gus returned to the camp with the rest of the mercenaries. They had set up a site just outside the city and erected a large bonfire to gather around. Gus sat amid the rest of the men, disappearing among jovial chatter and raucous laughter. The roar died down as Garret took up a position in front of the fire, where all of the men could see him. He addressed them clearly, his expression serious.

"I hope you have all had enough time to rest and enjoy yourselves," he began. "However, we are moving out tomorrow morning. Our next job will involve timeliness on our part and we have but three days to reach our destination and prepare." Garret began to pace back and forth as he spoke. "There will be a caravan traveling this direction, illegally carrying goods that belong to the rightful king of these lands."

Some of the men chuckled and laughed.

Garret held up a hand to keep them quiet. "Our job is to retrieve these stolen goods in the name of the kingdom by whatever means necessary. We are more than enough men to carry out this mission. Your orders will be dispensed to you in a few days. In the meantime, rest up and enjoy yourselves. You've earned it. Tomorrow morning at first light we march. Understood?"

The men raised up their fists and shouted in agreement. The captain dismissed himself and returned to his tent. When the men dispersed, Gus noticed a larger figure among the crowd.

"Snowball!" He called out, waving a hand up in the air. The Minotaur turned and waited for his companion to catch up. "Snowball, I've been looking everywhere for you. Where were you off to?" Gus asked.

The Minotaur smiled happily and told him the whole story. "Oh, Mister Gus Man! Always there is strawberries where you go. Snowball did not know there would be so many. It took Snowball this many hours to find them all." Snowball held up his four fingered hand.

Gus through up his arms. "How do you find all of these strawberries? It's not like there's a farm for them everywhere we go!" He rolled his eyes and headed to where he'd set up his tent.

Snowball followed close at hand, still full of delightful joy at his wonderful day. "Oh, but Mister Gus Man, there is a strawberry farm all over. Snowball found it today."

"So, you were gone all day, eating strawberries that you found on someone's farm?"

The Minotaur nodded.

"Okay. See, that's called stealing. You can't just eat food off a farm that doesn't belong to you?"

"Okay Mister Gus Man."

"You're not going to do it again?" Gus asked, looking at Snowball out of the corner of his eye.

Snowball nodded.

"And why is that?"

"Because Mister Gus Man says not to." Snowball nodded with a serious expression.

"NO! Gods... You aren't going to do it again because it's stealing. Stealing is wrong. Do you understand?"

Snowball shrugged.

"Great..." Gus mumbled. "Well, listen. We've got another job to do here in a few days. Don't go wandering off unless you tell me first, alright?"

Snowball agreed and the matter seemed settled. Gus retired to his tent for the evening and the night passed uneventfully.

The hard march over the next few days seemed grueling. Gus's feet ached terribly, and the few places the company stopped to rest he was more than happy to sit down to get off of them. On the third day they made camp just on the other side of a bluff overlooking a dirt road heading further north. Preparations were made and most of the men were busy sharpening weapons and tending the horses.

Gus was busy polishing armor by a campfire when he was interrupted by the captain. "You're needed, strategist. We have planning to do."

Gus looked down at the greave he was only halfway done shining. "Should I finish this first?"

Garret was mildly annoyed. "Come on. Leave that to the peasants."

For a moment Gus thought to remind Garret that he was a peasant but the thought of his newly found title as strategist made him reconsider. He followed Garret to the captain's tent and set about analyzing the map laid before him on the table.

It was a simple map, detailing the bluff and the road as well as the tree lines in the distance.

"This is a simple mission. We hijack the wagons from the thieves. Even you can handle something like this."

Gus swallowed and furrowed his brow. "Will we be taking prisoners?" He asked.

"What?"

"Prisoners. Are we taking prisoners? If we mean to attack, whether or not we intend to take prisoners changes things immensely."

"What difference would that make?" Garret asked.

"Well, you see, if we intend to let them flee, then we'll want to leave an opening for the enemy to run away. If we are going to take prisoners, we'll have to cut off all the escape routes. Are we going to take prisoners?"

"Hmmm..." Garret began pacing the tent as he gave it some thought. "I'd just as soon kill them as take any prisoners." Gus was shocked but Garret continued, thinking out loud more than addressing Gus. "Well, their lives still have some value. The main objective is to secure the cargo they're carrying. I suppose we can spare those who flee and kill the rest."

Gus tried to appeal as best he could. "If I might suggest, Captain. Perhaps we could let all of them escape and if there are any that stay to fight, we take them prisoner instead."

Garret wasn't pleased with the idea but he let Gus continue.

"As you said, the main objective is the cargo. What difference does it make if they escape or not? Their lives might have some value to this company." He said, picking up on Garret's comment.

"What are you suggesting?" Garret asked.

"Well, I'm suggesting we take prisoners instead of just killing everyone. We're not here to slaughter them all, are we?"

"Well, I..." Garret began, "no, I suppose we're not."

"Then let's take prisoners. We can avoid the risk to our own men as well if we avoid outright bloodshed. After all, the men are our greatest resource, am I right?"

"You have a point..." Garret said, rubbing his chin in thought as he paced. "We did take considerable casualties in our last fight. We can't afford to incur costs like that on a consistent basis or this company will fold."

"Exactly!" Gus agreed.

"Are you suggesting we sell these prisoners on the open market?" Garret asked, liking the idea.

"What?!" Gus exclaimed, "no!"

Garret didn't seem to hear him. "You are right! We can take prisoners and press them into service. They can work off their debt through labor and join our forces if they wish. That will help us build our ranks as well as reduce costs. Then, if they don't wish to fight for us, we can use them as bargaining chips. That will make him furious."

"Wait, what?" Gus asked but Garret continued to ignore him.

"He'll have no choice but to pay for their release. He can't afford not to. It's perfect!" He turned and leaned over the table at Gus, his face red with excitement. "We'll let them run for their lives and those who stay and fight we'll take prisoner! An excellent idea! So, what's the plan?"

"I, um, well..." Gus swallowed, deeply concerned about what was going through the Captain's head. However, uneasy as it made him, he pushed aside his concern for a moment to do his best as a tactician. "Alright. Well, first we need to get the caravan to stop here," he pointed at a place on the map, "Just beneath the bluff. This will give us a natural barrier so they can't escape that way."

"Wait." Garret interrupted. "I thought I told you we were going to let them escape."

"We are, just hear me out. We use this as a barrier so they can't go that way. You can station your archers here at the top of the bluff and that will give them the best vantage point. Next, we place a platoon right here in front of them, as well as some cavalry. That way they can't simply make a break for it. We'll also want to place men here." He pointed to a place just off the road. "Their wagons will have to make wide turns. If we place our men here, they won't be able to turn around. The only other option for them will be to go backwards. We station the rest of the troops here, just up the slope and out of sight. Then, when the caravan stops, we can sweep in from behind to prevent them retreating. That will leave an opening here between the rear troops and the forward troops for the enemy to escape. Without being able to make a wide turn, they'll have no choice but to leave the wagons behind if they decide to flee."

The Captain nodded as he considered. "A sound plan." Garret acknowledged.

"What do we know about these men?" Gus asked.

"What do you mean?"

"Are they well-armed? Do you think they'll stay to fight it out?"

"Well, um," Garret thought on it for a moment, "You see, they are armed and well-trained fighters. They will stay and fight if they can."

"These thieves are well trained?" Gus asked.

"Er, um, yes," Garret explained, "We've heard that they may be former soldiers from the kingdom up north. Word is they've abandoned their duties to pillage the countryside, you see."

"Ah." Gus said. "I understand. Well! That will make things a little more difficult. We need to find a way to convince them to abandon their cargo." Gus gave it some thought.

"And how do you propose we do that?"

"Hmmm... We need to scare them with something so they'll run instead of fight. Something they won't think twice about."

"Well, what did you have in mind?" Garret asked impatiently.

He gave it some thought and then suddenly a huge smile spread across Gus's face. "Oh, I've got an idea," he said, "Do we have any drums?"

Chapter XIV

The wagons rolled along lazily, their wheels skipping and jumping in the shallow ruts along the dirt road. The peaceful sounds of birds and insects gave the day a cheery atmosphere under the bright sun as the caravan passed the tree line. As they rolled along the drivers chatted merrily, unaware of the danger that lay ahead.

There were three wagons in all, each heavily laden with barrels and secure with ropes and canvas. Each had its own pair of drivers and a finely dressed, well-armed guard sitting idly on the back. Beside these bulging transports walked another twelve men, scattered several paces from each wagon. They kept their eyes out for signs of trouble but in the beauty of a radiant day their attention had wandered.

Two of the drivers conversed energetically, one with the reins in his hands, the other trying to speak through a mouthful of bread about the finer points of life.

"Listen, you're not listening. What I'm saying is that all things come to a point. You see? It's like how when you look down the road at the path it looks like it gets smaller and smaller the further away you look." He took a big bite. "Iff naw science, iff juff simmle troof."

The one with the reins sighed. "I *am* looking down the path and all I'm seeing is a bunch of dirt and grass. The further I look, the more I can't really see. It's all blurry. And you see, it's not that I'm not listening. It's that I don't want to listen to you when you're stuffing half a loaf of bread down your throat. Finish your food before you speak for gods' sakes."

"I'm noff stuffin alf a loaf of bread dowm my froat!" The first one said. "I'm juff hungry. A growin man haff a eaff somefin."

"What did I say about talking? You've got horrible manners." The one driving pointed out.

The first one stopped to chew his mouthful and spoke before he took another bite. "But they do come to a point at the end, they do. Look!" He pointed down the road. "The sides of the road way over there in the distance are no more than a speck apart, they are!"

"How the bloody hell can you see that far? There's nothing out there but a blur!"

"Well at least I still have my vision then." The man with the loaf of bread said before taking another bite.

"I wish we could say the same for your intellect." The driver muttered.

"Hey! Thaff naw nife oo fay!" The eater sprayed crumbs everywhere as he spoke.

"Finish your bite!" The driver groaned.

He swallowed. "Well I'm tellin' you that's how it is. You can't see but they grow closer together, and that's just what I'm sayin'. A man goes through life like we go down this road and as he goes on his possibilities grow smaller and smaller."

"Then how come when we travel down this road the path stays the same, eh? We've been driving since sun up and I haven't seen the path get smaller and smaller, have you?"

"How would you know? You can hardly see!"

"I can see the road right here. Look at it. Is it any smaller now as it was back where we started?"

"Well... no." The eater admitted.

"Then how does that make any sense?"

"Well... what if it did get smaller?" The eater proposed. "What if we've just gotten smaller with it as we went down the road. Like I was sayin', maybe a man's horizons dwindle with time. And look at how much time we've spent on this road. We've been driving all day, you said it yourself! What if we've just been getting smaller and smaller?"

"That don't make no sense either." The driver shook his head.

"Yeah. I guess you're right. But it does look smaller in the distance there. They call it something. Perspective, I think. Yeah. That's it. It's perspectively a lot smaller over there than it is over here. And a man's life is the same way. When a man gets old, he can't do as much as he used to, you see? His possibilities grow fewer. A man of let's say seventy years old wouldn't be able to go become a soldier. He's too feeble. And one that's been an idiot all his life wouldn't be able to become a fancy scholar, you see? They've just grown too much in one way and the possibilities are fewer."

"Who even lives that long? Nobody lives to be seventy years old!" The driver exclaimed.

"They do so!" The eater insisted. "Lots of people do."

"Oh, really? Who? Who do you know that's lived past the age of fifty?"

"Well... there's... There's lots of folks. I just don't remember right now." The eater stuffed another mouthful of bread in his face and folded his arms.

"You don't remember because you don't know any. I don't know anyone as has lived longer than fifty, and that was my grand mum it was. They either dies because they get sick, or get killed in war, or get in some kind of accident. That's the way the world works. And even if they did live to seventy, it's not like their body just gives out! If someone was to not get sick or killed or something who knows how long a person could live. Maybe an idiot can become a fancy scholar. Who are we to say?"

"Look, all I'm saying is we have to look to the road ahead." The eater rolled his eyes. "That's all we got to do.

"Speak for yourself, watching roads that get smaller staying the same size..." The driver trailed off.

"No. You got to look to the road ahead." The eater insisted.

"No, I don't. I'm just going to keep on driving and not listening to your ridiculous speeches."

"No. Look to the road ahead!" The eater said more loudly.

"Oh, shut up. Just drop it will you." The driver said.

The eater grabbed the driver by the shoulders and then pointed. "No! Look to the road ahead!" He shouted.

The driver quickly pulled back on the reins as he saw the line of well-armed men blocking the road bearing banners emblazoned with the dragon star emblem of Kismet. The men looked dirty and wore furs and crude clothing over their armor, carrying torches and snarling and sneering at the train. The caravan came to a screeching halt in a thin cloud of dust. The guards escorting the shipment drew their swords and formed up in front of the wagons to defend the precious cargo.

A burning arrow thunked into the ground at their feet, causing them to look up at a high angle to the top of the bluff, a good twenty-five feet above their heads. They saw the line of archers peering down at them, arrows nocked. They made no move to attack, however. Instead, they started chanting in a low rhythmic grunt. With each beat they struck the earth with the butts of their spears or beat their swords against their shields. As the chant continued the mercenaries grew louder and louder. The drivers looked to their left to try to turn but that way was blocked.

"Back up!" One of the drivers shouted over the din.

"We can't!" The guards at the rear cried. "They're blocking the way!"

Just as planned, the caravan was hemmed in. They couldn't turn, they couldn't retreat. The chanting grew louder and louder.

One of the well-dressed guards sprang from the lead wagon and ran to the front, commanding the other guards to defend the shipment. The men at the rear of the train did the same, with the remainder splitting their forces between each. One guard at the front of the line stepped forward, his head high and his shoulders back to issue a warning.

"We will not be intimidated by bandits! Remove yourselves from our path! We are members of his majesty's royal guard. Interfering with royal affairs is punishable by death!" He shouted, doing his best to look steadfast and unafraid.

The mercenaries continued their chant, louder and louder.

The caravan guards exchanged worried looks with one another, not sure what they should do.

"I said...!" The royal guard began.

Just then the Minotaur leaped from the precipice, landing with a thud in a cloud of dust a few feet from the lead guard, leaned forward to just a foot from his face and let loose a mighty roar that deafened ears and echoed across the countryside. He roared so loud the guard's hair flew and he staggered back a step.

The guards dropped their weapons and ran, screaming, as fast as they could through the gap left by the mercenaries, quickly disappearing into the tree line. The guard at the front of the train shook in terror as he fumbled to pull his sword from its sheath. Snowball was quick to give him a bop on his helmet, sending him to the ground in a heap.

The mercenaries moved in to claim their prize from the front as a commotion broke out from the rear of the caravan. While the majority of the guardsmen had fled for their lives, including those stationed at the rear, one of the members of his majesty's royal guard stood valiant, his sword drawn, fending off six attackers at once as they tried to overtake the rearmost wagon. He fought to protect himself and the cargo with staunch determination.

With his shield in one hand, his sword in the other, he parried blow after blow, delivering quick butts with his shield against the mercenaries in between sword clashes and near misses. As one man charged him with a downward sweeping blow, he hooked the blade with the crosspiece of his sword and turned, throwing the mercenary to the ground and bashing him in the side of the skull with his shield. The other five attackers formed around him to one side, each making quick jabs and darts at the fearless guard. He was not to be deterred, however. He read their movements with seasoned practice and every blow that reached him was easily brushed aside.

"I will not yield!" He shouted warning. "Even if you send a hundred men at me, I will never betray my allegiance to my king!" With a snarl he deflected a spear thrust, rushed forward and knocked one of the men to the ground.

The fallen mercenary crawled away, unwilling to tangle with the skilled swordsman. The other mercenaries backed away a few steps, forming a semi-circle at a safe distance.

"What's this? Afraid to fight me? Cowards!" The royal guardsman barked. He took a few steps forward and the mercenaries backed away toward the mercenaries grouped behind them. "Hah!" He laughed with audacity. "Come on. Who will fight me?! I can take any man! Fight me!" Suddenly a shadow fell over him and he spun around to face his next attacker. He saw a heavily muscled, furry chest instead and slowly raised his gaze upward to see the full form of the Minotaur standing over him.

"Dear gods..." He murmured. He dropped his sword and knelt down on the ground, placing his hands on the back of his head. "I surrender!" He said with dignity. "I surrender."

Snowball was about to swing his hammer but Garret's command stopped him. "That's enough for now. He surrenders. We shall take him prisoner. You there, bind him and take him back to the camp!"

The wagons were quickly seized and driven back to the mercenary encampment. The men packed up their gear and headed back the way they had come with their newly won spoils until nightfall. After camp was set up and a bonfire made the men celebrated their victory with cheers and laughter.

Though he was right in the middle of everything, the celebration seemed out of proportion to Gus. Sure, they had succeeded in their mission. They had only to deliver the cargo. There had been no casualties or bloodshed which was in large part due to Gus' clever strategy. However, they had outnumbered the enemy by an enormous margin. It didn't seem likely that they would have failed given the sheer number of mercenaries. So why were they celebrating so heartily? To Gus they seemed more like bandits, stealing precious cargo under the guise of mercenary banners. It was all a little much to take in. He'd been up above on the bluff so he hadn't witnessed everything but he was glad his plan had worked.

As the men caroused and carried on through the night, Gus left the warm glow of the fire light and took a walk around the camp to help him clear his thoughts. The tents and wagons seemed empty and quiet next to the revelry of the evening as Gus made his way from campsite to campsite. He kicked at stones on the ground and stared up at the stars from time to time. There was something overwhelming to him, being a part of the mercenary band. Being in so close with so many was a little much to take for so long a time. He was glad to be out wandering beneath the stars.

On his wandering path Gus passed by a pair of men standing guard with spears at the rear end of one of the covered wagons. Gus took notice of the iron bars on the end of the wagon. The men caught sight of him and nodded respectfully. It was enough to make Gus smile. Perhaps some of the men recognized his handiwork in planning the attack. He puffed out his chest a little, glad to have at least made some impression. He strode up among them and gave greeting. "Good evening, gentlemen," He said. "Why aren't you celebrating with the rest of the company?"

One of them shrugged and the other answered, "We've been ordered to keep watch over the prisoner."

"Ah. I see," Gus said. "A very important job. It's a shame."

"We'll be relieved soon enough." One said. "We've been taking turns every hour or so to guard him through the night."

An idea crossed the peasant's mind. "May I speak to the prisoner?" Gus asked curiously.

"I don't see why not. We don't have any orders one way or the other." The first guard said.

They let him approach and stand on the step up to the wagon to look inside. The man inside sat against the far wall, his legs outstretched and his hands bound together in his lap. His head was downcast but he looked up as the wagon rocked when Gus stepped in. He was clean shaven with imperious features, watchful brown eyes and dark hair that ran to his shoulders. He had been stripped of his weapons and helmet but he still wore his chain mail and a deep purple tunic. Gus noted the coat of arms embroidered on his chest of a sun above shining down seven golden rays of light onto a white crown.

"You, sir. What's your name?" Gus asked, doing his best to look like a person of authority. The prisoner looked at him and, after seeing his small stature and otherwise unimpressive appearance, laughed once to himself and then remained quiet.

"I'm talking to you, sir. I'd appreciate an answer." Gus felt a bit insulted.

Again, the man remained quiet.

"Why do you still bear the symbol of your kingdom, if I may ask?"

The guard gave him a quizzical look.

"If you've abandoned your own country to loot and pillage the countryside, why do you wear it?" He asked again.

The man's face turned to one of anger. "You presume much. Be careful what words you choose next." He warned.

Gus was a little intimidated but decided that the bars and bonds holding the man prisoner were enough to ensure his own safety. "It's a simple question. I wonder why you still bear colors that display your allegiance."

"I don't answer to you, rodent. Now leave me alone and go back to whatever hole you crawled out of. I grow tired of your voice." The man said lazily as he turned his head to one side to get into a more comfortable position in the wagon.

Taken aback and not sure of what to say next, Gus left the wagon and the prisoner. "It was a simple enough question," Gus muttered to himself in irritation. "There was no need to be so rude." As he continued his walk through the camp, he came across the spoils of their heist stacked high under a canvas on a heavily laden wagon. He disregarded the loot at first, still thinking about this life of warfare he had stumbled into, when curiosity struck and he backtracked a few steps. He couldn't help but wonder just what kind of cargo was worth so much trouble.

He thought perhaps it was gold or silver but the likelihood of a shipment of that value being escorted by so few men seemed unlikely. Whomever it was stolen from would no doubt have had several dozens of trained soldiers protecting it from robbers and thieves. It would have taken dozens more to overpower trained soldiers. If that were the case, where were they? Surely, they had not been killed in the attempt, leaving a mere fifteen men and six drivers to take the cargo elsewhere. At the very least, they would not be taking to the main roads. True thieves would have disappeared into the wilderness so as to better avoid pursuit.

His inquisitive nature got the better of him and he moved closer to inspect the goods. They were large barrels, as well as casks and kegs stacked neatly in wooden troughs to avoid rolling or tipping. Getting himself up onto the wagon's side, he rapped his knuckles on the wood. There was hardly any noise from the knock which told him there wasn't much hollow space within. He wondered if they were in fact carrying ale or alcohol of some nature. What else would be transported in barrels, after all? He jumped down from the wagon and headed to the front where he found the kegs and casks hidden underneath the canvas. He pulled up a flap and took a look inside. It was difficult to see in the dark so far from the bonfire but he could almost make out some sort of markings on the wood. He peered closer, trying hard to make out the lines stamped in black in the shadows but it was impossible. He wished he'd had a lantern to see by.

Suddenly, the wood was bright and he stumbled back in surprise. Someone was coming. He heard voices and the glow of lantern light grew brighter as two men came around the corner of a tent. He quickly stepped away and dove beneath the wagon, hiding behind one of the wheels. The footsteps grew closer until they stopped just a few feet from where Gus hid.

"You think we can sneak a bit without getting noticed before we deliver it. After all, nobody would miss a drop or two, eh?" One of them said.

The second one protested. "We'd better not. You know Curtis. He'd smell it on our breath before an hour was up. No. We'd best leave it be. It's a shame though. Perfectly good, eh?"

"Agreed. Come on, let's turn in for the night. He's going to make us march all the way back to Carath and I'd wager we aren't stopping until nightfall. I'd like to get a good night's sleep before then."

"Have it your way, but I'm heading back to the bonfire. I think there's still some roasted lamb."

The two men wandered away leaving Gus alone beneath the wagon. He had only half paid attention to what the men had said. His mind was preoccupied with what he'd seen in the brief glimpse he'd had of the symbol on the barrels. He stole into a nearby tent and found himself a small lantern, struck it with some flint and brought it to the wagon, careful not to let it shed too much light. He lifted up the flap of canvas once more and, holding his lantern aloft for a brief moment, confirmed what he thought he'd seen. The barrels bore the same sun and seven rays shining down on a crown.

He snuffed the lantern and returned it to its home before he headed back toward the prisoner's wagon. The guards were still there, so he hid in the shadows. He needed to speak to the prisoner, whoever he was. However, his gut told him not to arouse suspicion. Something was off. When it became apparent that he was not going to be able to sneak a moment alone with the prisoner as the guards maintained their positions at their posts, Gus decided he'd have to try again the next night. It was a two-day march if they kept their usual pace before they reached Carath to deliver their cargo. He had until then to figure out what was going on.

He stole back to his tent and retired for the evening, though his sleep was troubled with concern over the company he was keeping and the symbol on the prisoner's chest and the stolen barrels.

Chapter XV

"Mister Gus Man!" Snowball's voice broke Gus rudely from his uneasy slumber.

"Uhnnn... What? What is it?" He groaned.

"Mercy-naries are going to walk soon. Mister Gus Man should get up before he is left behind."

While Gus was grateful for the wakeup call, considering he had no desire to repeat his experience of his first day as a member of the company, his head throbbed and he was terribly thirsty. With great difficulty he got up and packed his things. He made sure to get some fresh water before he joined up with the front of the company.

For him, the day's march was uneventful, yet exhausting. His mind was full of suspicion and the more he walked along the more he thought about what kind of company he was keeping. If there was a secret to be had, who was in on it? Every man he walked beside was an enemy, each man a spy sent to find out that Gus was catching on to them. As the day wore on, he grew wearied of such thoughts. Most of the men were jovial enough and seemed like good people. Instead, Gus spent his energy figuring out how to get time alone with the prisoner to ask him questions. They made camp just where the road took a bend west around the base of a wide mesa once the sun had set below the horizon. While the men were busy erecting tents for the night and starting small cooking fires, Gus strode through the camp to the captain's tent. He passed Snowball snuffling around in one of the mercenaries' tents, his tail wagging with curiosity as the rest of the monstrous Minotaur was poking about inside. He called out and caught Snowball's attention, gesturing for the creature to follow. Snowball did and the two marched promptly into Garret's tent.

The captain was busy tabulating costs for his mission and making careful notes in a ledger when the pair arrived. He would have paid them less mind, but the Minotaur's horns got caught on the hem of the door flap and the whole tent shook as he tried to shake his head loose.

"Please. Do be careful. I'd rather you didn't destroy my tent." Garret said, his voice only slightly irritated.

Snowball stopped moving but didn't seem to have any idea what to do.

"Would you please?" Garret asked of Gus with a roll of his eyes.

Gus reached up on his tip toes to un-snag the tent.

"What can I do for you? I am quite busy, but I can surely spare a few moments for my tactician."

The comment made Gus beam but he quickly adopted a more serious expression. "Sir, I noticed that the men guarding the prisoner seemed a little restless and ill-tempered," he lied. "I thought, since there is little need for tactical advice at the moment with us on the move and all, that I could volunteer myself and Snowball to take watch for the night. Give them a chance to rest."

Garret nodded but had a curious look about him. "That would be fine. Might I ask what's put you in such generous spirits?"

Gus was ill prepared with an answer so he paused to think, giving no indication that he was anything less than genuine. "As I said before," Gus recalled, "I want to pull my weight around here and contribute my fair share. I don't see why the other men should risk their lives and work so hard and I should just lie in my tent resting while there are other duties to be performed."

Garret stood up from his seat at the table and placed both palms on the table with a serious expression on his face. His expression soon changed into a mocking smile. "You're just determined to prove me wrong, aren't you? Don't care much for being treated as a lowly peasant, I take it."

Gus swallowed, unable to formulate a response.

"I respect your attitude, though I doubt you'll ever truly be worthy of higher status. We are all born into this

world with different yokes to bear. Mine is of command, and
yours of toil and labor. But who am I to say what a man
should do with his time? Who knows? I've made you tactician
already. Maybe you'll change my mind. Very well. I'll have
Curtis inform the guards that they are to be relieved in an
hour. You can take over their watch then. Understood?"

"Yes, sir!" Gus said with his best military gusto.

Garret sat back down and waved them away
carelessly. "Now, please leave me. I still have much work to
do."

Gus turned and left before Garret could say more and
Snowball followed.

"Why does Mister Gus Man want to guard tiny cage
man?" Snowball asked a little while after they'd left the tent.

Gus kept his voice low as he answered. "Something
isn't right here, Snowball. There's more to this whole mission
than meets the eye and I intend to find out what that is. I think
the prisoner might be able to tell me more if I can get him to
talk.

"What kind of meat is in Mister Gus Man's eyes?"
Snowball asked.

Pretending for a moment that Snowball had actually
understood what he'd said, Gus continued. "There was a coat
of arms on the prisoner's garments that is quite curious. I saw
the same symbol on the goods we just recovered. I can't help
but wonder if these men weren't bandits or thieves at all but
the proper owners. All I need you to do is keep an eye out
while I ask him a few questions. Do you think you can do
that?"

Snowball nodded.

"Good."

The two reported to the prisoner's wagon an hour
later and relieved the watch stationed there. Curtis greeted
them brusquely and informed them that they were not to speak
to the prisoner or let him out under any circumstances.

"If anything goes wrong it will be your heads. Do you understand?" He said.

"Yes, sir." Gus said.

Curtis was pleased with this answer and turned to the Minotaur for his response. However, the towering creature gave him pause. "Well, then. Very good." He looked to Gus. "No mistakes. I'll be making a full report of your behavior to the captain if I smell so much as a hair out of place." He turned to leave when Snowball asked "Tiny hooman can smell hair that is out of place?" He paused mid-step briefly before he decided to ignore the question and continued back to his tent.

"Mister Gus Man, how does smelling hair out of place-" Snowball started to ask when Gus cut him off.

"Don't worry about it, Snowball. He's just trying to turn a phrase."

"What's a phrase?"

"Just keep watch, will you. Tell me if anyone comes close enough to hear us." Gus said, stepping up onto the wagon once he was sure no one was watching.

The prisoner was fast asleep inside, curled up against the corner of his cage with his head at a funny angle.

"Psssst." Gus hissed, trying to wake him. The prisoner didn't stir, so he tried again. Unsuccessful, Gus looked around for something to prod him with. Finding nothing readily available, he used his sheathed sword to poke at the prisoner's foot. The man grumbled and adjusted himself but remained asleep. Gus tried a second time, and a third, until at last the man's eyes opened and he took in a deep groggy breath as he woke.

"Oh. It's you again. I thought I told you to go away." He said.

"Shhhhh. I just wanted to ask you some questions." Gus told him.

"I'm trying to sleep."

"It's important. It's about that symbol you wear."

"What about it?" Asked the prisoner, disinterestedly.

"Where does it come from?"

Curiously, the prisoner answered, "it's the banner of the king. Do you not know it?"

"Oh." Gus was surprised. "No, I can't say I do. You came from the northwest kingdom then?"

"What? No. Do you know nothing?" he furrowed his brows.

"I don't understand. Why did you steal those barrels?"

"What on earth are you talking about?" The prisoner was baffled. "We didn't steal anything. You are the thieves!"

Gus held up a hand to hush him. "Shhhhh... Listen. I'm not your enemy. I'm just trying to figure out what's going on. You say you didn't steal the cargo you were transporting. What were you doing with it, then?"

"We were transporting it as a peace offering to the kingdom to the south when you attacked us."

Gus was shocked. It took a moment for him to process what the prisoner had just told him. "You mean to tell me that you were on legitimate business for the king and we've just stolen your cargo that was intended to serve as a peace offering?"

The man nodded.

"Then who are we working for?" He thought aloud.

"My guess is you work for a man by the name of Garret. Am I right?"

Gus nodded.

"Why don't you ask him, then?" The man scoffed. "You really are a fool to employ yourself in mercenary work without knowing who you're working for."

Embarrassed, Gus fumbled for a response but was interrupted before he could formulate a reply.

"Someone is coming." Snowball said quietly.

"We'll talk more later." Gus quickly told the prisoner. "What is your name?"

"My name is Duncan, royal guard and servant to the king." Duncan said.

Gus swallowed and paused. "Don't worry. We'll find a way to get you out of here," Gus said before he turned and hopped down from the wagon. He quickly returned to Snowball's side and leaned against the Minotaur in a casual fashion as if to say that he clearly wasn't up to any mischief. The three mercenaries happening by gave him odd looks but continued on their way without saying anything.

Gus was relieved and very glad his companion was over seven hundred pounds of muscled fury. He was growing used to his friend giving others good reason to think twice about interacting with him. He immediately returned to Duncan.

"Why would Garret steal a peace offering from your kingdom?" He asked.

Duncan shook his head in disappointment. "You really are a fool. That's the king's brother you're working for."

"What!" Gus said in alarm.

"Shhh." Duncan hushed him. "We had heard rumors but never had any solid report on it. It is no secret that the king's brother was after the throne and when he was denied it by the birth of his younger brother, he grew bitter. No doubt he seeks to weaken his brother's position so he can raise an army of his own and stage a coup. You should be ashamed of yourself, falling in with the likes of him. There is no honor in you at all."

That last comment made Gus angry. He'd never thought himself a fool and he certainly had no interest in allying himself with traitors and thieves. "I'm here, aren't I. I told you I wasn't your enemy and I stand by that statement. You'll see. I'm sure this is just some big misunderstanding."

Duncan chuckled and shook his head, relaxing back against his cage.

Seeing that the prisoner was no longer interested in conversation and himself lacking more to say, Gus left

Duncan where he was and took up his station next to Snowball. There he stood through the rest of his assigned watch, staring off into the night deep in thought as he considered Duncan's words and everything else he'd witnessed with the mercenary band.

When morning arrived, it slapped Gus awake with a vengeance as the camp was packed up amid clamor and robust conversation. The poor peasant hadn't slept well at all in the few hours he'd had after the night watch. Groggily he went to work packing up his own gear and falling into line to march over the countryside with the Kismet Mercenaries. He moved about in a daze that morning, his mind foggy and distracted. On several occasions he bumped into members of the company on accident which caused him to trip and fall into the dirt. The third time he fell, before he could pick himself up, a strong arm grabbed him up and lifted him to his feet. He was expecting Snowball's dumb grin but was surprised to find it to be one of the mercenaries. He thanked the man and immediately went to find Snowball amid the company.

As he walked along, brushing himself off he got to thinking about the company he was keeping. How many of the men were aware that Garret might be the king's brother? Certainly, these men were loyal to the company, but how loyal? He thought hard about what he knew of the company. A large number of them were former soldiers of Kismet, thus the name of the company. However, many were newer recruits and were more interested in coin than the dubious moral disposition that came along with mercenary work. Gus had a hard time believing there were no good men among them. Many of them were jovial, hardworking souls making a living in the only way they knew how. Granted, it was with violence and bloodshed, but who was he to judge?

Suddenly, Gus thought of Sir Ethan. In his gut he knew Sir Ethan was a good man. He wasn't sure how it was that he knew, but he was sure. There was something in his bearing, in the way he was that told Gus there was more to him than just fighting. Sir Ethan was a knight, after all. Surely that still meant something.

He snapped out of his daze, giving up his search for Snowball and searched among the men for the drunkard knight instead. Gus found him drifting about as he marched along. The sun was starting to climb high into the sky and it was getting hot. Grabbing one of the banners from a mercenary wagon, Gus marched up next to Sir Ethan, shielding him from the sun with the standard.

Sir Ethan didn't realize at first but soon looked curiously at his shade-bearer. "You have a strange way of carrying the colors, master tactician," he said.

"I have great need to speak with you. I was hoping you and I could talk."

"Lissen," The knight slurred a little, "if this is about that chicken and potato incident last night, I wasn't involved."

Gus laughed uncomfortably. "No, no. It's not about that. I want to know more about Kismet. About your kingdom."

"Huh." The knight grunted. "It's not my kingdom anymore. That place is dead."

"Right," Gus ignored the knight's pessimism, "but you were a part of it and unless I'm mistaken it's still a part of you." The knight's silence was cue for Gus to continue. "When we reach town let's you and I share a drink. What do you say?"

The knight eyed him warily but the sound of a drink was too tempting for him to pass up. He nodded and offered a hand to Gus. Gus shook it in agreement and then the two parted ways to continue the march.

Gus was careful to note the other men who might have heard his conversation. They seemed not to care but he didn't want anyone else to get pulled into his plan unless he was certain he could trust them. So far, the only creature he felt he could really trust was Snowball. He was taking a gamble on the knight, but such was necessary.

The company marched on through the day, resting every few hours, making slow but steady progress back toward Carath. The following day was much the same. Gus spent his time marching next to Snowball quietly, deep in thought. He formulated plans, threw them out, composed speeches in his head and forgot them. As he looked forward to his drink with Ethan, he gave great thought to what to say to the knight to get him to understand. When at last the company reached the outer wall of Carath he made certain to regroup with Ethan and remind him of their meeting that night.

Sir Ethan gladly remembered, insisting that a promised drink among friends would never be forgotten so easily and that he would hold Gus to it "by his honor".

By the time the men had found lodging and stowed their gear, it was already evening. Gus agreed to meet Sir Ethan at a tavern known as the Golden Gander, located on the south edge of town. It was a simple establishment with enough seats and tables for thirty if you counted the balcony overlooking the bar. The atmosphere was cheery and the establishment wasn't terribly busy. Gus entered alone, having left Snowball with explicit instructions to stay in a tent just outside of town with some of the other mercenaries. He ordered two tankards of ales, one for himself and one for Ethan, and took a seat at a small table with two chairs on the balcony above. He had just taken a few sips of his drink by the time the knight entered. Gus waved him over and greeted him warmly as Ethan took a seat.

"Glad you could make it. Please, have a drink." Gus gestured to the second ale.

Sir Ethan drank eagerly, wiping the froth from his stubble once he'd taken a large gulp. "What did you want to talk to me about?" He said before a small burp.

"I wanted to talk to you about Kismet, your home country," Gus began.

"I don't know," Sir Ethan hesitated. "It's not a pleasant story."

"Please. I would love to hear about it. I know it may be hard but I'm sure you have at least a few fond stories of the place."

With a nod, Sir Ethan became lost in memories as he spoke. "Kismet was a great kingdom. Wealthy, prosperous. Our king was benevolent and a genius when it came to enriching his people. You should have seen the great plains ripe with golden wheat on a midsummer's eve. It was something to behold. Like fields of gold fire in the setting sun." As he spoke, his slovenly speech seemed to vanish and for a moment Gus could almost imagine the knight's homeland. "Kismetian people were good people. Honorable, strong, generous. It was a dream for a time."

"What happened to it?" Gus asked.

"We were a peaceful people, for the most part. Our brotherhood of knights patrolled the realm for bandits and the like that would pray upon our people in the countryside. We had a small army, you see. Kismet made peace with other nations far more readily than we waged war." His tone grew dark as he continued, holding his ale in his hands as though clutching at a precious stone. "Then they came from the north. Soldiers in the thousands. They swept through the countryside destroying everything in their path. We held a war council to counter this unprovoked attack. When the enemy reached the king's castle, we held strong. By the gods we held them back. We fought off hundreds of soldiers as they tried to breach the outer walls. As the second knight under the king, I commanded the majority of our troops. It was our job to prevent them entering the kingdom." Sir Ethan paused and looked down into his ale, deep in thought.

"Second knight?" Gus could hardly believe the drunken knight but he seemed to be honest. "Did your defenses hold?" Gus asked, engrossed in the knight's story.

Sir Ethan seemed drained as he recounted what happened. "None of it mattered. Sure, the defenses held, but we were defeated just the same. A viper made his way into the castle and assassinated our king. A poisoned dagger in his side as the night set in. He was found in his chambers, the dagger nearby, dead upon the floor. Before long, our forces collapsed and surrendered. Without a king to lead us, our men did not have the heart to continue the fight. And now here we are, scattered and defeated." The knight pounded back another big gulp of his ale.

For a moment, Gus was speechless. There was little he could say of comfort and conveying his sorrow for the fallen kingdom seemed like it would be insignificant and impolite. What good were the sympathies of a peasant who had never known Kismet? He watched the knight finish his ale as he thought hard on what next to say. A few moments passed before he resolved to his original purpose.

"Sir Ethan, I asked you here to speak with you about this company and what you are doing in it." Gus stated simply. "What do you know about the commander?"

It took Sir Ethan a moment to think on it. "He's a man with a vision of some kind. He took us in when nobody else seemed to care. Kismet was in ruins and he offered us a place where we could put our skills to use."

Gus nodded. "I agree, that seems to be the case, but what do you know about the man? Do you know who he is or where he comes from?"

Sir Ethan shook his head.

"I spoke with the prisoner we took from our last successful robbery," Gus said with a note of disgust, though he lowered his voice so as not to be overheard, "and he told me that our Garret is none other than the King's brother. Does that ring any bells?"

Ethan shook his head. "No. I don't..." he trailed off.

"If that's true and Garret is the king's brother, it's more than likely he took part in the siege that overtook your kingdom," Gus realized as he spoke, "and now he sets you up to conquer his own brother. What if those were no bandits we fought, but the royal guards of his majesty. What say you to that?"

Sir Ethan fumbled for an answer but he did little more than stutter.

The more Gus spoke the more he realized it sounded like the truth. "Sir Ethan, you were once a knight, or am I mistaken?"

The knight shook his head, unable to answer.

"Or have you forgotten the tenants of honor and justice?" Gus knew he'd hit a sore spot with Sir Ethan, so he twisted those last words in like a knife.

"Justice!" Ethan slammed his fist down on the table. "It will be a cold day in Hell before I throw Justice and Honor aside!" The knight stood up suddenly, rising into a posture of imposing strength. Gus could see a small fire behind his eyes. "Did you say Justice?!" Sir Ethan didn't wait for Gus to answer. "There is no greater cause in this world."

"Then you will help me?" Gus asked quickly before the knight could continue his outburst.

Sir Ethan sat down once again, leaning across the table to talk in an intense whisper. "What are you proposing?"

"Well," Gus swallowed, recognizing the gravity of what he was about to suggest. "I mean to free the prisoner and return the stolen cargo to its rightful owner. Will you help me?"

Sir Ethan narrowed his eyes at the peasant. "You mean to fight Garret, the man who took me in in my time of need? And the whole company of mercenaries, many who were my former kinsmen? In the name of justice and righteousness against impossible odds that are nearly sure to end in our swift demise?"

"Er... um... well, when you put it that way..." Gus said meekly.

"Stay your courage man, I will aid your just cause."
Ethan clapped a hand on the peasant's shoulder.

"You would be betraying your entire company." Gus
pointed out; no longer sure it was such a good idea.

"Do you know who I am?" Ethan asked him gravely.

"Well... I... You're -"

"I am Sir Ethan Wallard!" the knight cut him off.
"Knight! Of the Silver Dragon!" He roared, setting a robust
foot on his chair and striking a heroic pose for all the patrons
of the Golden Gander to witness. "And I will see justice done
this day!"

It was clear Sir Ethan was intoxicated, both with
alcohol and visions of justice and honor. The knight broke into
a tirade about virtue, glory and the honor of the kingdom of
Kismet while Gus shrank in his chair, trying hard to remain
unnoticed as the knight's robust declarations rang out through
the tavern. It wasn't too long before the both of them were
tossed out of the establishment.

Gus fell to the dirt next to his swaggering new friend
who shouted taunts back at the tavern, teetering to and fro. He
wanted badly to hide himself in an alley but his new
companion grabbed him up by the shoulders and looked him
straight in the eye. "Tell me more of your plan."

"Um. You're drunk."

Sir Ethan checked himself and could not help but
agree.

"Take a walk for a few hours and then meet me back
at my tent. The company may not remain in town very long
and we need to act before the delivery takes place. We can
strategize once you get your head on straight." Gus suggested.

"Hey. What are you saying? Are you saying I'm
drunk?" Asked Ethan. "Another round!" He said, raising a fist
high, not realizing they were no longer indoors.

Gus stood up, shaking his head, looked Ethan in the
eye and told him, "don't be late." Ethan's merry but blissfully
inebriated expression gave him doubts so he sighed and left.

Chapter XVI

Gus was not surprised when Sir Ethan didn't show up on time. In fact, he had nodded off as he sat leaning his back against his gear inside his tent. Snowball sat nearby just outside the tent, munching on something or other quietly. It wasn't until after midnight that Sir Ethan stumbled inside.

"I'm here. Where is the-" He paused to belch, "What is the plan, sir Tat-tician...?" He swayed considerably as Gus stirred from his nap.

The peasant looked up at him for only a moment before slapping his own forehead in frustration. "For the love of... Have you no self-control?" He asked.

"I am ready to garrison the fort, sir!" Ethan said with a sloppy snap to attention. "How many does our enemy number?"

"No." Gus said, getting himself up off the ground. "That's enough out of you. You need to pull yourself together, man." He took Sir Ethan by the arm and guided him to his own bedroll. "You're drunk and you're going to sleep this off. You are in no state of mind to do anything productive. Now lie down and go to sleep."

"But your majesty, I am here to serve!" Ethan protested lazily. The former knight fought against Gus's insistence and continued trying to get up and salute.

Fed up with it, Gus popped his head outside the tent. "Snowball. I need your help."

"Oh." Snowball finished munching his grassy snack. "Yes, Mister Gus Man."

"Your majesty, I must protest!" Ethan said, stumbling belligerently around in the tent, trying to push past Gus to get outside.

"Our friend won't go to sleep." Gus said.

"Oh. Okay!" Snowball smiled.

Bonk!

A quick bop of the Minotaur's massive hammer and Sir Ethan collapsed in a heap on the floor of the tent.

Gus was about to express his shock at what Snowball had done but stopped short and shrugged. "You know, I think I'm alright with that."

The next morning went by unproductively. Gus had spent the night sleeping in a leaning position on his gear since Sir Ethan occupied his bedroll, and had to walk about town and stretch to get all the soreness out of his body. He left Sir Ethan to sleep until nearly noon, when at last the former knight awoke complaining of two distinctly different kinds of headaches.

Gus and Snowball spent the rest of the day moving about town to determine what was to become of the goods Garret and the mercenaries had stolen. It was some time close to sunset before the pair took notice of crates and barrels being moved to a stone courtyard near a watchtower on the outer wall of the city. The courtyard was a sort of enclosure, only about thirty-foot square, with a doorway in the stone walls to the north and south and a stair leading up the west wall to the tower. A storeroom was on the eastern wall and several Mercenaries carried casks down a set of steps and through a doorway to stow the goods.

Gus only had time to glance around before leaving for fear of looking suspicious. Several men stood guard to watch the procession as each piece of freight was moved from place to place. As Gus was leaving with his minotaur companion, he asked one of the men carrying a cask as he passed by "what is going to happen to all this stuff?"

The mercenary didn't seem to mind and told him "They're being stored overnight. The buyer will come by to pick them up first thing in the morning." He added over his shoulder as he continued on, "We're moving out at noon tomorrow. Make sure you have your gear packed, oh mighty tactician."

None too pleased with the guard's tone as it dripped with sarcasm, Gus continued on his way. Once he was out of sight of the mercenaries, he made haste with Snowball to get back to their tent as soon as possible.

Sir Ethan appeared to be busy cleaning a damp spot out of Gus's bedroll when they returned. He greeted them as they entered the tent and immediately apologized. "I'm sorry, sir. It would seem I made a bit of a mess after the drinks last night."

Gus tried not to think about the faint smell of vomit and instead focused on the task at hand. "Sir Ethan, we don't have any more time. They will be moving the goods first thing in the morning. If we don't do something tonight it will be too late. We have to act."

"What's the plan?" Sir Ethan asked, seeming decidedly sober for a change.

Gus shook his head and stared at the floor, trying to come up with something. "They've got the goods in a storeroom on the west side of the city. There's a watchtower nearby, so it may be hard to approach. Garret has guards posted to keep an eye on the goods."

"Perhaps we can go in quietly. That may be the best method." Ethan suggested.

Gus thought about it for a moment, then looked and pointed at Snowball. "I don't think that's going to work. As cunning as Snowball can be, it's hard not to notice someone of his size."

"You have a point."

"We're not going to get in without a fight. The only trouble we face is the chance that one of the guards will sound the alarm. If that happens, we'll have to fight off every guard and mercenary in town."

"Oooh! This is a good idea!" Snowball said, his tail wagging in excitement.

"No! It's a terrible idea." Gus exclaimed. "We can't beat an entire mercenary company *and* all the guards. Not only would we be horribly outnumbered and trapped in a confined space, but we would be made enemies of the town guard and therefore the crown. I'm not going to go through life as a fugitive!"

"Awwww..." Snowball looked disappointed.

"Let's not forget Duncan. The prisoner will be sure to lend a hand if we can free him. I know where they're keeping him." Sir Ethan volunteered. "I can take you there."

Gus nodded. "Once we have him freed, we'll need to get to the storehouse fast. If anyone notices that he's gone they may sound the alarm. When we were marching, they kept just two guards watch on him. If we're quick enough, by the time they realize he's gone we can have taken back the goods and made good an escape."

"How do you intend to move the goods once you've reached them? There's a whole wagon load of heavy barrels and crates." Sir Ethan pointed out.

Gus thumbed at Snowball. "He can move the whole lot like a pile of feathers."

Snowball smiled.

"We should make haste then. I will take you where they're keeping him. Come." Ethan didn't waste any time and led the way through the mercenary camp. He stopped by his own tent where he grabbed his weapons and gear along the way. When they reached the prison wagon and stopped just out of sight of the two guards keeping watch, he turned to Gus.

"What's the plan?" He asked.

"Well... I suppose we overpower them as quietly as possible. Perhaps we can sneak around from behind."

"From behind? That's cowardly." Ethan objected. "A man must live and act with honor. We should approach them from the front and declare ourselves. Then state our intentions. They are sure to see the justice and honor in what we strive to do and if not, they will have no choice but to submit to honorable combat."

"What?! That will never work." Gus said in as loud a whisper as he could manage. "These are mercenaries, not knights. They don't care about honor. They'll sound the alarm!"

"We must hold ourselves to higher standards." Ethan struck a pose of righteousness, "we must act with honor and dignity. Justice must not be kept secret or sneaking around in the shadows."

Gus wiped his face with his hand in frustration. "Even if these were former soldiers, you know that as mercenaries these men can be bought. There is no honor in that and there is no honor in them," he insisted.

"I have to believe in the greatest virtues of others or else they will not believe in those virtues themselves." Sir Ethan argued. "If we cannot live to better ourselves then why live at all?"

Gus looked around as he noticed that Snowball had disappeared as they were arguing. "I think my companion may have other ideas," he noted. He peered around the corner before he grabbed Ethan by the arm and pulled him over to see.

Snowball approached the two guards directly, not bothering to conceal himself in the least. He stopped directly in front of them and they both looked up at him, intimidated, but with a certain amount of respect.

"Hello." Snowball greeted them both with a friendly wave.

One of the guards worked up the courage to ask, "What can we do for you?"

"Sleepy time." Snowball said.

The two guards looked confused.

The Minotaur grabbed each one by the helmet and knocked their heads together. They collapsed to the ground in a heap. Snowball looked over to where his friends stood and smiled.

Though Sir Ethan stood dumbstruck, a smile crept across Gus's face. "How's that for honorable? Approached from the front and stated his business."

"I- I- I don't-" Sir Ethan fumbled for the words to say.

"Come on." Gus didn't wait for him. He quickly set to work searching the guards for the keys. Once he found them, he unlocked the cage and Duncan, who had been asleep until he'd heard the ruckus, stirred and gladly accepted his freedom.

"Had a change of heart, have you?" He asked Gus with an air of condescension.

"We're going to let you go and retrieve the stolen goods. I was hoping to enlist your aid in this." Gus said. "This is Sir Ethan." He gestured to the former knight.

"Knight of the Silver Dragon!" Ethan added.

"Right." Duncan raised an eyebrow.

"And this is my friend, Snowball." Gus gestured to the Minotaur who was standing in front of the wagon picking his nose.

"His name is what?" Duncan was surprised. "Wait. That creature is... your friend?"

Gus shrugged. "I've yet to meet a better companion. They're going to help me retrieve your goods. Will you help us?"

Duncan considered for a moment. "What's to stop me from escaping and warning the king?"

"Well. Nothing, really." Gus admitted.

"Your sense of honor and justice." Ethan pointed out. "We are men bound by duty to serve the kingdom."

"Right you are." Duncan agreed.

"Besides, you can always warn the king once we get back your cargo. You wouldn't want to go back empty handed, would you?" Gus pointed out.

Duncan said nothing but nodded. Then he asked, "What is your plan?"

"Well... We storm the courtyard and incapacitate the guards before any of them can raise the alarm. Then we load the goods onto a wagon and get out of here."

"Yes. I'm sure it will be as simple as that." Duncan said sarcastically.

"Have heart, lad." Sir Ethan encouraged him. "If our cause is just and our hearts true, we cannot help but to succeed."

"Right. What he said." Gus laughed. "Come on. We need to get moving before they wake up."

At Duncan's suggestion they bound the two guards and locked them inside the wagon before they hurried for the storeroom. Duncan made sure to grab a sword from one of the guards before they left.

They approached quietly under the cover of darkness, which amounted to much stumbling into things on the part of Gus, Ethan and Duncan. Snowball, in spite of his size, moved nimbly through the alleys with little trouble. Gus got the distinct impression he could see a lot better than they could. They remained just outside the torchlight near the entrance to the courtyard. From their position they could see little. Even the top of the watch tower was obscured to them.

Gus had been trying to come up with a solid plan but had thus far been unsuccessful. He turned to his companions with the only real idea he had. "Sir Ethan, Snowball and I can approach without too much suspicion since we are a part of the company. We'll get the guards talking. While they're distracted, we need to make sure the men in the guard tower don't sound the alarm. Do you think the two of you can take care of that?" He asked Snowball and Duncan.

"It will be difficult to approach the tower without entering the courtyard and being noticed." Duncan pointed out. "While that is fine for you and your companions, I will be spotted at once."

"Perhaps," Sir Ethan suggested, "it would be best for Duncan to procure for us a wagon on which to load the goods. Meanwhile, we three secure the courtyard. What say you?"

Gus nodded in agreement and Duncan gladly sneaked off into the shadows.

"Snowball can infiltrate the tower and make sure that nobody sounds the alarm. You and I can approach the guards and offer to relieve them of duty. How does that sound?" Gus asked.

Sir Ethan considered it. "That sounds like deception. I'm not keen on deception."

"It worked on the guards protecting Duncan."

"You have a fair point. While I may not like it, we shall give it a try." Sir Ethan grumbled.

"Snowball. Go up into the tower and knock out anyone you find." Gus ordered. "But do it as quietly as you can. We don't need to hurt anyone we don't have to. The less commotion we make the better."

"Okay." Snowball agreed eagerly.

The three moved into the courtyard and while Gus and Sir Ethan strolled casually toward the two guards stationed on the eastern wall on either side of the storeroom door, Snowball made his way up the stairs to the watch tower.

"Well met!" Sir Ethan greeted the guardsmen as he approached.

"What is your business here?" The first guard asked, with a vague air of suspicion.

"We were ordered to relieve you of duty." Gus said.

"You aren't properly equipped." The second guard noted Gus's lack of armor. "And we were not informed of a shift change."

"What?" Gus improvised. He knew they would not believe it if he told them Garret had sent them. "Curtis didn't send someone? That doesn't sound like him at all," he lied, knowing Garret's lieutenant to have a rough reputation among his men. "I'm sure it's just a big misunderstanding."

"Huh. I'm not surprised," snorted the first guard. "He always says he'll do things and never does."

"What is he doing?" The second guard pointed to Snowball as he moved up the stairs.

Gus shrugged. "I'm sure I don't know. He said something about delivering a message but he didn't say what."

The first guard thought he smelled something suspicious but he couldn't tell what it was. "Without formal orders we cannot leave our post," he said.

"Oh. Well, I understand." Gus had not expected such reluctance. "I..." He thought for a moment and played it off casually," I guess I'll have to go find Curtis and ask why he didn't send orders. It's awful late," he turned to Sir Ethan, "Curtis isn't going to be happy, us waking him at such an hour. Come on, let's go get this straightened out." Gus turned to leave and gestured for Ethan to follow.

"Wait." The second guard said. "There's no need for that. I'm sure he just forgot to send a messenger. Let him get his rest. He's very unpleasant when he doesn't get enough sleep. I'm sure we can let you take over from here, right?" He asked the other guard.

The other guard nodded. "Yes. I suppose it wouldn't hurt anything. Just don't mention it to Curtis. Carry on."

The two men left promptly. Just as they left the courtyard Gus heard a dull thump from the watch tower.

"I think that went rather well, don't you?" He asked Sir Ethan.

Ethan sighed. "I dislike deception. There is no honor in it. It did work, however, so we may as well make the best of it. After all, we are here for a just cause."

Another dull thump sounded from the watchtower.

"We can't be picky in the name of doing the right thing," Gus said. "Come on. We have a lot of cargo to move before someone finds out.

"And what of our companion? Should we not lend him aid?" Ethan asked, looking toward the tower.

Gus looked in that direction as well and thought on it. Another dull thump resounded from that direction.

"No. No, I think he's got it."

After a few moments Snowball reappeared from the watchtower and assisted Gus and Ethan as they labored hard to empty the storeroom of its contents.

Duncan drove up with a wagon and parked just outside the entrance to the courtyard and they began loading, barrel by barrel. Naturally, Snowball did the bulk of the work, hefting one full sized barrel over each shoulder, while Sir Ethan and Duncan rolled one along between the two of them and Gus was left to carry one keg at a time with his meager strength.

While Sir Ethan and Duncan stood taking a quick breather from all the heavy lifting, briefly discussing the best route out of Carath, Snowball finished setting two more barrels on top of the wagon and Gus was sat on the stairs to catch his breath for the third time. In that brief lull, Commander Garret, Curtis and twelve armed men entered into the courtyard.

Gus and his companions froze, all except for Snowball who stood dumbly in the middle of the courtyard scratching at his hindquarters.

"So, this is how you show your loyalty." Garret commented. No one responded, so he made a gesture to his men. "Apprehend them!"

Sir Ethan stood forth and raised a hand. "Nay. You will stand down!" He said with the air of command in his voice. The men stopped in their tracks. Ethan aimed his gaze at Garret. "You have disgraced yourself and your company in the name of selfish ambition. We know these goods to be the rightful property of the men you stole it from as witnessed here, all to smear the name of your brother the king! Have you no shame? How answer you?"

The other mercenaries looked to one another in confusion before directing their attention back at their commander.

"You heard your commander!" Curtis barked. "Get them!"

The men hesitated but acknowledged their orders. They turned and advanced on Sir Ethan.

Sir Ethan drew his sword with the practiced grace of a true knight and took up his shield. "You leave me but little choice. For I will defend justice! No matter the cost!"

Duncan drew his sword as well and they stood shoulder to shoulder as Garret's men hemmed them in against the storehouse.

"Snowball!" Gus called out. "Defend them!"

"But Mister Gus Man! Wobbly Slushy man and Mister guard want to take the strawberries away!"

Gus was a taken aback. "What? What do you mean, strawberries?" He looked at the barrels, then Snowball, then Curtis and Ethan.

"Didn't you know it's a shipment of strawberry wine?" Curtis mentioned.

"Traitor!" Sir Ethan called out at Snowball.

Gus went slack-jawed. "Strawberry... wine...?" Just when it mattered most, he'd stumbled on yet another batch of unintentional strawberries. "Oh, for the love of... Snowball, Commander Garret and his men want to take the wine too!"

"No, no, Snowball," Garret was quick to assure the creature, "we want to keep it out of the greedy hands of the king because he wants it all to himself."

Snowball recoiled in horror.

"Don't listen to him!" Ethan said, "he means to thwart what is right and just. You mustn't listen to his foul lies!"

"Trust me, minotaur." Garret added, "they mean to take it away and leave you without so much as a drop. But not me. I have given you the gift of glorious battle. Would I steer you wrong?"

"Heh. Steer is right..." Curtis chuckled to himself.

"He means to turn you against us, creature." Duncan added.

"Snowball... uh..." The monstrous creature turned back and forth between the respective parties, unsure of what to do. "Mister Gus Man." He turned to Gus.

Gus realized rather quickly that Snowball would do whatever it took to ensure he got what he wanted. He would not be able to convince the creature one way or the other. He had to come up with something and quick.
Suddenly it struck him. The solution was quite simple, though Gus was sure he didn't like it. "Sorry." He apologized to Sir Ethan and Duncan.

"Snowball, knock everyone out!" He commanded as he did his best to get out of everyone's way.

Everyone's jaws dropped.

Snowball's frustration and unsurety vanished almost instantly and was replaced with a joyful smile of purpose. With glee he wound his hammer up by his shoulder and charged into the group of mercenaries, swinging with merriment and wild abandon. Mercenaries flew left and right, each swing sending another soaring, toppling or spinning to the ground.

"Gus! Why-" Sir Ethan had no time to protest the peasant's command as he was quickly engaged with mercenaries and the Minotaur's massive whirling hammer.

Duncan did not fare much better, though he backed up to the doorway to the storehouse to defend the precious goods. He dodged what he could and parried several blows as two of the mercenaries made to put an end to him.

Curtis shied away from the Minotaur as best he could but he was caught between looking good in front of his commander and avoiding the one creature he feared above all others. His commander, Garret, moved in decisively to strike at Snowball with a strong thrust of his sword. The blow, aimed at the Minotaur's legs, was parried by the downswing of Snowball's hammer as the creature wound up to bat a mercenary halfway across the courtyard.

The men fought Snowball, Duncan and Ethan, and Ethan and Duncan fought Snowball and the mercenaries, and everyone was locked in a mad melee between friends and foes alike.

Finding himself to be the only one ignored through the battle and with a sigh of sheer disappointment at how things had devolved into senseless violence, guided by his own hand, Gus took a seat on a crate and conceded to watch the whole brawl unfold. He took up a tankard he found near one of the kegs and popped the cork, pouring himself a full glass of strawberry wine. "Oh well..." He shook his head before he took a sip. One of the mercenaries was thrown hard in his direction by the swing of Snowball's hammer. He face-planted harmlessly against the wall to the peasant's side before collapsing to the ground, only to get up snarling and throw himself back into the fray for another piece of the action. Gus had hoped to avoid violence altogether but if there was one thing he had learned in the last month it was that violence followed Snowball around like a playful puppy.

Chapter XVII

It's almost like a sort of dance, Gus thought as he watched. Like a violent ballet unfolding to the tune of some unheard symphony. In his growing amusement he noted how gracefully Snowball grabbed up two mercenaries by the leg, one in each hand, and spun around like a top, knocking men over left and right. He thought it so strange how everyone would rush in together and then be pushed back by the creature's fury like waves upon a shore. He started humming along as the mayhem unfolded.

"You know, this wine isn't half bad." Gus noted as he took another sip. In another moment, another mercenary, struck hard in the chest by Snowball's hammer, flew back and landed unconscious in a heap at Gus's feet. Gus shook his head and poured half the tankard of wine on the mercenary's face with another sigh. "It's good, but it's really not worth fighting over, you know." He said.

With a mighty sweep, Snowball used his hammer to fling one of the mercenaries high up and over the wall of the courtyard only to come crashing down out of sight. Seeing a brief opening, Sir Ethan caught one of the mercenaries off guard and bashed him hard with his shield, sending him to the ground unconscious.

Duncan, fighting hard to hold back now three of Garret's men, rushed forward and with a thrust from his shoulder bowled one of the mercenaries backward. While the blow was not enough to seriously hurt the man, his step back to keep his balance was just enough to put him in the path of Snowball's hammer and he was quickly smacked to the side of the courtyard where he crumpled up in pain. The other two mercenaries gave up their attention on Duncan and turned to hold back Snowball. By then there were only five men holding their ground against the Minotaur including Curtis and Garret.

Sir Ethan, being attacked from behind, spun to his aggressor and shouted "Coward! Fight me face to face!" He made to confront the mercenary but a quick tap on top of the head from the Minotaur's massive hammer while his attention was on the mercenary sent the daring knight to the ground unconscious.

Garret was determined not to be thwarted by the great creature. He took advantage of a momentary gap in the action to disappear into the guardhouse, paying Gus no mind as he stormed up the stairs. When he reappeared a moment later, he had in his hands a heavy crossbow, locked and loaded. He took careful aim as Snowball seemed to have his attention on the remaining four men that surrounded him on all sides. When he thought he saw an opening he squeezed the trigger and let the bolt fly.

With a roar of defiance, Snowball spun and whipped his hammer around, batting the bolt to the side angrily as if swatting aside a fly. Snowball's back-swing caught one of Garret's men over the shoulder and dropped him. Duncan seized the moment and caught a distracted mercenary in a grapple, wrestling him to the ground.

Garret quickly reloaded another bolt to take another shot. Snowball, angry at the source of the projectiles, moved to get to Garret before he could fire again. While his back was turned, Curtis made a great lunge and stuck the tip of his sword into Snowball's thigh.

"Hah!" He cried in triumph, having been the first to strike a successful blow against the creature. Although Snowball did roar in pain, Curtis's victory was cut all too short. When he had stepped out to thrust his sword, he had completely extended toward the creature. Before he could withdraw his blade and step back, Snowball turned and with his long, heavily muscled arm delivered a four fingered fist the size of Curtis's head straight into his face. Curtis landed hard on his back and didn't move.

In that moment, Garret let fly another bolt, which sank into Snowball's back.

"Snowball!" Gus cried out, dropping his tankard and jumping up from his seat to help his friend as the Minotaur roared.

Garret immediately dashed down the stairs while the Minotaur was wounded to strike before he missed the opportunity. Gus saw the commander and without thinking took action. He grabbed a nearby keg and rolled it straight at the foot of the stairs. Garret, who was solely focused on Snowball, hadn't paid the peasant any mind during the entire fight and stepped down that last step right onto the keg. It rolled out from underneath him and he fell backward against the stone steps. The fall knocked the breath from his lungs and the crossbow from his grip and out of his reach. He was stunned and before he could recover, Snowball grabbed him by the leg and hoisted him skyward. Garret's sword fell out of its sheathe and clattered to the stone floor as Snowball dangled him upside down so that only his cape brushed the ground.

The Minotaur roared in Garret's face furiously.

"Ahhhhh!" The commander screamed and thrashed around in an absolute panic as he completely lost composure.

Snowball thought to swing Garret around like a rag doll but Gus put him in check.

"Stop! Just hold him." He commanded. Snowball did likewise and everyone present froze, not sure what was going to happen next. "Drop your weapons, or else! We have your commander!" Gus added.

Curtis, seeing the panic in his commander's eyes, grew pale. "Stand down!" He said to the few remaining men.

The other men lowered their weapons and watched anxiously.

"Don't let him go, Snowball! No matter what." Duncan ordered. "He will return with me to answer for his crimes."

"Let him go," Curtis bargained, "and half of this shipment is yours."

Snowball's attention snapped to Curtis.

"Let me go, Snowball," said Garret. "You will be handsomely rewarded. I promise."

"Your promises are worth nothing, Garret." Duncan barked.

"Snowball, he's your commander!" Curtis reminded him.

The courtyard erupted in protest as everyone spoke at once to convince the creature to hold on or let Garret go.

"He's a criminal!"

"They want the wine for themselves!"

"You have to let him go!"

"You can't let him go!"

"Think of the strawberries!"

"QUIET!!!" Gus bellowed as loud as he could. For a man of such small stature, his voice filled the courtyard and echoed off the walls. To his surprise, everyone went quiet from shock and stared at the usually timid peasant.

Gus was at a loss as he struggled to find words to say. He hadn't expected his outburst to have such an effect. "Yes, he is a criminal," he said to Duncan, "No, he is not going to let go unless you order your men to stand down," he shot at Curtis, "and nobody is going to get their hands on this cargo if you all don't stop fighting and drop your weapons. Do you hear me?!" He yelled those last words as a challenge to everyone present. They were stunned.

Gus moved closer to his companion in the awkward silence and spoke quietly. "Snowball, do you want a barrel of strawberry wine just for you?"

Snowball nodded eagerly, somehow oblivious to all of the arguing that had just occurred.

"Do you trust me?" He asked.

Snowball nodded again with a smile.

"Good." He stood on tiptoes while Snowball leaned down to hear as he whispered in the Minotaur's ear.

"Oh! Snowball understands. Mister Gus Man is very smart." He smiled.

"Don't just stand there!" Garret cried out to his men. "Save me!"

The command was cut terribly short, however, as before any of Garret's men could act, Snowball threw the commander with incredible might straight at the group of men. He knocked over the mercenaries, Curtis and Duncan, sending all to the ground in a heap. Before any of the men could recover, Snowball gave each one a rap with his hammer, leaving all sprawled together in various levels of unconsciousness save for Gus.

Gus, of course, was both appalled at the violence but pleased with the results. He took a seat on the steps and let out a sigh of relief. "See. Now we have some time to think things over."

"Oh. Mister Gus Man was very right. So many talky shouty mans." He took advantage of the silence and stooped into the storehouse to grab himself a barrel of strawberry wine. Popping the cork, he poured a healthy gulp down his throat and wiped the rest from his lips with his arm. He sat down near Gus and asked, "What will Mister Gus Man do now?"

"Well, Snowball." Gus paused for a moment in thought. "That's a good question. I think Duncan is right. We should let him take Garret to the north to answer for his crimes."

Snowball grunted in assent.

"However, Curtis and the rest of the mercenaries are not at fault for their commander's orders. They were just doing as they were told. I think we can sneak out of here with the shipment and leave them be. They may follow us but with just one wagon and these supplies we should make better speed than an entire company of mercenaries deprived of their commander. As for Sir Ethan... well... I suppose he'll have to decide what he's going to do with himself. Why don't we throw him and Duncan on the wagon with Garret and get moving? What do you say?"

"Okay."

With that, they loaded up the wagon with the last of the strawberry wine, bound Garret and tied him to the barrels, and threw Duncan and Ethan on top of the pile to sleep off their injuries. They made haste from the city and steered the wagon northward.

The road was quiet and peaceful in the night and after several hours of travel the sky grew rosy with the morning light. Sir Ethan was the first to stir with a groan and great effort. He looked about, confused as to where he was and winced as the sun crested the horizon and his headache became manifest.

"Good Gods, my head." He grumbled as he took off his helmet and rubbed at his temple. "It feels like I've been struck by sixty-pound hammer..." He took note of the weapon resting heavily by Snowball's side. "Oh." And after a moment, "What happened? Where are we going? Can I surmise that we have come out victorious?" He asked.

Gus laughed. "Yes. Well. That's certainly one way to put it. We've been riding north to return the cargo. I suspect Duncan will stir any moment now. You may as well rest. It'll be a long ride."

True enough, Duncan stirred but a few moments later, the same questions and pounding headache as Sir Ethan.

"We're heading north to return the strawberry wine." Gus explained.

Duncan spoke anxiously, "What about Garret? What became of him?"

Snowball and Gus chuckled together before Gus explained, "He's tied to the back. Didn't you notice?"

Curtis and Sir Ethan both turned over their shoulders to look behind. Garret was bound and limp lying over the cargo. "Sir, won't he stir soon?" Ethan asked.

"Yes. Well. I don't think that will be much of a problem. He already stirred about an hour ago."

"Is he sleeping?" Duncan wondered.

"Nope." Gus smiled.

"Then..." Ethan swallowed, "is he dead?"

"No. He's still alive, don't you worry. We just gave him some "extra rest" when he woke up and started rocking the wagon in a desperate attempt to escape."

"Oh. Extra..."

"He'll have twice the headache you two have when he wakes up." Gus laughed. "We've got a fair ride ahead of us, gents. May as well get comfortable and take it easy."

Sir Ethan and Duncan took his advice and for a while they rode on peacefully. By afternoon they stopped to rest the horses and stretch their legs. Gus asked of Sir Ethan, "Now that you've sobered up and learned about Garret's treachery, what are you going to do? With Kismet gone and no mercenary band, will you offer your services to the king in the north?"

The former knight shook his head and looked over at his former commander who was at present bound by the legs and hands and sitting with his back to the wagon wheel looking stubbornly away from his captors.

"I'm not quite sure what my place is exactly but I don't think my place is there. I think once we've delivered him and the wine, I'll head back to Carath to find what's left of his men. You've made quite an impression upon me and I feel a greater calling. Though Kismet may be no longer, her knights still roam this realm and need guidance and a proper cause. I think they need the Knight of the Silver Dragon more than ever. I intend to round up whatever knights and soldiers remain and reorganize the Knights of Kismet. We will stand together in defense of this realm in the name of justice! Doesn't that sound like a sound good cause?"

"Sir Ethan," Gus smiled, "I do believe it does."

"As for me," Duncan broke into the conversation as he returned from a brief stroll, "I am eager to return. Are we ready to get underway?"

The journey was uneventful and soon the wagon and all its cargo were parked just outside the gates of a large walled city surrounded by stone battlements. Sir Ethan, Gus and Snowball disembarked as Duncan took the goods inside and within a few hours returned with a pair of horses and a heavy pouch. He presented the horses and the pouch to Gus, who accepted them gratefully.

"His highness presents you with a generous reward for your courage and the service to our kingdom. He offers you a hundred crowns and two of his finest steeds. He extends his gratitude and wishes you well on your journey." Duncan said, bowing with respect. He gave a half smile and added "I told him that I was aided by a noble adventurer and his barbarian companion," he nodded toward Snowball, "as well as a former knight from Kismet. He asked that I offer you a position here, Sir Ethan, defending king and country, though I know you will refuse. I will inform his majesty properly of your humble refusal."

Sir Ethan smiled and bowed respectfully. "I thank you, Duncan. Though the offer is certainly tempting."

Gus handed Ethan the reins of one of the horses. "Here. We don't need both of them. You can help yourself to half of the reward."

"Oh, no." Sir Ethan raised a hand, "Doing what is right and just is payment enough. I will gratefully accept this fine mount and continue on my way but keep the coin to yourself. It was an honor to help you all and I wish you great fortune in your travels. Now, if you'll excuse me, I will take my leave."

Sir Ethan climbed into the saddle and rode into the distance as Duncan returned through the gates of his kingdom.

Happy to have a hefty sum in his pocket, Gus got on his new horse with a quick boost from Snowball and they began heading east.

"Well, Snowball. It looks like we've finally had a bit of luck, wouldn't you say?"

Snowball nodded eagerly, his tail wagging behind him.

"A happy tale coming to a happy end, eh? Who knows, maybe we'll find even better fortune on the road ahead." He beamed.

"Minotaur!" Came a terror-stricken cry from the wall-top as a guardsman on patrol caught sight of them.

"Maybe not!" Gus cried before he snapped the reins and kicked his horse into a gallop. "Come on, let's get out of here before he calls for reinforcements!"

Without a moment's delay, Gus and Snowball rushed along on the road ahead to whatever adventure lay in store.

PART IV
The Return Policy

Chapter XVIII

Strawberries and friendship... well... you know the metaphor well enough by now. Like a great patchwork of vines, our friendships grow and grow and always together. The thing about such gardens, whether big or small, is that some things growing within are difficult to remove. Strawberries endure many pests but some things threaten to ruin the whole patch, like a returning weed that strangles the life out of everything.

Believe it or not, the hapless peasant was thinking of very similar things, though perhaps for very different reasons. Gus sat quietly on the trunk of a fallen tree as he contemplated a garden of his own. The soil had to be rich and black, like fine velvet, and there needed to be an adequate amount of shade to cool the flourishing plants wherever they grew. It would need cool, sweet spring water and ample sunshine. He imagined an incredible field stretching out beyond the horizon for just such a garden, with room for thousands... Nay, hundreds of thousands of plants all growing together. Each and every one of these ingredients would have to be perfect if he was going to grow a strawberry patch big enough to feed the gluttonous monster that sat next to him, picking diligently at its nose with a hairy finger.

Snowball, all seven hundred pounds of raw muscled fury, bound up in shaggy fur and a minotaur's frame, was also thinking of this same exact garden, stretching for miles in every direction. It was a blissful dream in which he frolicked through the sweet red delectables with unrestrained joy, picking berry after berry in an endless feast of delicious fruit.

Gus was pulled from his own imagination by the spatter of minotaur drool as it dribbled onto the ground. He returned to his senses and stood up to secure his pack to his horse. The mare stood by with not a care, un-intimidated by his human handler or Snowball. Gus had few of the oats left that had been packed for him and they would soon need to resupply if they were going to continue wandering across the countryside. While he was packing, he asked his companion, "Snowball, does it not bother you that people are afraid of you?"

Snowball's tail swayed back and forth; his mind still enthralled by the sumptuous daydream.

"Snowball!" Gus said forcefully.

"Huh?" The Minotaur snapped out of it. "Oh. Uh... Tiny hoomans do not scare Snowball." He said, thinking this a satisfactory answer.

"No. I was asking if it bothered you that *they* were afraid of *you*."

Snowball scratched at his hindquarters. "Hmmmm..." Snowball thought on it. "Nope. Snowball does not care. Snowball just wants to find more strawberries. Or maybe smash something."

"Great... Well spoken." Gus muttered. He was growing used to the Minotaur's eloquence little by little as they traveled across the realm. He suspected that any poetry written by the creature, if Snowball could actually write, would contain more sounds and images of breaking things than actual subject matter.

"Does it bother Mister Gus Man that Snowball makes tiny hoomans run like scared little mouses?" Snowball asked.

"Mice," Gus corrected. "And yes. Yes, it does. How am I ever going to succeed in this world if everyone I try to interact with runs for the hills screaming?"

Snowball thought on this for a while before coming up with an answer. "Mister Gus Man just needs to be more scary so that tiny hoomans are too scared to run away."

Gus sighed. "Right." The Minotaur's logic was incredible. "Well, I don't think that would work very well for me. Maybe for you..." He put a foot in the stirrup and lifted himself up onto the horse. "Come on, then. The only way you and I are going to find our fortune is to keep moving."

Gus rode off down the path and Snowball followed close behind.

"I'm surprised this horse is so calm around you." Gus commented as he rode along. "You would think it'd go running off. It's very well trained."

"She just wants oats. She knows Snowball would smash anything that tries to get her." Snowball replied disinterestedly.

"Wait. She? I guess I haven't even checked." Gus realized. "Wait a minute. Can you talk to horses?"

Snowball burst into deep laughter. "Oh, Mister Gus Man is funny. Of course, Snowball cannot talk to horses."

"Oh, good," Gus said, "that's a relief."

"Horses do not talk. Snowball just listens and horse just listens."

The comment caught Gus off guard. "Wait, what? So, you can communicate with it?"

"Her." Snowball corrected.

"Yes, her. You can communicate with her?"

"What is moonicate? The moon is very high up." Snowball puzzled.

"Communicate." Gus repeated. "It means to talk... er... it means to share ideas with someone else. Talking is communicating."

"Oh! Yes. Mister Gus Man is right. Snowball moonicates with horsies."

"Wow! That's incredible, Snowball!" Gus marveled at his companion. "What is she saying now?" He asked excitedly.

"Oh. Horsey is glad Mister Gus Man is tiny and pathetic like a shaking feather."

"I... er..." Gus was at a loss for words. "Forget I asked."

"She thinks pathetic hoomans would be easy to stomp on if -"

"All right. That's enough for now. Thank you, Snowball. Let's just focus on the journey ahead." Gus tried to keep his gaze on the path but he couldn't help a feeling of uneasiness as the horse turned its head, looking back at him as they rode on.

Traveling was tiresome over the uneven forest hills, so they stopped frequently to rest. When at last the sun was beginning to set, Gus made sure to find an appropriate patch of land amid the trees to make camp. As he was assembling the tent, he noticed a silhouette in the distance perched atop a ridge. It was very small but Gus could make out a pair of antlers atop its head.

"A deer?" He wondered. "Hey, Snowball. We haven't seen many deer around here lately, have we?"

Snowball shrugged.

"Some venison would be a real treat. We could eat for..." He looked at Snowball, whom Gus was sure was a strict vegetarian, "Well, at least *I* would be fed for a while." He said with a grumbling stomach. They had some supplies from their last stop but it was quickly running out and he had grown tired of nuts and dried berries. Of course, Gus realized that he had no idea how to properly dress a dear and only had a vague idea how to prepare dried meats. Without the proper implements, he was sure he would fail spectacularly so he pushed visions of venison steaks from his mind.

The following morning, Gus got up early and packed up camp aside from a small cooking fire. He boiled up a meager breakfast and then He and Snowball continued on their way.

By late morning, Gus could see thin wisps of smoke drifting up from among the trees. Up ahead lay a modest village and by the time it was in sight they could hear the sound of lumberjacks hard at work among the trees.

"Careful, Snowball. We don't want to cause a stir up here. I have an idea. Why don't you take a look around the area and gather firewood and berries." He handed Snowball an empty sack for the berries. "I'll head into town for information and supplies. We can trade some firewood for food and we've got plenty of coin now. Just try to stay away from anyone you see and that will help us avoid any unnecessary trouble. What do you say?"

Snowball happily agreed and wandered off.

Up ahead a simple village stood on the bend of a small river. Aside from the sound of axes striking trees and the normal hubbub of a sleepy forest village, the air was quiet. A main road ran through its center, past a stable and blacksmith as well as a tiny inn and general store, and onward deeper into the forest. Gus stopped just outside the village fence and readied himself for society's pleasantries. He had been riding for some time and it had been days since he'd spoken with anyone aside from Snowball, whose conversation could hardly be called normal.

To his left he noticed a wooden sign bearing a detailed carving of heavy pines that read "Timberfell". He chuckled to himself, "oh, my. How original. Who would think? A town named after trees falling down..." He did his best to put on a friendly smile and rode into town.

As he did, he got uneasy stares from the village folk. They continued about their daily chores, tossing laundry on the line and herding the chickens back to their coups, but as he passed by there was a noticeable effort on their part to shrink away warily. He met a young boy's gaze and smiled pleasantly. The boy could only stare with mild fear in his eyes. For a moment, Gus remembered what Snowball had said about scaring people and thought to raise his arms up and say "Roar!" but thought better on it. Instead he nodded politely and continued on his way without saying a word. Passing into the center of town, Gus led his horse to the general store and tied the reins to the hitching rail outside.

"Welcome." Came a friendly man's voice as Gus wandered in through the door. The voice belonged to a heavy-set fellow with a burly beard. When the shop keeper saw that his customer wasn't one of the townsfolk, he immediately became uneasy. "What business bring you here?" He asked.

"Oh. Well, I am passing through and need to resupply. I don't suppose you've got enough oats to feed a horse for a week or so?"

The shopkeeper, seeing Gus's unimpressive stature, relaxed and shrugged. "Yes. I suppose we have some available if you've got the coin. Whereabouts are you headed?"

"Uh... well..." Gus struggled, "I guess the next town. To be honest I've been traveling the countryside. How far is the next town heading east?"

The shopkeeper tugged at his beard as he thought about it. "Well, supposing you took the logging trail southeast, you could reach the next village in about three days, two by horse. Otherwise it's another five days heading northeast through the pass."

"Hmmm. I don't think I'd like to head through a pass." Gus considered.

"I wouldn't either if I was you. These woods are dangerous these days." The shopkeeper mentioned. "That your horse out front?"

"Yes, sir."

"I'll bring the feed around from the back. Is there anything else you'll be wanting for the road?"

"No," Gus said. "Are there wolves?" He asked.

"Wolves?" The shopkeeper stroked his beard.

"You said the woods were dangerous. I was just wondering if there were wolves."

"Oh. No, nothing like that, I don't think," he said. "There's been word of bandits roaming the countryside and heading in this direction. I've heard they've been attacking the roads, robbing people and leaving no survivors."

"Huh." Gus was a little concerned but wondered, "If there are no survivors, who spread word that they were roaming the countryside?"

The shopkeeper stroked his beard once more. "You know, you have a fair point, sir. Either way, be careful out there if you're traveling. I'd make camp far off the main road and travel by day. Have you any companions with you? Strength in numbers and all that."

Gus shrugged. "Well... I think I can handle myself but don't worry. I'll be careful. However, now that I think on it, I could use some dried meats and provisions for a few days."

"Very well, sir. Very well. I'll bring the feed around front for you and get your horse loaded up. Feel free to have a look around and if there's anything else just let me know."

After accepting payment, the shopkeeper disappeared into the storeroom in the back of the shop and Gus took his advice, spending a few minutes perusing the goods. When he left his horse had already been loaded with a few sacks of oats and he was quick to head out of town.

A few minutes down the road his hulking companion came crashing through the brush, eager to greet him. Gus was about to tell his friend that they should get going but he noticed the load Snowball carried with him. The sack he had handed the Minotaur for berries was bulging with firewood and had small tears with sharp bits of wood poking through. Additionally, there was a subtle smear of red on the creature's mouth and at first Gus alarmingly thought it to be blood but, after considering the other clues, recognized it was most likely raspberries.

"Snowball, I told you to gather firewood and berries."

Snowball nodded with an enthusiastic grunt. "Snowball did find berries and wood."

"You used the sack I gave you for berries to collect the wood." Gus noted.

Snowball nodded emphatically.

"Where did you put all the berries?" Gus asked with a raised voice.

"Snowball put them in his mouth. They were very tasty."

Gus rubbed the bridge of his nose. "You were supposed to put the berries in the sack and carry the wood, not eat the berries."

Snowball put on a confused expression, looked first at the now torn and bulging sack and then at the front of his snout, then back to the sack, then back to Gus. He paused for a moment as his mind contemplated what Gus had said, then "Oh! Mister Gus Man, Snowball did not mean to. Snowball thought Mister Gus Man wanted Snowball to eat the berries. Snowball is very sorry."

Gus groaned. "Ugh. Never mind. Listen, next time I send you out, try to bring at least some of the berries back so we can both eat them. Let's get moving while we still have daylight. It's still a few days before we reach the next town and there might be bandits in the woods. We'll need to be on the lookout, alright?"

Snowball nodded and they set off down the road.

Chapter XIX

Evening approached and they made camp just out of sight of the road in a small clearing. Once the tent was up and they had a small fire going, Gus took a seat on a fallen tree. While Snowball poked lazily at the fire, deeply amused by the sparks, Gus took out his locket and absently thumbed it. He drew deeply into a thoughtful mood and began to contemplate their situation. His mind wandered from his companion to the locket, to the town and all the misadventures they'd been on since he'd left his own sleepy little village.

Out of nowhere he asked the Minotaur, "Snowball, what are we doing? What is our goal here?"

Snowball grunted. "Strawberries," he answered simply.

"No, that's not really enough." Gus explained. "We've been wandering the countryside, getting into all sorts of trouble along the way, and I can't really say there's been a point. I feel like I'm missing something in my life. You see, that's why I left my village in the first place."

Although he knew his concern rose far above the head of the Minotaur, Gus continued thinking aloud as he absently toyed with the locket. "If we look at this objectively, I'm traveling the countryside with a veritable monster without even so much as a plan. At first I thought we were looking for strawberries..."

Snowball grunted in agreement, apparently oblivious to being referred to as a monster.

"...but there are always going to be more strawberries. It will never end."

Snowball grew more excited as he listened.

"And maybe that's good enough for you, but it certainly isn't my goal in life. There is more to a man than filling one's belly."

The Minotaur was drooling once again.

"But then again, look at you." He gestured. "You know what you want and you go for it. And you're happy. Happy to just endlessly chase a never-ending field of strawberries and smashing things to pieces along the way."

If the Minotaur's tail could have wagged more furiously it may very well have split a rock in two.

"So, what is it? What is my purpose? I left my home, my family, everything I've ever known to wander aimlessly with a monster, nearly get killed on several occasions and all just to make a mess of things and waste what little time a man has on this earth. And what for?"

"Strawberries!" His companion nodded vigorously and exclaimed.

"Damnit, Snowball!" Gus said slamming his hands down on the fallen tree.

Snowball didn't seem to mind. He continued poking at the embers with a stick, laughing to himself with each puff of sparks.

Gus shook his head and resumed fiddling with the locket and soon realized it had popped open when he'd slammed his fists. There inside sat the little lock of hair. He stared at it for a while, thinking about all the memories he had wrapped up in his childhood.

Fiona was the only one who ever showed him genuine kindness growing up. He had always been the runt, the butt of jokes and a convenient scapegoat for the other villagers. He thought back as far as he could to how the two of them had met. He remembered that morning when he had accidentally let the pigs out of their pen and was chasing them all around the village. He was such a small child and the pigs were almost more than he could handle by himself. He had managed to chase all but one back into the pen, but the last one was the largest and wasn't about to budge as it munched on the feed set aside for the horses. The ground was muddy from the rain the night before and Gus could remember how drab and cold that day had been.

He'd put his shoulder against the large swine, pushing with his whole body, but the fat pig wouldn't budge as it ravenously devoured the oats hanging in a sack on the side of farmer Ben's stable. He'd pushed and pushed with all his might but he wasn't strong enough. His feet slipped in the mud and he fell. He'd struggled to get back up but the hog, in its gluttonous frenzy, stepped carelessly over him, pushing him even further into the mud and badly bruising his back. He remembered sobbing and crying to get out from under the pig. Eventually the hog finished its feast and moved on to find some other meal to stuff its face with. He remembered laying there in the mud with tears and dirt all over his face. He remembered how it had started to rain and he'd just laid there crying.

Then someone leaned over him and offered him a hand. It was a young, well-dressed girl with a radiant smile. At first, he hadn't known what to think as she held her hand out to him, but then she grabbed his muddy hand on her own and pulled him up anyway. He'd been scolded for letting the pigs out later that day and she'd been chastised by her father for getting mud on her dress but neither of them had cared back then. They'd become friends.

"Mister Gus Man just needs to mate." Snowball concluded.

"Huh? What?" Gus snapped out of his daydream. "No. That's..." He looked down at his locket.

"Mating is good." Snowball agreed.

"No!" Gus groaned.

The Minotaur didn't seem to understand.

Gus shut the locket and held it tightly in one hand. "Haven't you been listening to a word I've said?"

Snowball still didn't understand but he smiled happily anyway. Then he wondered. "What is Monster?"

"I just…" Gus shook his head. "You're a monster. Well... You're a..."

Snowball waited for Gus to answer.

"A monster is a scary creature that people want to avoid at all costs," Gus said forcefully, "even if they have to kill it."

"Oooh! Snowball *is* a monster!" The Minotaur declared with excitement.

"No!" Gus said. "Wait... Yes. Yes, you are a monster. Well... you're a Minotaur anyway. And most people think a Minotaur is a monster," Gus muttered. "But it's not a good thing!"

"Wait. If tiny hoomans want to avoid monster, does Mister Gus Man want to avoid Snowball?"

Gus stood up and busied himself with preparing dinner. "Sometimes, I just don't know," He admitted. "You're a lot of trouble."

Snowball went quiet. When Gus noticed the silence, he looked over at his companion. The Minotaur looked hurt. "... You're a lot of trouble to your enemies!" He said with hollow enthusiasm, pumping his fist in encouragement. "I'd hate to be the bloke who runs into you alone in the woods."

"Oh!" Snowball said. "Like Mister Gus Man!"

Gus realized that was how they'd met in the first place. "Uh. Yes. Just like that. Boy, was I scared back then. What a fierce... uh... friend."

"Is Mister Gus Mans thinking that being a monster is bad?"

"Ugh…" It was getting difficult for Gus to explain to such a simple mind. "It's more like, people… humans are afraid of strong, aggressive, dangerous creatures like yourself. They want to be as far away from things like that as possible."

"Like the plague?"

"What? Yes. Yes, like the plague." Gus nodded. "Wait, how do you know about plagues?"

"They sound fun at first, but then hoomans get all white and fall down. Why do hoomans put the word play in plague?" Snowball asked.

"Ah, that's a good question." Gus had never drawn such a strange connection. "Hoomans-" He cleared his throat, "Humans do lots of strange things."

"Like run from monsters?"

"Well, that's… that's different. That's just survival." Gus said. "And that's what makes traveling with you…" He carefully considered his words for fear of hurting his companion again. "Traveling with you is…" He decided to play to the Minotaur's ego. "Challenging!" He pumped his fist once again. Snowball wagged his tail with excitement so he continued, "I mean, just think. We could easily get *jobs* to make money, or stay in comfortable *beds*, or eat good food at an inn. But not us! No. We…" Gus swallowed how painfully depressing he sounded, "We... we rough it! We're regular adventurer's, we are. We don't take the easy way out!"

"Yes!" Snowball agreed.

"We stick to the hard route." Gus gave a stern look to Snowball, "And we don't give up like… like pansies! Tiny little flowers that are good for nothing!"

Snowball nodded energetically.

"We have to figure out how to make money without taking... pathetic... jobs. We have to sleep on the ground like… like… well, men!" He said stoically, pounding a fist on his puffed-out chest. "And it isn't easy!"

"Nope!" Snowball chimed in.

"It isn't fun!"

"Nope!"

"But it's what we gotta do." Gus slumped down on his seat on the fallen tree in defeat.

Snowball roared with excitement. Gus had him fired up.

"Mister Gus Man is right! Snowball and Mister Gus Man are going to make money without stupid jobs or tiny little beds inside tiny little inns. Because we are friends and we do all the stuff together!"

Gus groaned to himself but smiled at his companion. Snowball wasn't wrong. They had become friends. The only trick was figuring out what they were doing wandering all over creation together.

"Is hoomans monsters?" Snowball asked once he had settled down.

The question caught Gus off guard. He scratched his chin for a moment. "What makes you say that?" He asked.

"Lots of tiny creatures want to avoid hoomans. Like deer and rabbits and fish."

"I... huh. You have a pretty good point, Snowball. I guess I've never thought of it that way.'

"So hoomans is monsters just like Snowball?"

"Heh. Well, maybe not just like you..." Gus chuckled. "But perhaps you're right. I suppose humans are monsters in their own way. Taking land for themselves. Hunting down creatures and killing any pests along the way. Torturing and killing one another. Hunting each other down. Starting wars. Writing terrible fiction. Humans are certainly complicated creatures. But they aren't nearly as big or strong as a minotaur. That much is certain."

Snowball flexed his muscles. "Yeah. Tiny hoomans."

Gus returned to preparing a meal and shook his head. "Well, at any rate, let's get some food and some sleep. We still have a fair bit of travel ahead of us."

They supped and slept after dousing the fire and soon the day had ended.

The following day was uneventful as they followed the old logging road. In spite of the mild weather, the forest was strangely quiet. Gus took notice as they traveled that there was little activity to be had. He attributed the quiet to the overcast sky, thinking that perhaps a coming storm had spooked the wildlife.

It was mid-day, just after they had stopped for a short rest. Rather, Gus had stopped for a short rest. After all their time traveling the wilds, Gus was beginning to wonder if Snowball every actually got tired or if he could go for days on end without stopping. Snowball had wandered off to forage for berries, or terrorize forest creatures, or perhaps scratch his backside on a tree somewhere, as far as Gus was concerned.

The peasant had sat down on a low stone just by the road to get off his feet for a moment when suddenly he heard a rustle in the bushes. He called out once, thinking it was Snowball snuffling around when a rough looking man dressed in unwashed clothes sprang out of the bushes, brandishing a knife. He was a scraggly looking ne'er-do-well with a homely face and a patchy beard and was about six feet tall. Gus held up his hands to show that he was unarmed.

"Alright, you. Put yer hands up!" the bandit said.

"But they're already up..." Gus pointed out.

"Shut up, you! Empty your pockets. Give me all of your money! C'mon now. On the double." He ordered.

Gus could tell he wasn't the brightest sort. "But you told me to put my hands up."

"What?" The bandit was confused.

"You told me to put my hands up. I can't empty my pockets with my hands up, now can I?"

"I... er..." The bandit was at a loss for words. He hadn't expected Gus's response.

"So, which is it? Put my hands up or empty my pockets?"

The bandit had to think for a moment. "Give me your money. Go on, now. No funny business."

Gus did as he was told and untied the purse from his belt. He tossed it on the ground in front of the bandit. The bandit reached down and snatched it up. However, by the time he had untied the pouch, he looked up and went pale.

Snowball stood over Gus's shoulder with his usual dumb expression. He eyed the newcomer with disinterest.

The bandit dropped everything and fled, screaming for his life.

"Did I tell you I was traveling with a friend?" Gus called out after him as the bandit disappeared around the bend.

"Oh! Mister Gus Man. You are a scary monster!" Snowball decided after seeing the bandit flee.

Gus chuckled. "Well, I don't think it was me he was running from but thank you anyway."

"Mister Gus Man was right. Hoomans *is* monsters!" Snowball said, ignoring Gus's comment. The Minotaur was so proud of his companion.

Gus laughed. Having the strange creature hanging around hadn't turned out so bad after all. Snowball was certainly a deterrent for any trouble along the road, and since Gus would otherwise be wandering the roads alone in search of something he couldn't quite name, having his own makeshift bodyguard around was a blessing. Gus shook his head. How could he, of all people, become so fortunate to have the most terrifying creature by his side? It wasn't like he was an important figure or a brave warrior. He was a clever little nobody who had fled, terrified for his life, and only happened to survive due to the most unlikely circumstances he could think of.

He took out the locket from beneath his shirt and thumbed it absently. He wasn't one to believe in fate and all that. However, if it wasn't fate that had been set up ever so perfectly, he had stumbled into perhaps one of the most improbable of coincidences of all time. What were the odds that he would have been in the woods at the same time as his monstrous friend? Carrying a locket with a faint smell of strawberries wrapped into the lock of hair it contained? And the monster having an unhealthy obsession with strawberries on top of it all?

"Ugh!" Gus groaned as he got up and started walking while leading the horse. Thinking about it had him frustrated.

He didn't believe it was fate. However, if that were the case, what in the Gods' names was it?

They continued well into the evening before they pitched camp. Gus had paid no attention to the aching of his feet or the tiredness of his step. He was too preoccupied. He hated the weight on his mind all the more as he threw down his pack and hitched his horse to a nearby tree. These sorts of existential crisis were exactly why he had left in the first place. He didn't really feel like he belonged anywhere. Heavy thoughts like this made him miserable and he wanted desperately to get away from them. He busied himself setting up the camp, doing his best not to think at all while he did.

The night crept up and soon they were sitting beneath the stars, surrounded by black forest and lit only by the orange glow of the campfire. Gus poked at the fire with a stick, once again deep in thought. He was about ready to call it a night when the hairs on the back of his neck stood on end and he noticed Snowball suddenly snap his head toward something in the distance, his ears alert for something only the Minotaur could detect.

"What is it, Snowball?" Gus asked.

"Someone is following." Snowball said calmly.

"What?" Gus yelped.

"Oh, do not worry, Mister Gus Man. They have been following for days now."

Gus went pale. "Days? You mean there's something out to get us?"

Snowball shrugged. "They did not get us so far. Maybe they are scared because Mister Gus Man is a ferocious monster."

Gus just shook his head. "Can you tell how far off they are?"

Snowball pointed off in the distance. "Just past that rise. They can see the fire."

Gus immediately wanted to put it out. He stood up and grabbed a branch he could use to scatter the fire. Before he could push aside more than a branch, however, Snowball grabbed him firmly by the arm.

"Do not put out the fire, Mister Gus Man. This is how they know where we are." Snowball said with seriousness.

"But don't we want them to not know?" Gus whimpered.

"If they do not know where we are, they will not come." Snowball pointed out. Then his expression turned to sinister confidence. "We will let them come. And Snowball will break them to pieces."

Gus swallowed nervously. Snowball had never seemed so serious before. "They? Are you saying there is more than one?" Gus asked.

Snowball sniffed at the air. "There is many," he said definitively. He paused, then added, "Snowball does not know how to count."

Gus slapped his forehead.

"There is one with horns." Snowball noted. "One who is taller than the others. He is one with the wild."

Feeling uneasy, Gus asked "What does that mean? One with the wild?"

Snowball looked at him with a stern expression. "Tiny hoomans do not have the smell of wilderness on them. Too clean. The horned one comes with that smell. Like wild thing."

Gus didn't like the sound of that. The "Horned One". It gave him the chills. "Snowball, we need to put out the fire. Maybe even move camp, or else they will kill us in our sleep."

Snowball laughed from his belly. "Let them try. Snowball will not be killed by tiny hoomans so easily."

"Right." Gus sighed. "It's not you I'm worried about."

"Try to get some sleep, Mister Gus Man. Snowball will watch until morning time. You will see. The Horned One will not come.

Gus had his reservations but decided to trust his minotaur friend. He left the fire going and disappeared into his tent to try to sleep. In spite of his fears, he couldn't help but feel confident that he would sleep safely with the Minotaur guarding him. Even if they were attacked, chances were whoever came would fare poorly against such a beast in the middle of the night. Snowball had an uncanny way of perceiving, even in the dark, and with what Gus had seen of his battle prowess, his opponents would be foolish to try anything without a solid plan. It took some time but eventually Gus was able to drift off into a restless sleep.

Chapter XX

The morning was cold and misty when Gus crawled from his bedroll. The forest felt sleepy to him. He went about his business without making too much noise and kept quiet as he finished packing up the camp. His horse seemed on edge so Gus spoke to her gently to calm her down. Snowball was in an equally quiet mood, which was unusual for the creature. The Minotaur had a habit of tromping about, sniffing the air and rummaging around in the bushes for goodness-knows-what most mornings. It gave Gus the willies. Something was strange that morning.

They headed out without saying so much as a word and continued down the path for most of the day. By late afternoon they had reached the end of the narrow trail leading down into a small misty vale. Within, spread through the trees, a small, run down village lay. The morning mist had collected in the valley and made the slowly rotting buildings seem the more forlorn and forgotten.

Thinking it best to leave his companion in the wilderness while he took a look around in town, Gus told Snowball to gather some firewood and find a secluded place they could rest out of sight of the townsfolk. Gus saw not a soul as he passed through the pines and onto the main road through town. The mist made it difficult to see and everything was eerily quiet. "Hello?" He called out; afraid the town had been long abandoned. He passed a rather poorly maintained wooden sign rotting in the overgrowth off the road. It read "Welcome to Hogwash", though it had severe cracks running through the grains. He snorted. "Nice name for a town..."

He felt somewhat relieved when he noticed someone heading off the street and into a nearby house. He waved but the figure only glared over its shoulder before disappearing through the door. A little while later he passed a small tavern and got the glances of a few men of the village. They wore thick beards and dark expressions, eyeing Gus as he passed by. "I should be used to this by now..." He told himself. "I suppose with bandits about there's good reason to be wary of strangers."

Gus swallowed his courage and rode up to the men out in front of the tavern. "Excuse me, gentlemen. May I trouble you for a moment?"

The men seemed to glare but nodded to him.

"You see, I've been traveling round and was wondering where the nearest town might be. We just came from Timberfell..."

"We?" One of the men asked gruffly. "You mean you and your horse?"

"Did I say we? My apologies. It's been a long ride today. I just came from Timberfell. Heading east. Can you point a fellow in the right direction?"

One of the men with darker hair scratched at his beard. Another moved his mouth in thought as if chewing something, and the third simply grunted. "There's bandits moving through these parts. The roads aren't safe. You'd be smart to stay in town a while," one of them said.

"Yes. Well, I will certainly keep that in mind. Perhaps you know where I might find some means of employment to earn my keep while I'm here."

All three of the men sized him up and chuckled. "I don't know there's much here for you," said the one.

"Right." Gus said, feeling a bit frustrated. "Well, I may not look like much but believe me, there's plenty of hard work I can get done if given the opportunity. You see..." Just then Gus spotted Snowball down the alleyway behind the tavern, waving his arm to get Gus's attention. The Minotaur gestured for Gus to come over to him silently, as if to tell him an important secret. Gus wasn't sure what made him more uneasy: The fact that the Minotaur was just around the corner from three grown men and could be spotted any minute, sending the town into a panic, or that the Minotaur was actually attempting to remain inconspicuous.

"Go on, boy." One of the men urged him in an irritable tone.

"Uh. Right. Well then, what was I saying?" Gus drew his attention back to the three bearded men.

"Do you want work or don't you?"

Snowball made stronger gestures, indicating the severity of his need for Gus to follow.

"I er... Yes, well you see..."

"Go on. Out with it, lad!" One man growled.

Gus's attention was divided.

"Well. Yes. I would be glad to work any..."

Snowball had picked up two small branches and was waving them around like signal flags desperately trying to get his attention.

"I... Uh... Hold that thought, gentlemen." Gus said before turning his horse down the alley and galloping in Snowball's direction, leaving the men confused on the bench in front of the tavern.

Gus followed Snowball through the brush until they were well out of earshot of the town. "What is it, Snowball? What's the matter? I was right in the middle of securing some work for us."

"Mister Gus Man needs to come with Snowball. There is something Snowball needs to show."

Gus was feeling quite frustrated. "Well, it had better be important."

Sure enough, it was. Snowball led Gus to the foot of a great pine tree in the middle of the forest where a body lay strewn on the ground, pale and rigid. It took only a moment for Gus to recognize the body as the same bandit that had tried to rob him on the road the day before. His clothes were in tatters and there were signs of struggle everywhere; broken branches and drag marks in the dirt. The bandit's face was screwed up in an almost comical expression as if saying "Ewwww..." as its hands clutched at a wooden spear penetrating his heart.

Gus blanched. "By the Gods..."

Snowball waited patiently for Gus to collect himself.

"Well, on the one hand, he got what was coming to him, robbing people along the roads and all. But at the same time, I can't help but feel sorry for him. I wonder... What happened to him." Gus shook his head.

"The Horned One." Snowball told him.

"What?"

Snowball pointed at the spear. "Smells like him."

"Oh." Gus shivered. He didn't like the sound of "The Horned One" at all. He stood there for a while trying to figure out what he should do. It was unnerving to see someone killed in cold blood like that and certainly gave Gus reason for concern for his own safety. After a while, Gus nodded to himself and said "let's at least bury him."

Snowball nodded vigorously and picked up the body by the shoulder and letting it hang limply as they looked for an appropriate clearing. Gus thought to tell Snowball to treat the body with more respect but then decided he didn't really care. It was only a body anymore, and one belonging to a ne'er-do-well at that.

When they had found a good spot, Snowball quickly tore the earth apart with his hands and casually tossed the body in the hole before covering it up with soil.

"Should we say a few words?" Gus asked as they stood over the fresh grave.

Thinking on it for a moment, Snowball nodded in agreement.

"Well..." Gus began, not sure of what he could say about the former bandit. "His struggles in life are now over. May his spirit rest in peace."

Grunting his approval, Snowball added, "and may his tiny body grow into tasty strawberries."

Gus sighed, knowing he should have expected as much from his companion. He chuckled a little to himself as he suddenly wished he had some strawberry seeds to plant over the grave.

They returned near to town before parting ways once more and Gus headed toward the tavern. He still had some coin in his pocket to pay for a room for the night. To his relief, the three men on the bench out front had left by the time he returned. He suspected they'd be leery of giving him any sort of employment after he'd left so abruptly. The man at the tavern afforded him a room for a few copper pieces and Gus was glad to spend the night once more in a proper bed.

Gus awoke with a headache well before the sun had risen. He laid there for a while feeling miserable, debating if he should get up and get started with his day or just stay in bed pretending the rest of the world didn't exist. He decided on the latter, feeling unwilling to deal with yet another difficult day with people too afraid of strangers to give him a fighting chance in the world.

When at last the light peeked through his window, Gus got up and prepared for a hard day. He grabbed a quick meal in the tavern for a few more copper. When he stepped outside, he was keenly aware of the dreariness of the day. The sky was a blanket of gray settled heavily through the town. The earth was damp and misty, the smell of earth wafting up from the puddles of mud, made fresh with the morning's moisture. The town was quiet throughout, even as still as the forest. Not a bird chirped or creature stirred in the brush. It was as if the mist had formed a gentle cocoon around the muddy town of Hogwash.

He wandered around for a while leading his horse, looking for signs of anyone, but every door was shut and the townspeople were not about with their usual chores. When he made his way back to the tavern, he was surprised to find that it too had been shut tight. Feeling a bit out of sorts, Gus decided to find his companion. Something strange was happening and it made him terribly uneasy. He climbed into the saddle and rode out of town. Not entirely sure where Snowball had wandered off to, Gus called out several times, hoping Snowball was in earshot. His shouts went unanswered as they dissipated into the mist. Given that he had no other real means for finding his friend and his tracking skills not being terribly sharp, Gus took out his locket and thumbed it open. Snowball had followed the scent of the strawberries on it before, perhaps it might work again.

After half an hour of wandering, disappointment set in. It wasn't working. Gus called out once more but to no avail. "What do you think, girl?" Gus asked the horse. "Any ideas where he might be? You don't think that something happened to him, do you?"

Gus waited for a response. The horse snorted. He almost wondered if it had understood him. He was mostly talking to himself and using the horse as an excuse, so he played along with it. "You've got a fair point. What could have possibly happened? He's got more muscle than a field of farm-hands, and that ridiculous hammer. A man couldn't sneak up on that beast if he was the southern wind, huh girl? I once saw him squash a mouse that tried to get too close while he was sleeping, and he never even woke up!"

The horse snorted.

"He's got an uncanny sense of direction, so it's not like he's lost. He must be off getting into trouble somewhere, or he found a strawberry patch and hasn't finished devouring everything in sight." He said the words but didn't really believe them. The forests they'd been traveling through weren't quite right for strawberries. Not that he was an expert on the local ecology. It just didn't seem like the right environment for them, which meant that more than likely Snowball had wandered into some trouble.

After seeing the dead body the day before, Gus felt that the chances were good the bandits he'd heard talk about were in the area. They were clearly violent and out to cause trouble, and if they ran across his companion there was no telling what might happen. Snowball wasn't the type to refuse confrontation. Of course, Snowball wasn't the type to always use sound judgment either. What if he had joined the bandits? Was that even possible? Snowball might but he needed proper motivation... Like violence...

Gus gulped. He needed to find his friend.

The horse stamped in protest and came to a stop at the top of a small rise.

"What is it girl?" Gus asked, not sure why the horse wasn't responding to his commands to move onward.

The horse shook its head and let out a small whinny.

"Can you seriously understand me?" Gus wondered aloud. When the horse calmed down and turned its head to look back at him, he could not help but feel surprised. "We're trying to find Snowball. Shouldn't we keep moving. You've been doing so well up until now." He pleaded with the horse but it stayed put and started munching on some plants. "Would you please just listen to me and do what I ask?" He begged. Then he noticed a set of hoof prints pressed into the dirt near where the horse was grazing. He dismounted and investigated.

The soil was soft and the prints deep. There were more leading off northeast. They were distinctly bovine in nature, Gus noted, which would be unusual from what he'd seen thus far. There hadn't been any cattle in the area and certainly no ranches. This forest had seemed to him to be lumber territory and not terribly good for ranches. He followed the prints for several yards before he noticed a large red smear on the trunk of an old tree. *Had something happened here?* He wondered.

He turned back toward his horse. "I see. You wanted to show me these hoof prints, didn't you? Clever girl."

The horse snorted and immediately turned and galloped off into the woods.

"Oh, great!" Gus threw his hands up into the air. "Thanks a lot!" He shouted after the horse. He was about to turn and investigate the smear on the tree, which he took to be fresh blood when he heard movement in the bushes and five men appeared, clad in animal skins and armed with clubs and daggers. *Bandits*, Gus thought.

"You sure make a lot of noise." One of the men said as he moved closer and the others made to surround Gus.

Now, like any sensible peasant, Gus carefully analyzed the situation. He noted the advantages and disadvantages before him and was able to arrive at a sound course of action.

He turned and ran like the dickens.

Certainly, if he could outrun a rampaging minotaur, he could outmaneuver a ragtag bunch of bandits, couldn't he?

Outrunning a single creature had been difficult but outmaneuvering five men proved to be a whole other beast. Gus was quick, but every time he tried to shake his pursuers, they spread out to hem him in. He turned left around a dense cluster of trees but the bandits anticipated and went around in both directions. He went right past a rocky outcropping but they followed right behind. He ran and ran for all he was worth but he could hear them close on his heels. He was small and quick to turn but his shorter legs weren't good for long distances. They were closing in on him and if he didn't think of something fast it would be over. Climbing up a tree would do him no good and they'd catch him before he was half-way up. He had no idea where he was even headed and he couldn't use the unfamiliar terrain to his advantage. Gus could hear their steps just behind him. He chanced a quick glance over his shoulder just in time to see one of the bandits reaching out to grab him by the collar. He yelped and ducked into a little ball to protect himself. The sudden stop caught the bandit by surprise and he ran right over the top of Gus and tripped, tumbling headfirst into a thick tree trunk. Gus seized the opportunity and before the bandit could recover or his cohorts could catch up, Gus darted forward and pushed his way through the dense brush...

... and over the edge of the steep slope hidden behind.

Had he known it was there, Gus surely would have skidded down the slope and nimbly continued on his frightful chase. Instead, he plummeted down the slope like a sack of potatoes only to come skidding to a stop, the bark along the forest floor digging into his skin. He tried his best to ignore the pain and scrambled to his feet to resume his flight. He heard shouts at the top of the slope as the bandits caught sight of him.

Oh, Gods! Gus thought. *I'm going to die!*

The sounds of bandits clumsily sliding down the slope behind him put vigor in his step as he pounded across the forest floor. He managed to keep ahead of them for a few moments as he tried to think of anything that could help him to escape. That's when he caught sight of a massive bank of dense brush just to the left of the path ahead. He zipped around the corner as quick as he could and turned back, changing directions and diving underneath the bushes and out of sight. The bandits ran past a moment later, dashing further down the path before they realized they'd lost sight of their quarry. Gus felt a fist sized rock underneath his hand and decided to pick it up. Careful to remain hidden, Gus poked his head up while they were searching for him in the opposite direction and hurled the rock as quietly as he could into the woods. The noise caught the bandits' attention and they all turned and ran in that direction and out of sight.

Gus rolled over on his back and breathed a sigh of relief. He'd escaped, at least for the time being. It wouldn't be too long before they realized he'd given them the slip. He'd need to put some distance between them. He paid no mind to his scrapes and scratches and scampered off, careful to keep low and not make too much noise as he went. Before he knew where he was, he found himself breaking through the mist behind a log cabin just off the main road through the town. He felt a little relieved to be nearer to civilization, hoping for a greater amount of safety from the bandits.

"Hogwash!" A gruff voice shattered the quiet air.

The voice came from just the other side of the cabin. Gus went quietly to investigate.

"No, it's not." Another voice argued.

"And I'm telling you it is!"

Gus peered around the corner of the building to see two rough looking fellows dressed in tatters and animal skins, armed much like the men who were chasing him. He decided to remain out of sight.

"That's the name of the town. Hogwash."

"That's a stupid name. Who in their right mind would ever name a town Hogwash?"

The one man shrugged. "Beat's me, but that's what it's called."

"First thing we're doing is renaming it. I'll talk to the boss about it."

They were moving further away, and against his better instincts, Gus decided to follow.

"The Horned One isn't going to rename this mud hole." The other one insisted. "He's got more important things to do. Besides which, we're not staying."

"We're not?" The first one asked.

"Yeah. Boss says once we're done here, we're gonna kill everyone and head south. Says there's goods ripe for the taking that way."

Gus went pale. *Kill everyone? And were they seriously calling their boss "The Horned One?"*

Whatever was going to happen to the town, he needed to know. He followed for several minutes, remaining just within earshot but out of sight, keeping behind the buildings and low to the ground. They went on and on about imaginary loot they were going to pillage and how they were going to have a great big feast someday soon. They were mentioning The Horned One in little bits and Gus quickly gathered that "boss" and The Horned One were one in the same, and that whoever the man was, he was ruthless and violent. The pair disappeared into the tavern and Gus sneaked around from the back to find a window he could peer in through. There was one just next to a wood pile and Gus stood on tiptoe to peek above the sill. What he saw inside gave him the chills.

Five of the townsfolk, including an old housewife, the owner of the tavern, one of the men from the day before and a young couple were huddled on the floor in the far corner. Towering over them was a large man dressed in deer skins, half his face obscured by a deer-skull mask complete with stag horns. He was heavily muscled and held a short spear with a wicked looking spearhead as he menaced his captives. The two men Gus had been following stood nearby, laughing and talking among themselves quietly. At first Gus feared for the lives of the captives but it didn't seem like they were in immediate danger. The man with the horned helmet seemed to want something from them. He would gesture with the spear and assume a more threatening posture and the women would shake their heads in response and the owner of the tavern would say something in reply. Gus couldn't read the man's lips but Gus could tell that he didn't have whatever it was the boss wanted.

Just then the five bandits that had chased Gus through the woods came in through the front door, one of them massaging his swollen face. Gus ducked as they entered to avoid being seen and waited a moment before risking another look through the window. The men addressed their leader, who turned to face them and Gus could only see an angry scowl beneath the deer mask.

He ducked down and pressed his ear to the wall to try to better hear the conversation.

"We couldn't find 'im, Horned One." One of them explained.

Wow, Gus thought, *they really do call him Horned One.*

"Well, we found a peasant," another one chimed in, "but he got away."

The first bandit turned and elbowed his companion in the gut. The Horned One remained still, awaiting an explanation.

"Right. Well, we found someone and he ran and Brian here let him get away."

"Hey! It wasn't my fault!" Brian objected.

"Well anyway, it was just one peasant. Hardly worth your time, Horned One. I know you told us to round up everyone but surely one tiny peasant won't make much difference. We have this town under our thumb." He explained. He was cut short as the tip of The Horned One's spear was suddenly at his throat. The Horned One said nothing.

The bandit gulped and held his hands up helplessly. "We're sorry! We're sorry! It won't happen again. We'll find him and round him up like the others. We swear!" The bandit pleaded. When The Horned One didn't let up, the bandit begged further. "We'll go right now. Right now. And we won't come back until we find him. Promise!" The Horned One paused before withdrawing the spear and nodding his consent. The five turned and flew from the room to search the woods and Gus ventured another glance in through the window.

With only two men and The Horned One in the main room, Gus sorely wished he could find his companion. Snowball would make short work of them, he was sure. Well, at least of the two. The Horned One had an aura of malice about him that was nearly palpable.

From the sound of things, there were probably more bandits skulking about. If the whole town was "under their thumb", did that mean they had everyone confined indoors? That would take a substantial force, Gus thought. And here he was, powerless. Well, perhaps not. Maybe Gus wasn't as strong as the Minotaur, but he was clever. It would be dangerous but perhaps he could find a way to free the captives without Snowball's help. All he needed was a sound plan... and to not be terrified out of his wits.

First things first, Gus needed to find out just how many townspeople were being held against their will. It was all well and good to try to rescue the five in the tavern but there were more out there and with a larger force of bandits it would be difficult for them to escape without being noticed. Next, he would have to create a distraction in order to draw The Horned One and his lackeys out of the town long enough to escort their captives to safety.

He left his position at the window and stole through the mist to investigate the other buildings.

Now, if this were a typical story, Gus would have undoubtedly sneaked through town, checking windows and doors, remaining out of sight all the while. Then his clever plan would have been formulated with the greatest of care, executed with a few hiccups along the way and at last brought to fruition in some sort of climactic display of cunning and guile.

However, Gus had an uncanny ability to defy proper tales of valor.

As he sneaked up to the nearest house, he checked the window to see if anyone was watching. Seeing no one, Gus approached quietly and used a small wood pile as a step so that he could reach the window. The side of the house was on a down-slope and so the house rose up a bit higher than usual. At the same moment that he popped his head up to see inside, a patchy-bearded bandit had gone to the window and was yawning and scratching at his armpit. For both Gus and the bandit, it took a moment to register that they were both staring at each other in the face. Surprised, Gus smiled sheepishly and waved. The bandit instinctively waved back, only to realize what he was doing and scowled instead.

Not waiting around to see what the bandit would do, Gus turned to run, forgetting that he was standing on a small pile of logs. The logs rolled from underneath him and he crashed to the ground before sliding down the slope. The logs continued rolling as Gus scrambled to get upright and they hit a wooden chuck beneath the wheel of a wagon of stones. The chuck dislodged and the wagon began lazily rolling down the slope, slowly picking up speed as it headed right for the tavern. Gus went pale and ran after the wagon to stop it hitting its target. By the time he could reach it, the wagon had already reached an unstoppable speed and Gus was carried along with it as it his feet dug into the mud. By then, the bandit had rushed to the door and was chasing behind, shouting at Gus. Gus paid him no mind and looked around for anything that might stop the wagon. He caught sight of a large branch in the road and decided instead to jam it into one of the wagon wheels. He rushed to pick it up and with a mighty thrust caught it in the wheel spokes. The wagon was far too heavy however and instead of stopping, merely changed direction and was now heading toward an open front door.

Even the bandit stopped to watch as the wagon went right in through the front door and crashed in a cacophony of splintered wood, pots, pans and all manner of implements and breakables.

Gus turned toward the bandit, who turned toward him. They looked at each other for a moment before the bandit remembered what he was doing and continued running toward Gus. The peasant turned to run but by that time the loud noise had alerted the whole town to his presence and there were already seven men barreling toward him. He was surrounded and desperately looked for a way out but all exits were blocked. They pounced and brought him to the ground in a dog-pile.

Gus didn't bother struggling as they brought him to his feet. It only took two of them to hold him by the arms and they were more than strong enough to restrain him. The others made way as the boss strode up to investigate the commotion.

The Horned One said not a word and seemed to radiate an almost overwhelming aura of dominance and malice as he approached. When he was just a few feet away from Gus he stopped and stood, bearing over the short peasant like a towering monolith. The men went quiet, watching and waiting to see what The Horned One would do. The town was completely silent.

The Horned One slowly lifted his spear, savoring the sensation of the deadly weapon moving through the air as he brought its point to rest gently against the soft spot underneath the peasant's jaw. The horns on his mask looked extremely sharp as Gus tried to look at them or the trees or anything other than the pale deer skull or the glowering eyes of the person concealed beneath.

Suddenly, The Horned One spoke and his voice seemed to shatter the air... And Gus's impression of the malevolent figure. "Well, well, well, if it isn't Gus the Fuss." He said with a certain air of satisfaction. The voice was all too familiar and it took only a split second for Gus to recognize The Horned One as his childhood tormentor and lifelong antagonist, Ian MacBrody.

The Horned One leaned in close, so that Gus could get a good look of what was visible of his face. "Look familiar, do I?" He hinted.

Gus said nothing. He was too terrified and at Ian's mercy.

"Perhaps I should jog your memory," He continued. "Not so tough without your minotaur friend, are you?" When Gus didn't respond, he rammed his fist into the peasant's gut, knocking the wind out of him. "Recognize me now?"

Gus coughed and wheezed, so desperate for breath he could do little more but make a 'one moment' gesture with his hand and lift his head to try to get some air.

"No?" Ian whispered. "Still don't recognize me?"

Of course, Gus knew exactly who he was but the dim-witted bandit thought himself all too mysterious and intimidating. So, he continued trying to lead the peasant along to realize who he was.

"Perhaps this might help." He reached toward Gus's neck and though he looked as if to choke him, he snatched the locket from beneath the peasant's collar instead. "I think this rightfully belongs to me." He dangled it from his fist for Gus to see. "Still no? Well, last time I took it you had that monster with you. Now you don't, do you?"

Gus mouthed something inaudible.

"What's that?" Ian asked, leaning in slightly.

Gus mouthed it again, only slightly louder.

Ian leaned in close, angling his ear to better hear him.

"I already know who you are, idiot." Gus wheezed.

Ian grew angry but didn't say anything lest his men should hear. Instead, he stepped back a pace and punched Gus right in the face.

The men immediately laughed with their beloved leader. He accepted their applause graciously and then rammed the butt of his spear into Gus's stomach, causing the peasant to double over. They applauded more and Ian held up his arms as if to say "You like that? You want to see more?" So, he brought his spear-butt up, whacking Gus's skull and knocking him unconscious.

Chapter XXI

The black world slowly blurred into a fuzzy swimming light as Gus came around. He wasn't sure how long it had been but the sun was still up. Light came in through a roughly window-shaped blur somewhere on a vaguely wall-shaped blur across the room from him. His head pounded painfully with every heartbeat. He needed to lie down somewhere for a while, so he tried to lean over to find the ground but discovered that his hands couldn't move from where they were. Confused, he looked over to his left and right and after a few moments, when he could actually distinguish shapes, he could see that he was bound by ropes to a wooden pole. He drooped his head in defeat and saw that his feet had been bound also. He was inside a small barn tied to one of the roof supports and though his vision was still adjusting, it was clear there wasn't anything nearby that could help him escape his bonds.

"Well, I'm definitely not going anywhere now." Gus grumbled.

It wasn't much longer before the door was flung open and two men entered, both dressed in similar bandit fashion and carrying clubs. One had a somewhat swollen face and he approached Gus with a snarl. "This is for my face!"

The bandit walloped him in the head with his fist and then wound up to deliver a blow to Gus's stomach. Gus was getting rather tired of the pain in his skull and the lack of air in his lungs, but unfortunately for him the ordeal was far from over. The two bandits gave him a sound pummeling and stopped when they were tired and satisfied with the job. Gus felt a bit like a lump of painful jelly but he could do nothing but hang there by his ropes while the bandits took a step back to admire their handiwork.

"You think he's had enough, eh?" The first bandit asked the swollen one.

"More than enough to make up for my face, I think." He replied, feeling smug.

"You want to have a sit down and then give it another go in a bit?"

The swollen one shrugged. "Nah. I've got it out of my system. Besides, The Horned One says he wants him alive so as not to spoil him too much, you know?"

"Ah. I hear that." The other nodded. "I remember this one time when I was beating the tar out of some bloke and I accidentally hit him too hard. We were supposed to hold him for ransom I think, and I splatted his brains all over."

"Oh, that's rough. Don't you hate that?"

"I sure do. I mean, sometimes you just get into it and you forget where your priorities lie, you know what I'm saying?"

"That I do, friend. That I do."

"I mean, I know we're supposed to be bandits and all, but it's not like we get the proper training for it."

"True, that is." The swollen one agreed. "Not even a proper orientation."

"I mean, maybe if we got a bit of practice in, or something. Then we might really go places, is all I'm saying."

The swollen one placed a comforting hand on his fellow bandit. "You have my sympathies, friend. I mean, there's not even a pension plan, is there? We don't get paid much and there's no retirement fund in place. Most of what we get goes to the rest of the gang or to the boss. And I'm not saying the boss doesn't deserve it. He definitely does, what with how well he's pulled us all together. But you've got a point. Maybe if we had a few practice sessions a week. Get in some mock robberies and proper pummeling lessons. And for the Gods' sake a step by step breakdown of the pillaging process would be nice."

"Oh, I know! When we pillage a town it's right chaos out there, it is. Absolutely no rhyme or reason to it at all. How does we know what houses have already been hit or what's good for stealing and what's good for leaving. It's a madhouse."

"Sure is. What a pity."

Gus shook his head as his abusers prattled on about the conditions in their bandit group. With a stroke of inspiration, he decided to work himself in on the conversation.

"Sounds like you could use a representative to address your needs, if you ask me." Gus said, a bit numbly through his swelling face.

"See!" The swollen one pointed a hand at Gus. "He gets it!"

"That's right he does."

"Perhaps," Gus continued, "What you really need is a proper resource for the human part of being a group of bandits. You know, dealing with conflict, scheduling training and setting expectations for the other bandits to meet."

The other bandit nodded in agreement. "You've got a good point. Remember Terry?"

"Oh, Gods. I remember Terry, all right." The swollen one shook his head with disappointment. "That man was a right lunatic. Didn't have a clue how to be a bandit!"

"Bloke should have been fired from the get-go. He actually tried to rob a carriage with a knotted rope. Can you believe it? A knotted rope!"

The swollen one shook his head. "The passengers was so surprised by it that they nearly laughed him off the road. Who frightens someone with a knotted rope? And then remember when we was all set up to ambush that wagon train? And he calls out and says to them 'aye, you best watch out! We're gonna ambush you, we are! We're the most fearsomest bandits ever!' What in blazes was he thinking?"

The other bandit sighed. "I don't think any amount of training would have set that guy straight."

"But everyone else could benefit, don't you think, from someone to represent your interests?" Gus said in an attempt to get the conversation back on track.

Both bandits nodded in agreement. "Oh sure," the one said, "we could use someone like that, sure as I'm standing here. But what would we call this human resource type person? They'd need a proper title for something like that, I think."

"Oh, aye." Said the swollen one. "A person like that would need a proper title. What do you think we could call 'em?" He asked Gus.

Gus thought on it for a moment as he stopped struggling to loosen the bonds holding his hands. "Well, I suppose that a human resource like that would do well if he were called... if he were... Well, I suppose a Human Resource Manager sounds pretty official, don't you agree?"

They nodded in hearty approval. This was sounding better and better the more they thought on it. "But that sure is a mouthful." The one pointed out. "Maybe we could shorten it."

"You mean, like when you shorten each word so that it's a smaller bit, maybe?"

"Yeah. Let's see. You take an H, for Human, and then an R and an M..."

Gus laughed to himself and shook his head with the utter ridiculousness of it all. "You want to call them a Herm?"

"Yeah. That's easy to say. But it sounds a bit off. Maybe add a bit at the end. Like... well... Hermit? We could call them a Hermit?"

"I think I've heard that word before, mate." Said the swollen one.

"No, no. You're thinking of something else. It's never been a word before, I'm sure of it."

"Well, that settles it then. If you're sure then I'm sure. We'll call this Human Resource Manager a hermit!"

"Great. You fellows are certainly smarter than you look." Gus flattered them.

"Aye! That we are!" The one agreed, feeling quite proud of himself.

"You should take it to your boss, get it approved. I'm sure he'd praise you for it. Taking care of all these men must be quite the burden. Take a bit off his shoulders, if you know what I mean." Gus suggested.

The two bandits looked at each other and considered it hard before nodding in agreement. "You've got a fair point. But who would we have do it? It's not something just anyone can do."

Gus shrugged. "Well, you need someone who is impartial, maybe someone from outside your organization."

"Uh huh. Yeah!" They agreed.

"Someone who's a bit smarter and maybe not as good at other bandit things, that way they can remain objective and handle things impartially." Gus continued.

"Right you are! Right you are!"

"Someone the men aren't afraid of, someone who doesn't pose much of a threat, you know."

The swollen one nudged his companion in the chest. "Look at this one. He's got the right idea."

"That he does."

Gus sighed. "Well, sounds like your best choice would probably be someone like me."

"That's a great idea!" The swollen one said. "You've got whole loads of those credentials."

Gus feigned disinterest and shook his head with a sigh before he paused and agreed. "It would be a heavy burden, but you've talked me into it." Gus said in a tone of defeat.

"Great! Don't you think that's great?" The swollen one asked.

"I do. I think the boss is gonna love it."

"Great. Well, I guess then if you think it'd be a good idea then there's nothing more to it. Just untie me and take me to the boss and we can pitch the idea together, what do you say?" Gus suggested.

The bandits nodded fervently and went to work to untie him but then the swollen one stopped. "Of course, The Horned One said not to let you go. Said we have to save you for something special later, he did. An execution or something."

"Eeep." Gus squeaked.

"Well... I guess we could wait until after and suggest it then."

"Yeah. I agree. That's probably for the best."

Gus sighed. He had been so close.

"You know, now that I think on it, boss was looking for a peasant, wasn't he?"

"Yeah," the swollen one agreed, raising a finger. "You're right. He was looking for someone like that. Said something about getting his revenge, he did."

"You think this is him?"

The swollen one shrugged. "If he is, it's a shame. Such a nice bloke. He could have been our hermit."

"Yeah. A right shame. But if he is then that means we get the lion's share of the looting this time 'round. Boss promised."

With an air of excitement, the swollen one nodded happily. "That's right. Wouldn't want to miss out on that. Let's go ask him if we can start the looting early, eh?" He turned to leave. "Well, it's been a nice chat, hasn't it?" The swollen one said in Gus's direction. "Take care and we'll see you later this evening."

They both waved a friendly goodbye as they left Gus all alone.

Many hours drifted by and Gus was left bruised and swollen in the barn. He had given up on escape by the time sunset rolled around. The ropes binding his hands and feet were firm and tight and there was nothing on his possession he could use to cut them. There was little in the barn other than some bits of straw. Certainly nothing he could use to escape.

As the light inside began to fade, the doors burst open and several men entered and removed Gus from the post, escorting him forcefully to the center of town. Bandits loitered about the muddy street as several hogs wallowed nearby. In the middle of it all stood Ian with his deer-skull helmet. He stood as still as he could to portray an intimidating presence, but Gus could see signs of giddiness as Ian bounced a curved sword slightly in one hand. Ian had been looking forward to this ever since Gus had bested him and his men back in Jagodwine. None of those men were present now and Gus was sure that they had abandoned their leader in favor of better fortune elsewhere, forcing Ian to recruit new members.

When they tossed Gus into the mud in front of his childhood tormentor, Ian smiled cruelly. "Well, then. Looks like you're just as pathetic as ever." Ian gloated. "But I can't forgive what you done to me. Nobody makes a fool out of..." He stopped himself before saying his real name loud enough for the other men to hear, "...The Horned One and gets away with it." He raised his sword high for all to see. The men cheered in anticipation. Ian prepared to strike just as Gus had managed to push himself to his hands and knees.

"Hey, boss. Does this mean he's the one you was looking for?" The swollen bandit interrupted.

Ian stopped mid-swing and looked dumbfounded at his cohort.

"Because I was just wondering. You know. You told us we could have whatever we could loot, isn't that right? And I was just thinking maybe while you're doing your decapitation here, we could have a go at the town. We've been awful patient, is all I'm saying."

"Yeah. I agree." Another man chimed in. "We done what you wanted. Wouldn't you rather savor your moment in peace while we busy ourselves with all the pesky looting and all?"

"Yeah!" said another.

"Oh, for the love of..." Ian muttered.

"Yeah, boss. Let us have a go at the town. You can do your executing on your own, I think. We've already seen plenty of people gettin' their 'ead chopped off. Maybe we could change it up a bit."

Ian growled. "Really? That's what you want? Fine. Go, do your looting. Just shut up and let me have this moment, won't you!"

The men cheered and scattered like the four winds to the houses and tavern and anywhere else valuable goods might be found, leaving Gus and Ian alone on the street.

Ian rubbed at his temples underneath his dear-skull mask. "Load of good-for-nothings. Can't even let a man do a proper execution..." He caught Gus trying to crawl away unnoticed. "And where do you think you're going?" He shouted. He delivered a vicious kick to the peasant's ribs.

Gus cried out, still trying to pull himself away to the side of the road.

"Go on then. Escape, you little coward!" Ian kicked him again.

Gus collapsed; the side of his face stuck in the mud. His body hurt all over from the bruises and swelling and the kicking only made it worse. He groaned in pain and looked up. Ahead of him two mud-covered hogs snorted and bullied one another. Something about it caught him off guard. Suddenly, the sight of it took Gus far away from that moment as though he was reliving another time altogether.

It was that same day with the overcast sky. Gus had been trying his best to watch over the pigs while his father was out gathering wood and his mother tended to the house. He'd tapped a stick absently on the fence while he stood there lost in imagination.

"Hey, Gus the Fuss!" A voice called out. It was one of the older boys in town. He was thin and wiry back then but he stood a head and a half taller than Gus. There weren't many kids in their quiet little hamlet but Ian was bigger than all of them. He came jogging up and stopped just in front of Gus. Ian shoved his shoulder. "What's the matter? Too weak to fight back? Huh?" Ian shoved him again, this time harder. "Go on, then. Fight back." He goaded.

Gus was too small, and when he tried to push Ian back, Ian grabbed him by the arms and threw him sideways into the mud. Gus fell down and started crying, Ian walked over to the gate and opened up the pig pen. The pigs scattered and ran through the town eager to find something to munch on.

Ian had been a terror back then. He caused trouble for no reason, fought anyone and everyone he could and pushed Gus down every chance he got.

"Go on. Beg for your life, coward." Ian's words brought Gus out of his memories.

Gus stared ahead at the pigs as they snorted and snuffled in the mud. He didn't seem to hear anything.

"Go on. Beg!" Ian kicked him again. "Weakling."

Gus slowly pushed himself to his knees and turned to face Ian. His eyes on the verge of angry tears. "No." He said defiantly.

Ian was taken aback.

"I am done being afraid! If you want to kill me, go on. Go ahead and kill me!" His voice grew in intensity as he spoke. "I am not your plaything anymore. You are a rotten human being and always have been. I would rather die than live another moment suffering your ridiculous savagery!" Gus was surprised at his own outburst, but he'd had enough. He meant every word of it. It was true that he was small and weak. It was true that he couldn't really fight back against someone like Ian, but if he was going to die at this monster's hands, he would do it on his own terms.

Ian grew angry and kicked his heal into Gus's chest, knocking him down. "You're pathetic, you know that? Just pathetic." He spat the words. "Not so tough without your minotaur friend, are you? Can't even fight your own fights. Relying on others to survive. You're like a parasite."

"You're the parasite, Ian. Preying on others..." Gus shot back, but Ian didn't let him continue.

"Shut it!" He stomped on Gus's stomach. "That's enough out of you."

Gus coughed and wheezed for a trace of breath.

Ian puffed out his chest. "You've always been the loser. Can't do anything yourself. Can't even make any proper friends. Look at me. I've got people begging to follow me around. And you... Nobody wants to be around a pathetic little whelp like you. Makes sense the only thing that will follow you around is that stupid monster."

Ian was right, Gus thought. He'd never made friends in the village. Everyone thought he was strange and wanted nothing to do with him. And he was right about Snowball too. Against all odds he'd befriended the inhuman creature. Perhaps Ian was right and something was wrong with him.

"Well then," Ian said, bringing the tip of his sword to just under Gus's chin, "Looks like this is the end for you." He brought his sword up high and struck without mercy.

His sword clashed against another.

"Guess again." Came an all too dramatic voice as Sir Ethan Wallard, Knight of the Silver Dragon, blocked Ian's attack. The blonde knight, dressed in his shining chain armor with breastplate and crest, kept his fearless gaze on Ian who was taken completely by surprise. The two paused, locking stares and sizing each other up.

"Who the bloody hell are you?" Ian snarled.

"I am Sir Ethan Wallard. Knight!" He announced with a flourish. "Of the Silver Dragon! And I will not let you harm my friend."

Ian gaped.

"Now stand down or I will cut you down, vile bandit!" Ethan challenged.

Gus took the opportunity to crawl a few feet away on his back to give them space and he was glad he did. Ian swung his sword but his blow was blocked by the impervious defense of the knight of the Silver Dragon. Ethan quickly returned the attack and delivered blow after powerful blow and it was almost too much for Ian. The bandit leader fell back a step before renewing his assault with savage overhead strikes. However, Sir Ethan was more than a match and deflected each attack with precision and skill. With a quick parry, the knight stepped in and delivered a sword butt into Ian's face, cracking the deer-skull helmet and revealing a part of Ian's face. The Horned One's facade partially broken, Ian retreated and shouted for his men as he headed for the tavern to regroup.

Rather than pursue, the knight turned his attention on Gus. "Come on, let's get you up and get out of here." Sir Ethan took Gus by the hand and pulled him off the ground.

The peasant didn't object and soon the pair were through town and out in the countryside where a campsite and Sir Ethan's horse waited. He helped Gus to a seat on a stone and gave him a moment to collect himself.

"Are you well, sir?" Ethan asked, studying the injuries Gus had sustained from his beatings.

Gus shook his head, a tear in the corner of his eye. "Sir Ethan!" He cried. "Thank you! Thank you from the bottom of my heart!" He tried to get up to thank the stolid night in gratitude but Sir Ethan held out a hand to stop and steady him. "I'm sorry, I'm sorry." Gus apologized. "I nearly died back there. I don't... I..." Gus was so worked up he could hardly speak. Sir Ethan waited for him to calm down some before he continued. "You are truly a knight, sir. Truly a knight. How can I ever repay you?"

Sir Ethan held up a hand in protest and averted his gaze, staring dramatically into the distance. "Please. You needn't thank me. It is the duty of a knight to offer aid wherever he is needed."

"Oh, shut up." Gus shook his head. "You're a good man and I owe you my life. That's all there is to it." He let out a small laugh and that brought a smile to Sir Ethan's face. After a deep breath, Gus asked, "What on earth are you doing here? I can hardly believe it's you."

Sir Ethan struck a noble pose and explained. "I have been wandering the countryside in pursuit of a most villainous group of bandits. After our separation with the mercenaries, my men and I swore to seek out and destroy all evil within the kingdom and beyond. This led to an epic journey in the name of... Justice!" He said with added emphasis on his favorite word.

Sir Ethan continued at length in a story of (perhaps somewhat exaggerated) heroism and daring as he and his men had traveled from town to town to seek out trouble. He explained how they had caught wind of bandits in the area and had agreed to split up in order to catch their trail and how Sir Ethan hadn't had the opportunity to send word to his men, due in part to the isolated region not affording a messenger service of any kind, but also due to the fact that Sir Ethan had only just caught up with the bandits when he had seen them chasing Gus through the forest.

"But we tarry too long here." Sir Ethan concluded his story. "Are you well enough to move? We have great need to find your monstrous companion. There's still a town in peril that needs saving."

"Yes. Yes, I think I'm well enough to move. Everything still hurts but I think I'll be alright. Wait. The town?" Gus asked. "You mean you want to save it from all those bandits?"

"That's exactly what I mean to say. But we are severely outnumbered. We'll need the strength of your friend and a cunning plan if we are to take her back and save her people."

Gus nodded and stood. "Alright. I'm with you. Normally, I think I might be glad just to be alive, but this time it's personal. Trouble is I have no idea where Snowball is. He's been missing all day and I haven't any clue where he's gone to. He's always been fairly easy to spot. I mean, how can you miss him? He's the size of a house."

"Well, let's start from his last known location. If we can follow his tracks, we may be able to find him before the bandits find us."

"Agreed."

Sir Ethan and Gus set off into the woods and kept a weathered eye for any trace of Snowball. After an hour of searching, Gus couldn't help but express his gratitude to the knight. "Sir Ethan, your fighting skills are incredible," he said. "The way you handled Ian, that bandit you saved me from, was amazing."

The knight waved him off. "That was nothing. My skills are keen, surely, but no more than any knight of this realm. Your assailant was a bandit. Men like him are only dangerous because of their strength and aggression. When it comes to honed skill, they have very little. What he has in aggression and strength he lacks in technique. It's no wonder I was able to fend him off."

"But why didn't you chase after him? You had him at a disadvantage."

Sir Ethan shrugged. "Now, why would I chase after a cretin like him only to leave you to the others? I fight not to destroy evil, but to protect what is good. Men like him are as common as grass, but people like you... well. I couldn't allow such a tragedy to befall such a noble man, now, could I? Besides," he added, "I've a feeling our paths will cross again, and the next time I'll have my chance to put him down."

Gus swallowed the gravity of Sir Ethan's statement. "Do you mean to kill him?" He asked.

Sir Ethan's expression grew grave. "There is little else to do, I'm afraid. Men like him do not change. If he is allowed to live, then he is allowed to cause more trouble. There is no sense sparing men like that. He has a complete disdain for the laws of men, so there is no point to a trial. And if we were to lock him up in the lowest dungeon, we would only waste food and resources keeping watch of him. There is indeed no sense in it at all. You see, dear Gus, there is a reason bandits are hanged promptly in this kingdom."

"Well spoken." Gus agreed. He had never really had much dealing with the law, but he couldn't argue with Sir Ethan's logic. It would be best if someone put a stop to Ian MacBrody once and for all.

"Shhhh." Sir Ethan warned suddenly.

Gus stopped in his tracks and listened. He heard rustling in the bushes. Hope flooded through him as he thought for a moment that it might be Snowball. He rushed ahead toward the source of the noise and Sir Ethan hissed after him "Gus, no!" But it was too late. He burst through the bushes to find himself confronted with two bandits.

Gus smiled his usual sheepish "whoops" smile but before anything else could happen, Sir Ethan crashed through the brush, brandished his sword and pointed it as he challenged them to combat. "Ye shall see justice, vile bandits!" He pronounced.

The bandits, not terribly keen to fight the knight after witnessing his bout with Ian, decided that turning and running was in their best interest. They fled to warn the others, shouting loudly through the woods to alert their comrades.

"Oh, great." Gus frowned.

"Well, we won't stand much of a chance fighting all of them at once, will we?" Sir Ethan pointed out. "We haven't much time before they return. We must hurry to locate your friend."

Gus agreed and the two pressed hard through the woods in the opposite direction, away from the town. It was difficult to spot anything moving at such a pace but they needed to put some distance between themselves and Ian's men.

After a good bit of running, Gus and Sir Ethan stopped to catch their breath in a grove of trees.

"If it wasn't for this infernal mist," Sir Ethan said between breaths, "this would be much simpler."

Gus held up a hand and nodded but said nothing in favor of breathing as he put his other hand on his knee to steady himself.

"Right. Good idea. We'll catch a breather and then strategize a search plan." Ethan agreed.

Not a minute later, both of them hushed and listened as they heard something nearby through the mist. It took a moment to register the noise but soon they could hear the grumbling of someone roaming about. Amid the grumbling, they heard wet sounds of something being slapped on the trees.

"... Stupid... just here for... waste of time..." The voice complained. It was one of Ian's men carrying a bucket. "Just who do they think I am? Eh? 'here, take this'" he said mocking someone else's voice, "'and go about wasting your time', filthy blighters. Like my talents are well spent out here doing this nonsense. I've robbed fifteen wagons for the Gods' sake. I'm wasted out here. But do they see that? No. Of course not. 'You're new, so you need to do the stupid jobs'..." He continued griping. He walked on for some time before he stopped and reached a hand into the bucket to smear some of its contents on another tree. "Under-utilized!" He announced to all who could hear. "I'm under-utilized. That's the word. I've got gobs of talent. More than everyone else, anyway. As if The Horned One," he voiced the title with disdain, "could ever understand my talents. I give him my best and he has me doing this!" He flicked his hand, spattering the ground. "And now my hands are all sticky. What kind of gobbledygook is this? 'Go paint the trees with this. It's very important. Just wander around and put this gunk on the trees as you go.' I mean, come on! It's strawberry jam. Who the hell puts strawberry jam on trees? Waste of time, if you ask me. Who bloody cares!"

Gus and Sir Ethan who had followed the lone bandit along as he whined and complained looked at one another. They nodded in agreement and rushed him, knocking him to the ground. The bandit never stood a chance and with a fierce blow with the pommel of his sword, Sir Ethan knocked him unconscious. As he fell the bucket turned over, spilling its contents on the ground. Gus took a finger to taste a sample.

"He was right. Strawberry."

"Strange," Sir Ethan remarked. "What would a bandit be doing with a bucket of strawberry jam?"

"Luring away a strawberry obsessed minotaur," Gus explained. "Snowball is in love with the stuff. Now it all makes sense! No wonder we can't find him."

"I'm afraid I don't understand." Sir Ethan said.

"That man with the horned mask, Ian. He's the leader of these men. I ran across him a while back and in a bizarre..." Gus rolled his eyes as he remembered the whole ordeal, "idiotic turn of events, Snowball helped me defeat him. I thought that was the last I'd seen of him but now he's back and it seems like he's out for revenge. He must have been luring Snowball on a trail through the woods to get him away from me. That's why the strawberry jam. It's not like they have a cage that could hold Snowball, after all."

"Well, that certainly explains the jam, but I still don't quite understand fully. You say that the two of you defeated him before. Not to put your morals in question, but you don't seem the type to fight off a group of bandits, Gus."

Sir Ethan was right. Gus wasn't one to seek out trouble like that. He nodded. "No. The truth is, that was how Snowball and I became friends. Ian stole something very valuable to me. I'm too weak to fight someone like him by myself, not to mention all his men. If it weren't for Snowball, I never would have gotten it back."

Sir Ethan put a comforting hand on Gus's shoulder. "You sir, are certainly a mystery. I cannot imagine how you managed to befriend such a beast. Tell me," he added, "what was it he took from you? I don't imagine a man of your status to be in possession of anything of value."

Gus paused before he decided to confide in the knight. "He took a locket. One given to me by a girl I cared for deeply when we were children. I know it sounds silly, but it's true."

Sir Ethan stuck another stoic pose. "It's not silly in the slightest. The memory of a childhood love should be held dear with all the strength of one's soul."

"Well, that sounds a little over the top..." Gus said, though Sir Ethan did not hear.

"It touches my very heart, noble Gus. Surely, you were not in error."

"And now he has it again," Gus groaned as he buried his face is his hands.

"What! That vile fiend!"

"It's just a locket..." Gus insisted, though in his heart he knew it meant more to him than that.

"How dare he trifle with the purest of love."

"I never said we were in love..."

"I dare say, he should be struck down this very instant!" Sir Ethan was in a passion and shouted forcefully into the woods. "You hear me, cretin! I will not stand for this injustice!"

"Calm down." Gus hushed his friend. "Calm down. It's just a locket."

"Nay, Gus! It is the principle of the thing. This man has violated the very soul of the human heart, terrorized the countryside and now has laid claim to the lives of these poor townsfolk."

"But what can we do?" Gus asked. "We still haven't found Snowball and they outnumber us at least ten to one!"

Sir Ethan leaned over with his hands-on Gus's shoulders and looked him straight in the eye. "We must do what is right. I mean to take back this town and liberate its people, bring this monster to justice and retrieve your locket. But I need your help. Will you lend me your aid?"

"I... well... when you put it that way..."

"Hah! I knew I could count on you, sir. We'll win the day yet!"

Gus sighed and gave in to Sir Ethan's indomitable spirit. "Alright," he agreed, "I'll help you. But if we're going to do justice for these people, we'll have to be subtle..."

"Did you say Justice!" Ethan exclaimed a little too loudly.

"... Which is something you lack, Sir Ethan."

"Knight of the Silver Dragon!" Sir Ethan added.

"Right." Gus rubbed the bridge of his nose. "Sir Ethan, Knight of the Silver Dragon. If we're going to do this, we need to keep quiet and figure out a plan. Ian and his men are out looking for us as we speak. If they find us, they'll overwhelm us. Meanwhile, the people are being held hostage in town and if we act too rashly, we'll get them all killed."

"What are you proposing?" Sir Ethan asked a little more quietly in his best attempt at subtlety.

"Well..." Gus thought aloud, "the first step is... hmmmm..."

Sir Ethan waited patiently for Gus to formulate a plan.

"Snowball is more than a match for the bandits, but the two of us would have a hard time defeating them all without him. Ian and his men are searching for us and will try to kill us if they find us. But that puts the majority of them away from town while they do. If we can be quiet about it, we might be able to double back to town and free some of the townsfolk ourselves while they are away. That would allow us to focus on Ian and the rest of his men. Which leaves us to the problem of finding Snowball." Gus looked down at the spilled bucket of jam. "Then there's the question of how best to strike Ian and his men. You said they've been traveling the countryside. Do you know any more than that?"

"They've been traveling on horseback for the most part." Sir Ethan remarked. "And likely they made camp outside of town before they captured it."

"Which means they have supplies and horses. Good. That could work in our favor. Here, help me scoop this back into the bucket." Gus said, using a hand to scrape the ground of the filthy strawberry jam.

Sir Ethan lent a hand. "Do I take this to mean you've come up with a plan, sir?"

Gus nodded. "Most of one. But we're going to need as much of this as possible."

Chapter XXII

The succulent smear of strawberry jam made a colorful addition to the backside of the tavern, Gus thought as he wiped the sticky remnants on his fingers on the hem of his shirt. He still had a good few scoops of jam left in the bucket, which he intended to save. Satisfied with his handiwork and with Sir Ethan close behind he made his way through town, keeping behind the buildings and sticking to the side paths to avoid detection. Not that there was much need. The majority of Ian's men had looted their fill, leaving most of the town a mess, only to have The Horned One order them to hunt down his lost quarry. As such, those few who remained were feasting on whatever food they had scavenged from the houses and were sitting fat and happy, glad to be left behind while the others did the hard work.

One such man, known as Barry "the Butcher" (at least that's what he imagined they called him), was thoroughly enjoying a piece of roasted chicken, holding his crude sword in his hand carelessly as he kept watch of the town baker and his family. The lowly baker and his homely wife sat huddled in the corner shielding their only child, quietly awaiting their fate as the bandit leaned on the dining table. He thought the meat a little flavorless but he was happy to have it. It had been a while since he'd had a decent meal. Barry happened to take notice as his quiet captives looked over at something by the door behind him. When he turned to look, however, he caught just a glimpse of a figure disappearing around the door frame. Thinking that maybe it was one of his gang he went to investigate. As he peered around the door, he was surprised to find the short little peasant standing there as plain as day, smiling. His expression, one of both disgust and surprise, didn't last terribly long, as a swift blow to the back of his skull turned his vision black and sent him to the ground.

"You see," Gus beamed, "I told you it would work. They're not the brightest bunch of people."

Sir Ethan frowned. "I don't like all of this sneaking around. It seems dishonorable. A man should fight his opponent face to face, not with his enemy's back to him."

"Ugh. Listen," Gus told him, "there is a time for honor and chivalry and all the rest but not when other people's lives are at stake. Now help me find something to tie him up."

They bound and gagged Barry "the Butcher", leaving him in the small storeroom at the back of the house. The baker and his family were grateful and left quickly by the road out of town at Sir Ethan's suggestion.

"Do you suppose they have their own knight out here to protect them?" Gus wondered to Sir Ethan.

The knight shook his head. "No. Most likely just a lord. This is such a quaint town with little in the way of resources, no military advantages and likely secluded up here to avoid the abuse of nobility altogether. If they did have a protector knight, he would have been the first to investigate and that villainous cur you call Ian would have gone after him first. No, with the lack of wealth here, there's likely a lord and if he hasn't been slain already then he has either secured himself in his manor for safety or is being held prisoner. Either way, our objective remains the same. We need to save and secure every man, woman and child."

"Let's get moving then, with less talking," Gus cut him off. "There's still plenty of men out there and people needing saving, as you pointed out."

The pair set about it, with Gus drawing out Ian's men and Sir Ethan utilizing his muscle in a "dishonorable" yet highly efficient fashion. It made short work of a half dozen men and Gus was beyond thrilled at the success of their endeavor. However, when they made their way back to the tavern, Gus's heart sank.

The tavern was filled with peasants and Gus thought he could even see the aforementioned lord through the window. Keeping a watch over all of them were ten men, armed with swords, clubs, and distasteful countenance. The furniture had all been pushed to one side to make room for everyone and the townsfolk were all crammed into the opposite corner where it would be easy to keep watch of them.

Gus ducked down and put his back against the tavern wall. "That's a lot of men."

Sir Ethan knelt down beside him and asked "How many?"

Gus turned to him with a bleak expression. "Ten. Versus our two."

"That's not what I meant." Sir Ethan corrected. "I meant how many people are in there?"

Gus scratched at his head. "I didn't count the others. There's probably three people for every one bandit."

"By the Gods! How did they cram all those people into such a small space?" The perplexed knight wondered aloud.

"The pushed all of the furniture to one side but it is still quite crowded in there."

"That certainly complicates things."

They sat pondering the situation for a moment before Gus spoke up. "Uh... well... I've got an idea. I don't like it but I've got one."

"Are you certain it won't put anyone in danger?" Sir Ethan asked gravely.

The hapless peasant sighed. "No... in fact I'm certain it will..."

From inside the tavern, while The Horned One's men ridiculed and terrified their prisoners, came a rapping at the window. Everyone looked to the source of the sound to find a head peering in and a hand waving 'hello.' Ian's men immediately recognized the bruised peasant that had gotten away. Gus ducked down from the window and ran. The majority of Ian's men made chase, scrambling to get out the door and be the first to nab the escaped prisoner. Only three stayed inside the tavern to guard the captives.

Before long, a swift blow to the back of the skull sent one of the guards to the ground as Sir Ethan made his move. The sound of the body crumpling to the floor alerted the other two who were completely unprepared for such an assault. The first was foolish enough to back too close to the crowd of people who immediately took advantage of the moment and seized him, giving him a sound drubbing until he was a curled-up whimpering mess on the floor. Before the other bandit had a chance to prepare himself, Sir Ethan flourished his blade and brought its tip to touch the soft spot beneath the bandit's jaw, forcing him to stand on tiptoe lest Sir Ethan run him through. The bandit's sword clattered to the floor and he held up his hands in surrender.

"Don't you dare make me do anything dishonorable, rogue!" Sir Ethan snarled. "I've had enough of that today already."

As for Gus, he was enjoying a lovely romp through town. Or at least, something like that...

"Ahhhhhh!" He cried as seven bandits chased after him with their weapons raised high.

He turned between buildings, skirted around trees, ducked under branches, his lungs on fire. "I'm... not... made..." he huffed between breaths "For long... distances..." But it made no matter, for the bandits were clumsy and unable to keep up with the fearful peasant's maneuvers.

Gus would have given anything to have his minotaur companion at his side. Without him, the hapless peasant felt powerless. All he could do was run in fear for his life. Being the bruised, purpled, huffing mess of panic simply did not suit him. He needed his friend. Fortunately for him, Ian's men were competing with one another as they chased him. This made their pursuit all the slower and gave Gus just enough room in his exhausted state to escape them. After several minutes of dogged running, Gus had lost track of where he was and ended up running right back into the middle of town.

He prayed that Sir Ethan had taken care of his half of the plan. When he saw what awaited him, Gus's heart leaped for joy.

The bandits chasing Gus came to a screeching halt as they came face to face with the town mob. The villagers had armed themselves with pitchforks, clubs, axes and hatchets. The butcher even had his cleaver and carving knife. At the front of the mob stood Sir Ethan in noble defense and in short order Gus. While the stoic knight readied himself to draw his sword, Gus did his best to look ready for a fight, while inside he was quivering right down to his boots.

Severely outnumbered and unwilling to slug it out with an angry mob of people, the bandits turned and fled into the woods.

After they were long gone, Gus gave up his strong demeanor and collapsed, laying right down on the very ground, his energy nearly depleted. He was tired beyond measure and hurt all over. His spirits were nearly at their limit and after the last few days he'd had, he could lay there forever for all he cared. He stared up at the lazily drifting clouds and breathed a sigh of relief.

Sir Ethan advised the townsfolk to make their way along the main road to get as far away as they could from Ian and his men. It would be safer if they stuck together. Trying to barricade themselves in their homes would ultimately prove futile if the bandits tried to take the town once more. They were glad to follow his suggestion after their ordeal and Sir Ethan promised them all that he would not rest until their land was safe from Ian's clutches. It didn't take long for them to gather what was necessary and head out of town.

As they were leaving by the main road, Sir Ethan returned to Gus who lay resting on that very same spot.

"Are you aware, sir," the knight began, "that you are laying in the mud?"

Gus frowned slightly. "Oh." He said, rather simply. Giving it some thought, rather than move he said, "You know, I don't think I care at this point."

"I see. Well, sir," Ethan said, "what's next?"

Gus sighed. "Well, step one is complete. The townspeople are saved and should be a bit safer now. Next is step two."

"Step two?"

"Yes. Step two is we have to get Snowball back."

"Yes... Your furry companion. He would certainly come in handy at a time like this, though he's a dangerous friend to have, to be sure."

"Well, if we're going to defeat Ian and all of his men, we're going to need some muscle. The townsfolk would be a huge help but we can't ask them to risk their lives after everything they've been through. After all, Ian is after me, not them."

"Yes, well it wouldn't be honorable, to say the least. Just how many steps are there to this plan of yours?" Sir Ethan asked.

"Three." Gus told him. "Step one, save the townsfolk. Step two, find Snowball. Step three, drive the bandits out and get my locket back."

"Your locket?"

Gus blushed. He was about to open his mouth to explain when Sir Ethan interrupted him.

"No doubt such a trinket was given you by a wealthy maiden?"

Gus was surprised. "How did you know?"

Sir Ethan chuckled and shook his head. "There aren't many men in this world with such trinkets and those who have them are wed and have started families of their own. Not to mention such an item is quite valuable. No offense intended, sir, but you strike me as rather poor. It makes sense that it was a gift from someone with wealth."

"Ah," was all Gus could think to say.

"So, step two. How do you plan on finding your monstrous friend?"

Gus finally decided to sit up. Mud stuck to his back as he did but he didn't seem to mind. "It's already in motion, but we can speed things up a bit. Can you gather some firewood and set up a cook-fire? I'll see if I can locate a proper pot."

Sir Ethan did as he was instructed and, after he had a good fire going, watched with fascination as Gus approached with a large soup pot and a bucket. Gus placed the pot on the fire, leaving the bucket behind and then returned once more with his water-skin. He poured its contents into the pot and began scooping the bucket clean, dropping large dollops of beautiful red jam into the pot. As the contents began to simmer the smell of strawberry hung on the steam issuing from the pot and filled the air.

"Aha! Quite clever!" Sir Ethan remarked. "You mean to draw the creature here by smell! Brilliant idea. And quite a strong smell it is!"

Gus plopped down on the ground, his energy failing him. He was still exhausted. His body desperately needed to heal and it felt like he'd been going nonstop all day.

"Are you all right?" Sir Ethan asked with concern.

"To be honest," Gus told him, "my body feels more like that strawberry jam than anything else. I feel like I could lie down for a week and still not feel quite right. I mean, look at these bruises!" Gus lifted up his shirt to show the knight the purple splotch the size of a melon on his ribs and abdomen.

Sir Ethan's expression became grave with sympathy. "You never deserved that rough treatment." The knight said. "The Horned One... er.... Ian, I think you called him... he's a despicable man. The lowest sort. I'll have you know that I won't hesitate to kill him if the opportunity presents itself."

Gus nodded quietly. Truth be told, he hated the idea of killing on principle, but even more so now he found himself confronted with violence on all sides since he'd encountered the Minotaur. "I just hope the smell reaches him before Ian and his men come back. I'm afraid I'm no good for a fight.

Without him, I'm practically powerless and I'll never get that locket back."

Sir Ethan suddenly grew quite angry. "That's enough of that!" He said quite forcefully. "You get that chin up and toss that despair to the wayside. We haven't lost yet. Cheer up, good sir! There will be cause for celebration soon. Mark my words."

Gus decided to change the subject. Sir Ethan's heart was in the right place, but his determined spirit was uncomfortably overwhelming. "What ever should we do with all of these bandits anyway? Are we just going to leave them tied up?"

"I've secured them in the barn for the time being. When my men arrive, I'll have them moved to the city to await further judgment."

"Ah. You mean execution."

"Nay!" Sir Ethan cried. "I mean Justice!"

"Oooooh!" Came a deep and excited voice from down the road. "Snowball loves just ice!"

"Snowball!" Gus exclaimed, overjoyed at the return of his monstrous friend.

"Very chilly but very good on a hot day." Snowball explained as he walked up excitedly. Gus stood, ready to embrace his good friend, but the Minotaur went right on past him and took the pot from the fire before reaching a hand in to scoop out the delicious contents. The watered-down jam was, however, still quite hot and Snowball shook his hand, blowing on it which sent spatters of hot jam everywhere. Rather than wait for the contents to cool, however, Snowball continued this exercise and endured the pain of bubbling jam to consume it in a rather savage manner.

Gus, a little put off by his companion's reception, instead just shook his head and sighed. "Why do I even bother..." He wondered, wiping a gob of hot jam from his forehead.

The jam devoured, Snowball sat lazily on the ground and properly greeted his friend. "Oh, Mister Gus Man! Snowball has had such a good day. There are trees through the forest that make strawberry sap!"

Sir Ethan, in earnest sympathy for Gus, slapped his own forehead for the hapless peasant. "By the Gods..." He muttered.

"Snowball, I cannot tell you how happy I am that you are here. Listen, we haven't much time. Do you remember Ian? The man who took my locket?" Gus asked.

Snowball pondered for a moment, before he said, "Eeyan BackBrokey?"

"Er... Yes. Ian MacBrody."

Snowball nodded emphatically.

"Well, he's back. He's taken my locket and is threatening the village."

"Oh!" Snowball exclaimed at mention of the locket. "Not the shiny strawberry."

"...The shiny...?" That was a new one by Gus. "Yes, the shiny strawberry. We need your help."

"Shiny what?" Sir Ethan was at a loss.

"Please," Gus pleaded, "I know I don't have much to offer but I'm begging you."

Snowball held up a four fingered hand to quiet his friend. "No. Snowball will do it no problem. Free of char."

"Uh... char?" Said Gus.

"I think he means 'charge'," Sir Ethan said under his breath.

"But..." Gus was perplexed. Snowball was a fickle creature. It had taken incentives to secure his aid when first they'd met. Even when they'd signed up with the mercenary band, there had been something in it for the creature. Yet here he was offering his aid freely.

"Snowball's friend is in need and Snowball wants to help. Mister Gus Man is like Snowball's brother."

"Even through you're half-bull?" Sir Ethan marveled at the creature's apparent kinship with the small peasant.

"Oh!" Said Snowball with enthusiasm. "Snowball is full of bull!"

"Sometimes..." Gus shook his head.

"Okay. Snowball is half-brother of Mister Gus Man. But shiny strawberry is important to Mister Gus Man, so Snowball will get it back."

"Wow. Thank you!" Gus could almost have given the beast a hug right then.

"Besides, Snowball get to re-smash up Eeyan BackBrokey and all of the bandit hoomans."

Gus got a feeling that was Snowball's real motivation, but he didn't question it. He smiled inwardly to himself. Snowball really was a good friend, in spite of it all.

"Right, well. Touching as this all is, we haven't a moment to lose. The longer we wait, the more time we give Ian and his men to regroup. I suggest we strike while the strawberry jam is hot." Sir Ethan said with robust encouragement.

"He's right, Snowball," Gus agreed. "We need to get moving. I'll try to come up with a plan of some sort and with any luck we can catch them with their pants down."

The Minotaur giggled.

"Not literally." Gus corrected. "Let me get my horse and then we're off. Sir Ethan," he addressed the knight.

"Yes, good sir?"

"Well... you see, I'm not terribly useful in a fight, and I doubt I'd be of much use..." Gus said, feeling a bit sheepish.

"Fear not, young lad! For we have Justice on our side. Just stay on your horse and let us handle the rest. At the first sign of trouble, get to safety. You've done your fair share already. It's time to let us have a turn. What say you, Minotaur?" Sir Ethan asked.

Snowball raised his hammer high and let out a mighty roar.

"Whoo. Alright then, that settles that." Gus marveled at Snowball's enthusiasm. After a quick search through town he managed to find his horse tied up near the barn. He saddled up and followed Sir Ethan and Snowball as they made their way from town, following the careless tracks left by the bandits.

As they were moving along, Gus wondered. "Say, Snowball. What about her?" He indicated his horse. "Do you think she'll be alright with all this fighting?"

Snowball nodded. "Do not worry, Mister Gus Man. She is not afraid of tiny hoomans fighting."

"Does she think we'll be okay?" Gus couldn't help vent his fears. He was feeling afraid and tired and desperate to see his locket returned to him once more.

"She isn't worried but she does think you're ugly and stoopid." Snowball told him.

Gus was a little taken aback. Could the Minotaur really tell what his horse was thinking? He looked down just as his horse turned to glance at him. "That's not true. Right? You don't think that, do you?"

The horse snorted and turned its attention back to the road ahead.

"That's not true, right Sir Ethan?"

The knight shook his head. "You worry far too much, lad. Stay sharp. We have one hell of a battle ahead of us."

And so, they did. As they saw smoke rising through the trees, they knew that they were close. They slowed to a halt as they caught sight of the encampment through the trees.

"Remember, our objective is Ian, the one with the horned mask." Gus reminded everyone. "He's the one with my locket. If we can take him down, the rest will most likely scatter."

"It'll be best if you hang back." Sir Ethan instructed quietly. "I'll make a racket and try to drive some of them your way, Snowball. You circle round and see to it they can't get to their horses. Alright?"

Snowball nodded in agreement.

"If things start to go south, I'll shout and try to make my way to you. We may be outnumbered but they'll lose their fighting spirit if they have to deal with the both of us at once."

The Minotaur and the knight shared a moment of silent understanding as they steeled themselves for the coming fight. In truth, Gus was somewhat envious of their courage but counted himself lucky to have such companions by his side.

Sir Ethan quietly made his way toward the center of camp and Snowball seemed to vanish into the woods, leaving Gus alone on his horse.

The bandits were ill at ease, bickering among one another after they'd heard Snowball's frightening roar through the trees. Some were saying they should stay put and defend the camp. Others were too scared to stay and desperately wanted to leave, not wanting to tangle with that monstrous beast. Either way, spirits were shaken and the camp was generally in disarray.

One particular bandit, known as Skull-Smasher (or at least that's what he wished people would call him) was fidgeting with his crudely crafted club (which he liked to also call Smasher) as he paced back and forth by the fire. Skull-Smasher was on the fence, as the expression goes. On the one hand, he was keen to take back the village and show those peasants what was what. On the other hand, he'd heard stories about the creature. He couldn't help but ramble on with the nearest of his allies to alleviate his nerves. His audience was massaging his swollen face and poking at the fire with a stick. He was hungry and scared and had lost all appetite for aggression after his last encounter with the people of Hogwash when they'd run him and the others out of town. He only half listened as he thought about some of his more questionable life choices.

"I've heard stories," Skull-Smasher confessed. "They say it's over ten feet tall!" He paced back and forth as he recounted all of the tales he'd heard. "They say the creature is so big he can squash a man's head with one hand!"

"Yeah..." The swollen-faced one nodded, not really aware of what Skull-Smasher had said.

"What are we gonna do?" Skull-Smasher paced a little faster. "The boss said he had a plan to deal with it, but you heard it. We all did. It's out there somewhere in the woods, ready to eat us."

"You think it eats people?" The swollen-faced one wondered. "I heard it's half-man and half-bull. Don't cows eat grass?"

"What if the half-man part is a cannibal?" Skull-Smasher worried. "It'll eat us all for sure."

"Wouldn't that mean it eats other minotaurs?"

But Skull-Smasher didn't hear as he continued his panicked pacing. "They say the creature crawled out of the gates of Hell. That it isn't half-bull at all. That its horns are those of a demon, come from the fiery underworld to butcher and slaughter humans and steal their souls!"

"I don't think that's true. I mean, how can a cow steal a soul anyway? Besides, the boss dealt with him before and survived. Here we outnumber that beast by the dozens. I'm sure The Horned One will know what to do."

"Doesn't matter. I also heard a story about how it's so strong it can tear full grown trees right out of the ground." Skull-Smasher had himself all worked up. He had taken to wringing his hands around his club nervously.

"Well, look on the bright side," the swollen-faced one said with a touch of optimism. "At least, if the creature that made that roar is as big as you say, we'll be able to see it coming before it can get us."

Skull-Smasher sighed a bit of relief. "You're right. That's a good point. There's no way a beast that big could sneak up on the likes of us."

Just as he had finished those words, Skull-Smasher turned his back to the fire and his compatriot to gaze out into the dark of the wood. He became confused by the strange looking trunk of a rather thick tree, that he hadn't remembered being there before, standing right in front of him. It had... shaggy, fur-like bark... and as he looked up, he saw the wicked grin of the Minotaur who stood before him. He had time to gulp before the creature rapped his noggin with its hammer and Skull-Smasher crumpled to the ground silently.

"That's more like it. Don't you worry. The Horned One will look out for us." The swollen-faced one said to his companion as he poked at the fire. When he didn't hear a response, he looked over his shoulder and saw no one. His companion had disappeared. "Oy!" He called out. "Bill! Where'd you go?"

At that same moment, across the camp, Sir Ethan swallowed his chivalrous ego and crept as quietly as he could toward a group of men anxiously chatting and arguing among one another. To his advantage, their bickering masked his footsteps which weren't as quiet as he had perhaps thought. Then again, sneaking around had never struck him as an honorable way to conduct one's self.

It was evident by their conversation that the men were shaken by the furious roar heard echoing through the forest. Some of the men were even commenting on their leader's odd behavior and questioning their loyalties openly.

Sir Ethan didn't waste his opportunity. With dramatic flair he burst into the open, drew his sword with an added flourish, the steel singing as it swept from the scabbard, and shouted "Have at thee, bandits!"

The men were caught completely unprepared and when the knight charged into their midst they scattered like mice. Only the nearest of the men had the wherewithal to draw his sword to defend himself. Sir Ethan struck him down quickly with a single slash. He took but a moment's pause to nod respect for the life he'd just taken before he flew into pursuit of the others, taking care to check his steps in order to force the men to run due west in the Minotaur's general direction.

All it took was one shout, "We're under attack!" before the camp erupted into chaos.

Chapter XXIII

Meanwhile, Gus sat atop his horse watching everything. In truth he wasn't terribly sure what he could do to help. He saw the commotion erupt as Sir Ethan shouted dramatic challenge to all who stood before him. He couldn't see where his other companion had disappeared to but Snowball had an unnerving knack for stealth that defied common belief.

As he sat watching events unfold from a safe distance within the trees, he saw a particularly clumsy bandit paying little attention to where he was going as Sir Ethan chased after him and a score of others. The man accidentally stepped into a fire and yelped, stumbling around only to fall over the top of a short wood pile and into a tent. The tent pole snapped and the canvas billowed down and to the side, knocking another bandit off balance as he took aim at the courageous knight with a bow. The shot went completely wide. So wide, in fact, that it ricocheted off a tree trunk, a rock and finally grazed the rear end of Gus's horse. The horse did what any animal would have done and ran right under a low-hanging branch, which knocked Gus from the saddle and left him breathless as his back hit the ground. He managed to wheeze an "Ow..." before his horse disappeared into the woods.

After he caught his breath, he realized he would be an easy target if anyone noticed him so he quickly got up and looked for a place to hide where he could still be of help to his companions. With little alternative, Gus looked up and saw the perfect vantage point in the tree that had knocked him down. With painful efforts, he clambered up, branch by branch until he could see the majority of the camp from a stout branch. He was shortly glad he did, for from his newfound vantage he could make out Snowball's bulky frame skulking about on the south-eastern edge of camp, dragging a couple of bodies in one hand behind him.

"Snowball!" Gus cried out as he saw the men Sir Ethan chased heading in his direction. "The horses! Don't let them get the horses!"

Sure enough, the men were scrambling to get to their mounts. If they were to escape there would be no telling what kind of trouble they'd cause. Gus still couldn't see Ian but if the cunning villain got away, all of their effort would be wasted.

Snowball, who until then had completely forgotten Sir Ethan's instructions, dropped the two men he had been dragging and turned his attention to the horses. They were all lined up, hitched to a large fallen tree. The men were nearly there, eager to climb into their saddles. They caught sight of the Minotaur and their eagerness to mount and escape increased twofold. Snowball looked to the horses, then the bandits, then back to the horses. He moved fast and with his powerful strength he shoved the first horse over... which fell into the horse next to it... which knocked over the next one... and the next one... and the next one... until they had all fallen like a row of dominoes. The bandits came to a screeching halt and when they realized that the Minotaur was near and their means of rapid escape had fallen over, they screamed and scattered.

Thinking this all to be wonderfully exciting, Snowball gave chase, swinging his massive hammer with joyous zeal. He swept the feet right out from beneath one man and before he could come crashing down to the ground, the Minotaur kicked him up with a hoof in order to give himself a few extra seconds to wind up the hammer a second time. The second blow launched his victim across the camp.

Sir Ethan, who had since expended the shock and awe of his dramatic entrance, was forced to take a more defensive approach as Ian's men recovered and joined forces to take him down. There were at least a dozen men and he was hemmed in on all sides. Knowing he had reached his limit but unfortunately having lost his sense of direction, he glanced about for any sign of Gus's companion. "Snowball, where did you run off to?" He said to himself.

He saw a bandit soaring through the air in a wide arc as yet another screamed in an almost comical fashion as he flew straight up above one of the tents. "Ah..." Sir Ethan noted. "Snowball!" He tried to hail his ally but the sudden assault of Ian's men put his rallying cry on hold. He blocked a fierce blow from a heavy wooden club and responded in kind, careful to watch his back as he parried and tried to advance on one enemy after another. It was, however, quite useless. Whenever he forced one back another stepped in to attack and take his place. He was losing the fight and though his stamina was great, if he didn't think of something quick, he'd be done for.

Suddenly, over the fighting he heard Gus's voice. "Sir Ethan! Behind you! Head to the fire!"

He couldn't tell from whence the voice came but he did see the fire and without question made a dash for it. By the Gods the peasant was right! Using the fire as a barrier to prevent advance, the bandits were only able to come at him one at a time. Furthermore, a natural embankment of earth rose up behind him, making it difficult for Ian's men to surround him.

"Snowball's got the horses!" Gus shouted.

"Wonderful, sir!" the knight exclaimed as he parried a nasty blow from a pickaxe and threw a shoulder at his attacker, knocking him down. "What of their leader?"

Gus had been searching and searching for the horned mask the entire time but, for whatever reason, he hadn't caught sight of it yet. What was Ian doing? Surely, he would have joined in the fray once the commotion had started.

"I can't see him!" Gus called down. "Snowball! Use the tent!"

Snowball, who had until then been enjoying himself with familiar hammer techniques was spending most of his time chasing after individual men. When he heard Gus shout, he took note of the tent and had the same tremendous idea. He grabbed the corner of the cloth and easily pulled the whole thing down. There was a group of men who had ducked inside to avoid the terrifying creature. They looked up from their huddled position when their shelter was suddenly ripped from them. Rather than simply strike them one by one, Snowball whirled the tent fabric above his head and swung it wide, trapping and wrapping the five of them together as if in a massive net.

"Oh!" Snowball exclaimed. "Mister Gus Man has good idea!" He gleefully whapped the noggins of each bandit in rapid succession and they crumpled.

"Sir Ethan, above you!" Gus cried, and just in time. His friend looked up to see the bandit that had climbed up one of the trees in order to jump down on him. Sir Ethan nimbly sidestepped and the bandit flopped onto the ground with a dull thud.

"Imbecile." Sir Ethan scoffed at the bandit. "My thanks, good sir!" He called out to his friend.

And so, the battle continued as Gus issued direction while his allies fought Ian's men. However, the ragtag rabble soon caught on and two men rushed to the tree Gus was hiding in with a pair of axes.

"Oh Gods." Gus said as he realized he was trapped. They began hacking at the trunk of the tree and each blow sent a shock through the branches. "Uh.... Guys! Help!" He called out. However, both Sir Ethan and Snowball were engaged in the fight and could not come to his aid. The poor peasant looked around him for anything that might be of help but nothing caught his eye. Soon, Ian's men would fell the tree, he would fall to the ground, and if that didn't kill him, he'd become an easy target.

His mind went into a frenzied analysis of the situation. Suddenly, he became keenly aware of the situation. He realized that the branches of the tree would soften the fall and if he remained on the upward side of the tree trunk, he would remain unscathed. The branches also provided some measure of cover and the bandits chopping the tree would not be able to get at him right away, which would give him some time to escape. Snowball had already incapacitated ten of Ian's men and was engaged in a raging battle with about half of Ian's forces, who were frankly keener to run than to try to oppose the Minotaur's hulking might. Sir Ethan wasn't overwhelmed but would quickly tire at the pace he was fighting. Gus had about a minute before the tree fell. In that time, he could scan the surroundings and come up with a plan. The tree would fall toward the camp, placing him just on the edge of the first few makeshift shelters the bandits had built in addition to their tents. There was a spear just a few yards from where he thought the tree would fall. He could use it to defend himself if it got desperate. He glimpsed his horse milling around just outside the camp. If he could get to it, he would stand a chance. He could use it to swing by Sir Ethan and the two of them could make good an escape. Snowball would be fine on his own, except against the archer who was taking careful aim at the creature.

Hold on.

One of the bandits was standing on a nearby boulder and was aiming a fully drawn bow at his brutish companion. He was a bigger brute than all the rest and his countenance was one only a mother could love.

It was Ian!

The clever ruffian had taken off his horned mask to blend in with the others and during the commotion had made himself scarce. No wonder Gus hadn't seen him. He'd been looking for the horns instead of the man.

"Sir Ethan! Snowball! Ian, to the south!" Gus shouted.

The knight and the Minotaur looked.

"No! The other south!"

"Huzzah!" Sir Ethan spotted the scoundrel.

Snowball took a swing at a foolishly charging bandit as he looked in that direction as well.

The timing was perfect, and Ian let the arrow fly. Snowball didn't have enough time to move or deflect the incoming missile and the arrow buried itself in the meat of his arm.

Snowball roared furiously and angrily smashed a bandit into the ground with an overhead swing. He ripped the arrow from his flesh with a spurt of blood and roared challenge as his eyes went red.

The Minotaur went into a wild rampage, his hooves pushing into the earth with incredible force to propel him at one enemy after the next. No man in his path stood a chance. Each hammer strike hit home with nearly impossible speed and vicious precision. First a bandit's leg crunching at the wrong angle, next a skull reduced to a more two-dimensional shape. All the while the Minotaur roared a nearly unintelligible cry that to Gus almost sounded like "you! You took my strawberries!"

Fearing the creature's powerful rage, Gus called out. "Sir Ethan! To your left! Head that way!"

Sir Ethan moved just in time as Snowball came crashing through the camp in his direction. The knight headed to the source of Gus's voice, feeling that now was the time to regroup. Something inside told him the Minotaur had entered a primitive frenzy and would be a danger to everyone, not just Ian and his men.

At that same moment, the last blow struck the tree and Gus clung to the up-side of the trunk as it cracked and came crashing down. The trunk sort of bounced with the springiness of its branches and tossed Gus clear, landing him on a makeshift sleeping mat. It wasn't terribly soft but Gus was grateful for it all the same.

His plan went into motion. He snatched up the spear as the bandits tried to skirt around the tree to get at him. He was quickly met by Sir Ethan who immediately placed himself between Gus and his pursuers, which made them re-evaluate their strategy and head in the other direction.

"The horse is this way!" Gus told his friend, and they ran in that direction. There was only one flaw with Gus's plan. Their objective had been to neutralize Ian and he hadn't counted on Snowball losing control.

"We need to get out of here." Sir Ethan told him when they reached his horse. Gus didn't object and they both got on the horse and turned to ride off.

By then, what few die-hard men were left at Ian's disposal were all that was left of the bandit camp and they foolishly stood their ground as the Minotaur came charging. One particularly brazen man put himself right in front of the creature and set his spear in the ground to impale him. Snowball stopped but raised his hammer high, bringing it down on the ground with serious force. The blow was so strong it sent a shockwave that knocked the spear from the ground and made the man lose his footing. It was too late for the bandit. Snowball trampled right over the top of him, his weight crushing body and bone.

As Snowball devastated his men, Ian stood his ground. He had faced the creature before and he knew its insane strength. However, he was confident he could best the creature this time.

"I'm not afraid to fight the likes of you!" He shouted in challenge as he loosed another arrow at Snowball.

Impossibly, the Minotaur plucked the arrow right from the air between his thumb and forefinger, snapping it in half as he roared his challenge back. Discarding the broken arrow Snowball darted to the side where a bandit had been trying to sneak up on him and hit him so hard with his hammer that the unfortunate soul's body flew into a young tree and splintered its trunk.

"How about now?" Snowball's voice was filled with joyful malice.

Ian swallowed nervously.

Snowball charged.

Ian's few remaining men moved in.

Ian... fled.

The men didn't stand a chance. The mighty hammer broke three of them in a single swing as they had charged in together. The fourth man did little more than collapse as Snowball used him as a springboard, charging right over the top of him and launching himself into the air. When he came down, the fifth bandit was caught in a downswing of Snowball's weapon and on the back-swing, Snowball swatted the sixth man like a ball. His aim was impeccable. The body flew like a rag doll through the air and knocked Ian's feet out from underneath him from twenty yards away. Ian fell to the ground with a groan of pain. He got up as quickly as he could and ran. He ran for his life. The Minotaur had the upper hand and it was clear he wouldn't survive if he stood his ground.

Ian could hear the heavy hooves pounding the ground behind him and the snorting of the Minotaur's breath. He flew from the camp not daring to look behind lest he lose his footing. Branches snapped behind him as he moved into the woods, trying to put as many obstacles as he could between himself and the creature to slow it down. His efforts were in vain. No matter how he ducked or weaved or slipped between the trees the Minotaur was always close at his heels, destroying everything in its path.

Ahead he saw a dense cluster of thick trees with just enough room to maneuver through and made fast for them. He knew there was no way his pursuer would fit through and after he'd cleared them, he risked a glance to see if he had succeeded.

Snowball swung his hammer hard as he ran and blasted apart an entire tree trunk to make room before he continued after his quarry. Ian yelped in surprise as he ran. He knew he needed to outsmart the creature. Surely there would be some means of escape for him, some trick he could pull, some obstacle the monster couldn't pass.

Ahead he saw his salvation. There was a steep slope littered with dry needles and loose soil. The Minotaur would never be able to scale it but Ian was confident he could scramble up. He drew his sword and stuck it into the ground ahead of him as he leveraged himself up the slope as fast as he could. The Minotaur's hammer smashed the ground just inches below him as Snowball caught up. When he reached the top of the slope, Ian looked down at the enraged monster. Snowball's eyes gleamed red with fury and steam flew from his nostrils in angry jets.

"Hah!" Ian laughed triumphantly as the Minotaur failed to climb the crumbling slope.

This only served to make Snowball angrier and instead of trying to scale the slope, Snowball took a nearby pine tree in his hands and with a deep rumbling growl he dug in his hooves and pushed it over, the trunk snapping as it gave way to his strength. The tree fell against the slope and it was all Snowball needed to get a sure footing. He flew up the slope as fast as if it were level ground and resumed the chase as Ian cried out in fear.

The mad dash to preserve his life continued but Ian was quickly running out of stamina. If things kept up at that pace he'd be caught. The slope had put some distance between him and the monster but it wouldn't last forever. He needed to find someplace to hide. With a desperately clever idea, Ian made use of a bend in the terrain around a stone-studded rise in the earth. It put him temporarily out of sight and gave him just enough time to clamber up a tree where he'd be hidden by the foliage.

He waited, his pulse racing as pounding footsteps grew closer. He held his breath.

The Minotaur passed beneath.

Ian let out a sigh of relief. That brutish beast was certainly strong and fast but he wasn't smart enough. Ian felt a touch of pride at his accomplishment. He'd outwitted the Minotaur!

Or so he thought.

Sounds of snuffling grew louder as Snowball moved beneath the forest canopy. Ian's heart leaped up into his throat and he stifled his own breath.

Snowball stopped just at the base of Ian's tree and sniffed the air. He caught a whiff of the familiar scent of Gus and the locket. Suddenly, he looked up.

Oh Gods! Thought Ian. He stared down into the demon eyes of that creature and felt its gaze pierce his very soul.

The creature growled, letting go of the hammer and went to the tree, digging his hands into the trunk with such force that the wood crushed inward. With a seething grunt, the creature lifted… And lifted. The roots began popping, the ground sank downward and the tree groaned.

For a moment Ian thought, *this creature must be mad if it thinks it can tear this tree down.*

The ground started to give way and the creature's grunt turned to a groan, then a growl. The soil protested and the roots held on for dear life. The growl became a yell and then a roar and with the strength of a thousand men Snowball tore the poor tree from the ground and the soil gave way, roots snapping and breaking.

Ian wet himself in fear of the awesome spectacle and clung to his branch, afraid to let go. But Snowball would not have it. The Minotaur threw the tree down to the ground and Ian with it. The blow knocked the air out of Ian's lungs and he rolled and wheezed in pain. Soon the Minotaur was standing over him, hammer in hand.

He tried to crawl away but Snowball followed with a sinister glower. "Please," he whimpered, but the monster kept on coming. Tears streamed down his face as full terror washed over him.

The locket! He remembered the locket! That was what the creature was after. He shoved his hand into his pocket and took out the shiny bauble, holding it out by the chain for the creature.

"Here! Take it. This is what you want, right? You want this. You can have it. Just please, let me go!" He begged. The locket quivered in his grasp.

Snowball stopped and sniffed. Then he reached out his hand and Ian closed his eyes in fear. He plucked the locket from Ian's grasp and looked at it curiously.

"See. It's alright. You can just let me go. I won't cause any more trouble, I swear." Ian promised.

Snowball draped the locket on one of his horns.

Then a wicked smile spread across his face.

"What? No!" Ian barely managed the words before Snowball lifted his hammer high with both hands. Ian held out a hand to stop him, but that was the last thing he did before Snowball brought it down and Ian's world went black.

Chapter XXIV

The sky had started to clear and the mist thinned and faded. For a while the forest was quiet before the sounds of birds and forest creatures returned. Gus and Sir Ethan rode into town, though it was empty, and hitched the horse just outside the tavern. The townspeople had done as Sir Ethan had suggested and left. With many of the bandits either dead or scattered and their leader... well as far as they knew he was still out there somewhere being pursued by the Minotaur... but with him out of the picture perhaps things would return to normal in that neck of the woods. Gus went inside the tavern to sit down for a while. He was wearing pretty thin and he could use a little peace and quiet. He found a mostly clean cup behind the bar and helped himself to an unlabeled bottle of something that didn't smell too horrible. He normally wouldn't have taken anything but with everyone gone and the trouble he'd just been through he figured it would be alright with the tavern's keeper.

Sir Ethan entered in behind him but left the bar alone. He leaned against a table and sighed heavily. "We've done these people a great service." He said, trying to remain cheerful. "That monster... sorry. Your friend, the Minotaur, will likely kill your bandit adversary. Those who survived have fled and though they will cause trouble in their own time at least they won't be working together anytime soon. Bandits are notoriously selfish and untrustworthy by nature."

"I don't know what happened." Gus said quietly. "He's never been like that before. Never that angry. I mean, sure, when he and I were trying to get my locket back the first time, I made him think that Ian was going to eat all of the strawberries and he got kind of mad but not like that. Not that... that..."

"Monster?" Sir Ethan finished for him.

"I..." Gus struggled to find the right words. "I don't think of him as a monster. He's not. I mean, he's not a human. Not by a long shot. But he's..."

Sir Ethan was at a loss for what to say in return and there was an awkward silence between them.

"I brought this on them." Gus realized. "Imagine what could have happened if he'd done that with the villagers nearby. He would have slaughtered all of them. He's a dangerous creature. I brought that creature along with me and wherever I go there's always a chance that he'll... that he'll..." Gus shuddered at the thought. What if he'd gotten somebody hurt? Someone innocent. "I... I befriended a monster. That's what he is, a monster. And here I am traveling the world alongside him. I brought him with me to all these people and put them in danger... Oh gods..." Gus began trailing off into a pool of his own despair.

"He was wrong, you know." Ethan said suddenly.

"What?" Gus asked.

"He was wrong about you. That Ian fellow. You aren't alone in all this. You've made friends throughout, no doubt. Myself, Duncan, and the knights of Kismet. All of us were inspired by your genuine innocence and pluck. I would count any of us among your friends, and I have only known you for a short time. I cannot imagine the affect you've had on others prior to our meeting. Would that you could see that."

"Thank you." Gus said quite sincerely.

"And as for the Minotaur," Ethan continued, "I do believe you'd befriended such a beast not out of your ineptitude at real human relationships, but through sheer compassion that spans beyond humanity itself. I do not think that any of us could have accomplished such a feat without a stout heart such as yours, good sir. Had you not, Hogwash would still be overrun by those miscreants and that despicable Ian."

Gus was at a loss for words. He could barely manage a thank you. Sir Ethan was right. He had never thought of others as friends but looking back he could not help but see the fruits of his labors in the attitudes of many of the people he'd met.

"Think nothing of it." Ethan insisted. "I speak only the truth. Now..." He walked over to his companion and slapped him heartily on the back. "Are you going to spend the rest of the day wallowing in misery or will you join me in rounding up the villagers to celebrate our victory?"

"What about Snowball?" Gus asked.

"You do realize he has the strangest name, you know. I mean, he's not even white." Sir Ethan pointed out. "I'm sure he'll return in his own time. After everything I've seen, I suspect he has grown quite fond of you, Gods save you."

"What do you mean?"

"I don't think it was strawberries that threw him into a frenzy, Gus. I think it was for you. In spite of how unlikely it seems, I think he went into his rage on your behalf to get back what was taken from you."

"You really think so?" Gus wondered. "I always thought he only liked strawberries and smashing things."

"I think you've underestimated yourself, good sir."

"Well... there's nothing to me, really. It was you and Snowball that won that battle. All I've managed to do is get captured and beaten."

Sir Ethan slammed a hand firmly on the table in front of him. "That's enough of that! You have more worth than you think. It was you who figured out how to lure the Minotaur back to us. It was you who came up with that clever scheme to save the townspeople and it was you who led your friend and I to defeat Ian and his men. Do not short-change yourself! The Minotaur is strong and dangerous, surely, and skilled in battle, but it is your clever mind that makes you doubly dangerous. Without Snowball, you may not be able to defeat many foes, but the two of you together, his brawn and your brains, make a powerful combination. Never forget that!"

Gus felt embarrassed and didn't know what to say. Sir Ethan told him "enough of that" and roused him out of his chair. Together they left the tavern and did just as Sir Ethan suggested, following the tracks of the townsfolk to let them know their village was safe.

The townspeople were grateful when they'd been reassured that they were safe and returned to the village to celebrate. A feast was prepared and by evening there was singing and dancing in the middle of town.

While the revelry was in full swing, Snowball returned, dragging a bloodied hammer with the locket still dangling on his horn. The music screeched to a halt, the dancing stumbled still and all form of conversation went quiet as if the town breathed a gasp of shock.

Somewhat horrified, Gus did the only thing he could think of to assuage their fears and approached his companion. Snowball smiled and showed Gus the blood on his hammer. "Do not worry Mister Gus Man, Snowball took care of mister BackBrokey."

Gus shuddered and tried not to think of what Snowball had done to his lifelong tormentor. Before he could do or say anything, he caught sight of his locket dangling from the creature's horn. Snowball gladly took it down and offered it to his human friend. Gus was overjoyed but, realizing that the whole town was still holding its breath, afraid of what the Minotaur might do, he turned his attention back to the people.

"You may think that Sir Ethan and I helped save your village, but the real credit should go to him," he announced as he thumbed at Snowball. "Snowball here is the one who deserves your praise. He has slain Ian MacBrody, the man in the deer-skull mask that they called The Horned One. He was the one who brought his men and attacked your village. So, the real thanks tonight should go to him."

The villagers were silent.

Gus shook his head with a sigh. They didn't really understand. He suspected they could hardly see past the fur and the horns. "I know that he appears to be a monster, but he's..." He shuddered as he remembered Snowball's rage earlier that day. "He's my friend, and if you can find it in your hearts to praise me, then surely you can praise this strange and wonderful creature."

They didn't. They stood silently watching, some tiptoeing away from the creature. Others looked for some weapon to defend themselves with.

Gus gave up. It didn't matter to him if they praised him or not. He turned back to his companion. "Come on, Snowball. Let's go." He said.

They left the village together as night pressed in and made camp just in sight of town.

As Gus sat by the fire, thumbing his locket and deep in thought, Snowball plopped down on the ground. Gus didn't notice. He mouthed words of an imaginary conversation silently as the Minotaur watched him curiously. He didn't seem to be aware of anything else and so Snowball broke the silence.

"Talking works better with sound." Snowball pointed out.

"Huh? What?" Gus snapped out of it. "Sorry, old friend. I'm just feeling a bit out of sorts. What were we talking about?"

Snowball laughed and shook his head. "Mister Gus Man is funny. He was not talking about anything at all."

"You're right." Gus felt a bit silly. "I was just thinking about the town and you and what we're doing here." Snowball listened, which to Gus felt quite rare at that moment. He continued, feeling grateful. "It's just, I don't know what we're doing out here. I know we left looking for strawberries, at least that's what you've been saying this whole time, but what am I doing out here? I'm not looking for strawberries. You and I have been traveling about, getting into all sorts of trouble and I don't know why I keep doing this. Shouldn't I get a job, or find some sort of purpose for myself? I left my village to seek my fortune and the first thing that happened was I ran into you!"

Snowball's tail was wagging.

"What am I supposed to do with myself?"

Snowball shrugged and said "listen to the horsey. Eat and sleep, and then find a mate."

"The horse?" Gus wondered. "The horse wants to mate?"

"Oh yes! She will not stop talking about it."

Gus felt a little perturbed. He'd been riding on top of that horse for days. That's when it hit him. "Actually, maybe you're right, Snowball."

"Mating is good." Snowball agreed.

"No!" Gus groaned. "I need to find her. I need to find Fiona!"

The Minotaur didn't seem to understand.

"That's what I need to do." Gus shut the locket and held it tightly in one hand. "Fiona left the village a few years ago and I haven't heard from her since. She's out there somewhere, Snowball."

Then Gus remembered how uncanny Snowball's sense of smell was. He had followed Gus by the faintest of scents still lingering on the locket back when they'd first met. "And you're going to help me find her! Snowball, that's perfect! We don't have to wander aimlessly. With your sense of smell, we might actually be able to find her!" Gus was beside himself with excitement.

Snowball still didn't understand what had just happened but he smiled happily anyway.

"Oh! I am so glad I met you." He said. Gus ran it through over and over in his head. It was a long shot, sure, but what better to spur him onward. Fiona was the one person he'd ever felt that close to and if by some small chance he could find her, maybe things would work out in the end.

As Gus stared into the fire, his mind racing with thoughts of reconnecting with his childhood love, Snowball wondered something that had been on his mind as well. "Mister Gus Man is half-brother?"

The question caught him off-guard. "What?" Gus laughed and shook his head. "Sure, friend. Sure."

"What half is Mister Gus Man?"

"Huh? Beg pardon?" Gus asked.

"Mister Gus Man said that Snowball is half-man, half-bull. What is Mister Gus Man's other half?"

"Half-bad-luck-charm..." Gus said half-jokingly.

"Snowball does not care if tiny hoomans think Snowball is a monster. But if tiny hoomans want to avoid monster, does Mister Gus Man want to avoid Snowball?" It seemed that it had been weighing on the creature's mind for some time. Somehow, amid all the fighting and roving the countryside, all the times when he'd been treated as a monster had added up and he was becoming aware that he didn't fit in. Even stranger, this fact had started to bother the creature.

Gus stood up and went to place a hand on the Minotaur's big shoulder. "Snowball, you are the biggest, strongest, scariest, most dangerous piece of walking pandemonium to ever bring disaster wherever you go."

Snowball gave him a curious look.

"I can't think of any more worthy a companion to travel with. If I'm ever going to find Fiona, only a creature like you could make it possible."

Snowball felt honored and smiled with his large bovine teeth.

"Well then, my monstrous companion," Gus said. "What say we turn in for the night and tomorrow morning, we'll set out to find her."

The pair did likewise and turned in for the evening. The night was peaceful. Crickets chirped under a sparkling canopy of stars and treetops. Invigorated, Gus lay awake wondering late into the night just what lay ahead of him when at last he fell into a restful sleep and for one night, the first perhaps in all his life, all felt right and well with the world.

The End

www.ingramcontent.com/pod-product-compliance
Lightning Source LLC
Chambersburg PA
CBHW072350110726
47909CB00003B/665